Hey, White Girl!

Susan Gregory

HEY,

WHITE

GIRL!

W·W·NORTON & COMPANY·INC·New York

Copyright © 1970 by Susan Gregory
SBN 393 07450 1
Library of Congress Catalog Card No. 79-90978
All Rights Reserved
Published simultaneously in Canada
by George J. McLeod Limited, Toronto
Printed in the United States of America

2 3 4 5 6 7 8 9 0

To Carol, Carmella, Rudy, and Roose-velt, whose love and friendship have given me the courage and conviction to write this book.

Contents

	PREFACE	9
	AUTHOR'S NOTE AND	
	ACKNOWLEDGMENTS	13
1	THE PREPARATION	17
2	SEPTEMBER	24
3	OCTOBER	33
4	NOVEMBER	47
5	DECEMBER	59
6	JANUARY	88
7	FEBRUARY	111
8	MARCH	122
9	APRIL	140
10	MAY	156
11	JUNE	187
12	THE CONCLUSION	206

Preface

I grew up unaware that there was anything unusual about our family. Indeed, I never doubted that all American families were like ours. Only as my experience widened to include larger circles of people did I realize the Gregory family could not be called "typical." Stability and a strong unity of purpose combined with a sense of independence may explain the quality of our family life.

The stability our family enjoyed came from regular patterns of behavior that remained constant in the midst of change. Not one of us four children ever went to sleep without hearing a story read to us, until we ourselves could read. On Sundays Daddy took us on a drive, or we hiked to the beach near our home. After these excursions we gathered in the living room for popcorn or hot chocolate. There were family discussions at dinner that often lasted for hours and knew no subject limitations. On holidays, and especially at Christmas, we shared activities that gradually became family traditions. These and other practices acted as stabilizers—they could be relied upon as constants, no matter what our physical, financial, or emotional state happened to be. They were the cushions that absorbed the shocks, the fears, the uncertainties of our growing years and made it possible for us to bounce back into the struggle of our development with a sense of security and continuity.

I have two sisters and a younger brother. We were all blessed with a degree of intelligence, creative talent, and a drive to achieve. One might have expected fierce jealousy among us and aggressive competition for status and parental attention. While we experienced normal sibling rivalry, we were taught from birth to respect individual gifts and to be proud of the achievements of other family members. Mom and Dad regarded each of us as a unique personality, and we did not envy one another's talents because we knew we had our own particular abilities to contribute. Our parents saw their task not as one of shaping and molding our lives but as one of allowing our natural endowments to develop.

In turn we learned to view our parents as individual beings, with their own human strengths and weaknesses. We learned to share our thoughts, our joys and depressions. We were aware of and sensitive to each other's moods. There was a live dynamic at work when the Gregory family was together.

In an age in which children are protected from the realities of the world and from sharing any responsibility for the condition of man, our family was an exception. Mom and Dad believed that loving children did not mean removing all obstacles from their paths. Rather, loving children meant preparing them to confront and challenge obstacles, helping them develop maturity and self-reliance in the process. We began making our own decisions and accepting responsibility for them when we were very young. If, as a child, I stood on a high step and asked, "Mommy, should I jump?", the answer would be, "Do you think you can handle it?" I was left to consider the consequences and accept the results of my judgment.

Practice in formulating decisions enabled me to weigh the consequences of joining the final day of the march from Selma to Montgomery in 1965 and to decide that I wanted to go. I was fifteen years old, and my family permitted me to leave home for that historic event. Noting Mom's look of concern as we drove to meet the bus that would take me to Alabama, I could say, with the confidence of having made a responsible decision, "I can handle it."

Finally, our family shared common goals. We children were learning to make decisions in order to serve our fellow man. Although each of us had different capacities and separate areas of commitment, we shared a vision beyond ourselves. As Gregorys our task was to expend our energy on behalf of others. This corporate mission gave strength and cohesion to our family unit.

Each member helped to shape our family decisions and no decision was made unless each of us understood and affirmed it. Our move to Chicago's West Side came only after several years of consideration and preparation. Not until each member clearly saw why such action was important and what his part in it would be, not until each member willingly shouldered his share of the responsibility, not until each member said, "I can handle it," did the family act.

We had difficulties. We suffered misunderstandings, quarrels, disagreements, and clashes of opinion. But our struggles were dealt with openly and honestly, each person helping the other find alternative ways to deal with existing problems. Through our maturing process as a family we recognized the bond that united us—the uniqueness of our knowledge and respect and love for one another.

This is not a book about my family. But it is necessary for the reader to understand the part my family plays in the book. Without that foundation of Gregory support, I would not have been able to tell this story.

Author's Note and Acknowledgments

I have kept a daily diary since I was fourteen. It was only natural that I continue this practice during my year on the West Side. Whenever friends expressed an interest in hearing about my experience, I referred to this journal. One evening in our home Miss Eleanor Perkins, a lecturer and book reviewer who employed my mother as companion-secretary before Miss Perkins's recent death, asked me to read from the journal. She perceived in the material the makings of a book and encouraged me to contact her author-agent, Max Siegel. Mr. Siegel and his partner, Roy Porter, gave me a sympathetic hearing and agreed that my experience would be of general interest. While I was fashioning the raw material of the journal into book form, Mr. Porter worked with me patiently as advisor and editor. He gave confidence to an inexperienced writer and, through his exacting critique, pushed me toward high standards. My mother proved a source of stability and strength and relieved me of the burden of manuscript typing during the months of shaping the book. In periods of depression and doubt, she reassured me that the message of the book was significant and needed expression. Evan Thomas, Vice President of W. W. Norton Publishers, read the manuscript and agreed to publication. I am particularly grateful to these five persons for believing in me and giving me the opportunity to share with others my unique experience.

The reader should understand that the emotions expressed throughout the book were felt only in the context of my year at Marshall. The intense experience of being totally immersed in the black world produced what the reader may feel are exaggerated expressions of the beauty of blackness. However, the reader should realize that I was discovering blackness and should take this into account when reacting to pointed contrasts between white and black. Two years after Marshall my feelings have been placed in a clearer perspective with the dignity of *all* persons emphasized.

I have recorded the incidents in the book as I saw them. The only details altered are the names of the persons involved.

Hey, White Girl!

The Preparation

CHAPTER 1

As was often our custom, we had remained in the dining room of our nine-room house having a family discussion until late in the evening. I lay on my back on the rug, looking up at the eyes that were watching expectantly for my response.

"Well, Sue, how do you feel about it? How would you react to selling the house and moving to the West Side of Chicago to join the Ecumenical Institute?" Daddy's question brought an immediate smile, and I knew they would interpret this to mean, "Yes, I want to go."

To retrace the steps that brought us to this important decision on an April night: In the summer of 1964 the Gregory family traveled to Knoxville, Tennessee, to participate in the

Summer-Study-Skills Program, a six-week school sponsored
by the Presbyterian Board of Missions to aid in developing the
academic skills of southern high school students with college
potential. We lived on the Knoxville College campus with
sixty-nine students, all but four of whom were black. Daddy
taught English and Mom worked as a secretary by day and
assisted in the library at night. My job was to care for my
younger brother and sister.

But as a family we found ourselves drawn into the very
center of the students' lives. The problems of the black man
in the South, which had previously been distant and impersonal, became clear and immediate. The stories of jail, intimi-
dation, and brutality were real when told softly and bravely
by a young girl from Jackson, Mississippi. And the word
prejudice took on concrete meaning when a black boy from
Atlanta, Georgia, recalled the day a white friend's parents
removed their son from the swimming hole where the two
boys had frolicked and splashed together. "You can't play
with him anymore," they said. Segregation became a tangible
entity when another black boy from Alabama recalled the incident that closed the old movie house in town. "We had to
sit in the balcony, so we threw things down at the white audience, and they threw popcorn and paper back. One day the
fight got out of hand, so they closed the place."

Six weeks in Knoxville heightened our awareness of the
black man's struggle. But we learned something no one had
ever told us, something we had never read in books. We discovered the utter beauty of blackness and the amazing spontaneity and vitality of both black youth and their style of life.
We were awed by the suddenness of a wonderful joke, of a
dance step, of someone snapping his fingers. The energy of
the students around us seemed inexhaustible; their animation
and responsiveness contradicted their historical deprivation and
suffering.

When the study-skills program ended we returned home to
Wilmette, Illinois, an affluent northern suburb of Chicago.
Daddy continued to teach English at predominantly white

New Trier High School where I was a sophomore. But an interest in the civil rights movement became the central force in my life. I spent hours reading and clipping articles about the movement from newspapers and magazines. I arranged them chronologically into notebooks and soon had completed thirteen bulging with current history. I read books and built my own library devoted to the black man.

Mom and Dad were forming ties with the Ecumenical Institute in Chicago, and when the Selma-Montgomery March began, the Institute chartered a bus. Daddy and I shared the journey south and participated in the last day of the march to the capitol. The thrill of those seven miles will always remain vivid, for we were united with blacks and whites from all over the country who believed in freedom and justice. We massed before Alabama's capitol building, arms linked and voices strong in dignity, singing "We Shall Overcome."

The summer of 1965 gave me an opportunity to learn about the city and to gain practical experience in an urban environment. I became a member of the New Trier Summer Seminar in community relations—a seven-week course designed for high school students from Chicago and suburbs. Half of the students were black, and one Negro boy from Hyde Park High School on the South Side became my closest friend. Through this program my love for the city blossomed.

During this same period, an open-housing movement started on the North Shore. Daddy and I participated in rallies and meetings of the North Shore Summer Project, designed to break open the suburbs to black families. That summer Daddy taught inner-city youth in a program called REACH, and his students often mixed with the members of my seminar. Both groups marched with Martin Luther King when his End Slums campaign moved to Chicago. The climax of the summer was a rally on the Winnetka Village Green in the heart of the North Shore. Martin Luther King's voice rolled over the green into the cool summer night, and I stood behind his podium counting money collected for the movement. There so close to my own home, as in distant Montgomery, I experienced the thrill of his oratory, his beautiful phrasing, his power of conviction.

Daddy was still waiting for an answer to his question. I sat up and hugged my legs, laughing. Would I hesitate to leave New Trier and spend my senior year at an all-black high school on the West Side of Chicago? Would I refuse the opportunity to live in the city and find out for myself what it was like? Would I say no?

I laughed again, looking up at the members of my family. "Why, she's got her bags packed already!" Kathy responded. "You bet. I'm ready!" I grinned.

Our move would mean changing schools for Daddy, too. He would teach English at John Marshall High School, in addition to his duties at the Institute. Kathy would be a sophomore in college, so our decision to move did not affect her as directly. But Ann was twelve, and she would have to start seventh grade in a city Upper Grade Center. Never one to retreat from new experiences, she was willing. Douglas, who was always self-contained and required little other than a place to design and create his space-age models, seemed generally unconcerned about entering second grade in a city school. Mom, who had been a staff member of our local church, working in Christian Education for six years, had taken Institute courses regularly for some time. She was eager to bring her theological training and organizational skills to this new venture.

The Ecumenical Institute is housed in an abandoned seminary in the heart of Chicago's West Side ghetto. Its scattered buildings and courtyard take up one square city block, bordered on the south by the Eisenhower expressway, a key artery connecting the nearby Loop to the western suburbs. In addition to the main administration building, the upper floors of which contain dormitory rooms, facilities include a gymnasium, a chapel, a faculty residence hall, and an apartment annex.

The Ecumenical Institute has two main concerns. The first is as a training center. Both on the campus and across the coun-

try Institute staff conduct courses in religious and cultural
studies for laymen and clergy. These are concerned with a
contemporary, twentieth century understanding of faith and
church membership. Members of the Institute share a basic
understanding that to be a man of faith means to lay down
one's life—"die one's death"—on behalf of all mankind. Therefore, they take a comprehensive, futuric, and intentional approach to world problems.

Those who decide to join the Institute become a part of a
modern religious Order, bound by commitment to the larger
corporate body and its decisions. The Order is made up of
family units, single persons, college and high school students,
coming from all over the nation and even from foreign coun-
tries to participate in this significant experiment.

The Institute's second concern—practical research—finds its
expression in Fifth City, a sixteen-block area on the West Side
for which the Institute has developed a reformulation plan.
The most important aspect of the Fifth City plan is its attack
on the problem of self-image. The black man in the ghetto
often thinks of himself as a victim, and it is this "nigger" image
that has to be destroyed and replaced with a positive, creative
feeling of self-worth. The Fifth City model concerns itself
with all ages and all problems at once. Therefore, the Institute
coöperates with community residents in programs for tiny
babies, youth, adults, and the elderly, as well as in programs
affecting education, housing, health, life style, and all other
aspects of ghetto life in need of attention. Festivals and community celebrations, held every other month, are exciting
evenings of entertainment and image explosion. Gradually the
people of Fifth City are directing their own programs, making
their own decisions about what they want for *their* black community.

Joining the Institute means a willingness to put the mission
of church renewal above all else. Life is regulated by the rules
of the community and accountability is taken seriously. A
worship service is held every morning at 6:15, and breakfast
is eaten corporately. Sunday evening is set aside for House

Church, the most important symbolic meal of the week, in which the Order meets together, takes communion, and celebrates any birthdays, anniversaries, or arrivals of new members. One's family has therefore grown to a body of two hundred people. Parents of individual families may be assigned to work outside the Institute, but their income is pooled with that of other Order members and budgeted according to their family needs. A week's work may include such diverse activities as teaching courses across the country, stuffing envelopes for a mailing, and decorating the campus for a festival.

Did we as a family wish to become a part of this larger dedicated family? Did we wish to take a small apartment on the Institute campus and join in the task of church renewal and community reformulation? By the end of that long night in April, our family had made a decision and the answer was "Yes."

"Are you happy?"
"Aren't you afraid?"
"Do you *want* to go?"
Looking out the window of our four-room apartment into which we had crowded our essential belongings, I recalled the reactions of my New Trier friends when I had told them of our plans to move and my change of schools. On that first August afternoon after we had moved, I could hear the rumble of the El and the hum of cars on the Eisenhower expressway. A police siren screamed in the distance, and a child's laughter drifted up to me from the street.

Yes, I was happy. I had wanted to go. But I wished that school would start. My apprehension stemmed from numerous warnings and stories about what Marshall was going to be like. My boy friend from the South Side said I would have to be wary of accepting dates. A Fifth City resident took my hand and wished me good luck when I told him I'd be a senior at Marshall. "Are you ready? I feel for you," he sympathized. He said it would be a traumatic experience.

A member of the Order gave Ann and me a lecture about

going out alone. He said we should always carry our purses under our arms and never be on the street after dark. He warned us of the possibility of rape. Everyone was quick with a word of advice, a note of caution. Danger signs flashed everywhere.

Shortly after our move Daddy took Kathy, Ann, Doug, and me on a walk through nearby Garfield Park. We were waiting for a break in the traffic in order to cross the street when a police car drove up and stopped. A white officer stuck his head out the window. "Did you run out of gas?" he asked. "Are you lost? Do you need help?"

We looked at each other and laughed. Apparently it was unusual to see a white family strolling through Garfield Park.

"No, we're fine," Daddy answered. "We live at the Ecumenical Institute."

"Oh," the policeman nodded. I had no idea if he really knew about the Institute, but he drove away.

I grew weary of warnings, however. I wanted to find out for myself about Marshall and the West Side. The uncertainty was unbearable.

September

CHAPTER 2

"Hey, white girl!" Daddy and I were standing on the curb waiting to cross Jackson when I heard the voice. For a moment I felt a tight knot form in my stomach. But I fought to relax my muscles, look straight ahead, and ignore him. The light changed, and the street became clear. Trying not to feel the eyes I knew were looking me over, I stepped over broken glass and paper. I couldn't help comparing this walk to school with the drive Daddy and I used to take when we lived in Wilmette. For three years, each school day we drove past stately mansions and carefully manicured lawns. We went down Sheridan Road along Lake Michigan. We parked near the school tennis courts and football field. But now we were two pale figures in a sea of black, kicking cans and bottles along the sidewalk like everyone else. And instead of mansions, the streets were lined with squalid tenements, liquor stores, and an occasional empty lot.

John Marshall High School faced an empty lot littered with trash and dressed with one large stand-up billboard advertising the latest thing in Chevrolets. The school's tired red brick walls had a foreboding, prisonlike quality as I stood among the students milling outside the locked front entrance, waiting for the bell on that first day of the fall term.

All new students from outside the Chicago public school system were to meet in Room 129. Never had I seen a quieter group of people. I was the only white student present. Sue, now you'll know, I thought. You'll know what it was like for every Negro who ever integrated a white school alone. As that Negro represented all Negroes to his white fellow students, so you will represent all whites to the Negroes around you. You're on trial now. Yes, really on trial.

The registrars were all white. I thought that was odd. But we were told to go upstairs to take placement tests in the library so we would be assigned to the proper class level. Those tests remain vivid in my memory. Black students, most of whom were from the South, sat at spaced intervals at the library tables. A white counselor presided over us and distributed our materials. I didn't like him. From his first words it was obvious he had already judged us.

"Who doesn't have a pencil? Raise your hand now. Come on. . . ." Several girls' hands went up, including mine. I had lent my only pencil to someone in 129. "Never come to high school without any writing implements," he scolded us. "That's the lesson for the morning."

As he passed out tests he noticed that the boy next to me had pulled a transistor radio out of his jacket for a minute. "Don't ever bring that radio back, boy! They don't belong in high school!" The words had an acid tone, and I felt indignant at them. But we were being given directions now for the tests.

"Print . . . your *last* name, then a *comma*, your first name, and then your middle initial. If you don't have a middle name, make one up." Make one up? Was he serious? I looked up to find the counselor's face. "That way we avoid having seven Joe Johnsons, and we know who you are." He wasn't joking.

"Now, put down the school where you came from, the city. . . . Check whether you're a girl or a boy, and if you don't know, ask your neighbor." A few giggles were heard then. But he was looking at his watch.

"Now everyone hold their pencils up in the air." I was remembering the numerous college board tests I had taken, the complicated directions, the forms to fill in. And here I was, a senior in high school, holding my pencil up in the air, waiting for a counselor to say "go!" When he gave the signal, arms and lead hit table tops. Was I really a senior? I felt like a child.

I got lost on the way home that first day. I took a wrong turn and had no idea where I was. I tried to read street signs and watch out for strange people at the same time. I was wary of everyone. By the large Chicago Transit Authority barn I ran into a group of boys. "Hey, girl. . . . Hey, white girl. . . ." There it was again. I crossed the street as quickly as I could. But there I faced several Puerto Ricans. "Ooooo— I wonder where she goes to school?" I heard one whistle.

Were they all just waiting for me? How was I going to get home? I retraced my steps to the barn and turned the corner. When I reached Homan I knew Fifth Avenue had to be around somewhere. A black boy passed me smoking a cigarette. "You!" A woman was calling to him. "Where'd you get that? You give that back! I'll whip your ass!"

I crossed the street. The buildings began to look familiar. Finally I reached home.

The second day at Marshall I made friends with a white counselor, Mr. Hamilton, who greeted me each morning in 129 where new students waited while their programs were scheduled. Neither Daddy nor I had seen any other white students yet. I had the feeling this was going to be the most emotionally draining and lonely experience of my life.

"I don't know if we have your program yet, Sue. . . . Things work kinda slow around here," Mr. Hamilton said on the third day. I was becoming anxious to familiarize myself with the halls and find my classrooms. This certainly was discouraging. Anyone who didn't really care about school and happened to be transferring to Marshall might be tempted to give up.

The fourth day Mr. Hamilton was all smiles again. "Waiting for a program?" he quipped. "Have a seat on the other side of the room. It'll be three days!" I remember watching the clock, wishing I had brought along a book to read. I stared at the seat in front of me. "Love is what counts" had been scribbled on the back. The window next to me had three holes that looked as though they had been made by bullets. One was patched with masking tape. The other two were untouched. Cracks in the glass shot out in lightning streaks. Behind the pane was a heavy metal screen with crisscross wires like a fence—or a cage. "I'm sorry to inform you, but all juniors and seniors—your programs are not ready yet." We groaned.

Mr. Hamilton, knowing I was from New Trier, gave me preferred treatment. By fourth period of the fifth day I had my program and started going to class.

Lunch was by far my most difficult ordeal. There was no one to eat with, and I felt tight. I became accustomed to the stares. But was it curiosity or resentment I saw in the eyes of my fellow students? Boys approached me constantly. "Do you feel rich today?" one asked. He wants to borrow money, I thought. He thinks I'm an easy pushover because I'm new and white. "No, never," I shook my head. "What's the matter with everybody? Nobody feels rich. . . ," he walked off sadly.

"Have you got Jesus in your heart?" another boy inquired. He turned out to be a real clown hunting for a new girl friend. I had to learn to play along with the game and not take any words too seriously. I wasn't used to the long forty minutes to eat, the loud, noisy, interplay of students, and the faculty supervisors.

One supervisor reprimanded a boy for sitting on a lunch table top. "What would your old man do if you were sitting on a table at home? Would he hit you for it?" The teacher raised his arm in anger, and the boy skirted to another part of the room.

In my Contemporary American History class I recognized one of the boys who had attended an American Friends Service Committee meeting a year ago. He had been one of the loudest freedom singers. His name was Rudy Harris. "Negroes know they've been down too long. . . . They've been done wrong too long," Rudy said during a discussion. "The white man has so much that he doesn't have anything." Rudy was expressive and had strong convictions—definitely the most exciting element of my history class.

"Hey, this class is integrated!" a girl exclaimed when she came into my English class. Miss Dorn, a plump woman with her brown hair in a page boy, spent the first days of class giving us vocabulary words. "These words are the words used in the *better* schools," she said. "They are used on all those tests you have to take, and you'll want to know what they mean. . . . You want to succeed? This is it!" I cringed. Again we were like small children, wide-eyed at the feet of an all-knowing master. Her condescending manner was proof of her judgment of our ability.

When Miss Dorn had finished with vocabulary she went on with a book list of classics. She insisted on reading each title out loud and giving us her own brief summary of the story. Benjamin Franklin's autobiography told "how to be successful in life." With a patronizing smile accompanying her tiresome voice, Miss Dorn concluded the period with the observation, "Aren't you pleased with yourself when you've read something you *should* have?" I had to get out of her class.

Fortunately I was moved to Honors English where Mrs. Vashka charmed me. Of Russian descent, she was petite and hauntingly beautiful. Outlining our reading assignments, she said we would cover works of world authors—Koestler, Voltaire, Turgenev, Shaw, and several American playwrights. This was the top senior English class, and I felt challenged.

New Trier was one kind of draining experience and Marshall was another. I used to come home from New Trier tired of thinking. Intellectually I would be completely worn out. But Marshall was *socially* draining. There were 5,000 black students, and I had never had contact with so many people before. I was constantly alert to where I was and who I was with and what others' eyes were telling me. I felt most self-conscious in the hall. I tried not to let anyone's glance unnerve me. But sometimes I felt so alone. I couldn't wait to get home, close myself off in our small apartment, get something to eat, and turn on the radio.

Music was important on the West Side. Everywhere you went someone had a transistor blaring WVON, the large soul station in Chicago. In order to understand what Marshall students sang in the lunchroom, you had to listen to VON. Soul music permeated every part of Marshall and played a significant part in the lives of the students. On your way to class it was not unusual for four boys in front of you to "blow" a chord in perfect harmony, imitating the Temptations. Singing was a regular part of any lunch period, and portable record players were brought to school and set up on a table.

So I listened to the radio every afternoon to learn the newest "jams," and to pick up language. As a newcomer I was the equivalent of a foreigner in a strange country. Marshall students and I did not speak the same language. Someone said, "I'm hip!" What did he mean? "No jive, for real." What was that? "He got a strong rap." Define rap. "Where you cribbin' at?" That meant, "Where do you live?"

"What jam can I mash on you?" the disc jockey asked. "What record can I play for you?" I translated it. "Keep your game uptight." "Handle that action, baby," "You cut in on my play." The words, the phrases were endless. But I learned them, and slowly they became my own.

"Dudes" and "studs" were boys. "Blow your cool" meant to lose face. A "humbug" was a fight. A "box" was a record player. "The hawk" referred to the wind. "Hammers" and "y-l's" were girls. "Get a gig" meant get a job. "Gig" was also a dance. Marshall and WVON helped me build my vocabulary.

Senior girls were leaving the gym and running downstairs to the locker room when I felt someone push me. "Hi!" The voice was loud and brassy. "My name is Shirley. Want to share lockers with me?" She was the first girl at Marshall to invite friendship, and, relieved to have the burden of choosing a locker taken from me, I accepted her offer. "Have you got a gym suit yet?" I shook my head, responding, "I don't know where to buy one."

"Well, why don't you come shopping with me!" We made an arrangement for Saturday afternoon. Shirley agreed to meet me at my apartment.

It was warm out Saturday. Shirley brought a twelve-year-old friend, and the three of us waited for the bus on Homan Avenue. Shirley instructed me about how to buy a transfer, teasing me because I was ignorant of the city. Boarding the bus she continued to badger me. "Wouldn't it be funny if I just left you?" Looking out the window, I didn't think it was at all funny! I had never seen any of the buildings before and had little idea how far we were from home.

The bus rumbled to a stop. Shirley pushed me off, and I followed her, weaving my way through the crowds of black shoppers on West Madison. We purchased my gym suit first. Then Shirley said, "We're going to Madigans to look at some blouses." We entered a large department store and headed for the elevator.

"Three please," Shirley said. We went up, and Shirley's eyes began to roll. She held her stomach. "Three!" she cried, watching the arrow as it moved to four. "I said three," Shirley glared at the operator. We went down again. "Thank you,"

Shirley sneered and defiantly stuck out her tongue as we stepped out.

Then we were looking at clothes. "Hold these, baby." She dumped several blouses into my arms. "Come on, honey." She beckoned me into a dressing room.

"Unzip me." Shirley pulled off her dress and fumbled with the blouse's pins. "Ouch!" she jammed her finger into her mouth.

"Let me do it." I took her clothes.

"You're sweet." Her face puckered into a wry smile, and she pinched me.

Shirley turned toward the mirror, buttoning the blouse. "Ooooo, I like that! Give me that other one." I shoved it at her open hand, and without taking her eyes from the glass, she accepted it. "Ooooo, I like this one, too," she exclaimed, moving about in the second blouse.

"But, they cost too much. Let me see. . . ." Shirley held the two up before her, trying to decide which to buy. Finally she picked the beige. It was $6.00. "What we'll do is take the $2.00 price tag off that one, and switch it to this." She dangled the beige blouse in front of me. "Now take this $6.00 tag off. Come on! Help me." Shirley bent over her work.

The twelve-year-old was diligently pulling off a price tag. I couldn't move. I just stood there, watching. It had never occurred to me that anyone would consider switching price tags on a store's merchandise. Frantically, I began sorting through reactions that ran through my mind. I had always stood up for what I believed in and never faltered about making a decision. Yet, I suddenly found myself questioning if I could risk my first move toward friendship with what certainly would be considered a rebuff, if I raised any protest. I couldn't ask Shirley to properly replace the tags. She represented my first girl friend, and she had offered to help me.

In a few minutes the three of us were at the sales counter. "You'd like this?" the clerk asked.

"Yes, ma'm," Shirley smiled. I cringed when she took the package and winked at me as we walked away.

Even after several weeks boys still bothered me considerably at school. But gradually I learned how to handle their remarks and passes. I knew that "What's happenin'?" was a standard greeting and could be answered with a nod and a smile. I knew that some boys were sincere about their concern for me.

I was walking home, and a car stopped along the sidewalk. A dude stuck his head out the sidedoor and yelled, "How are you?" I didn't answer, thinking it wise, because I had never seen him before. But he persisted.

"How are you?" he asked again. I remained quiet.

A third emphatic "How *are* you?" followed, and, realizing that ignoring the situation was not the answer this time, I responded with a hearty "Fine!" To my surprise, the car sped away.

Most boys, however, were not genuinely considerate, and I had to assert myself to make my feelings clear. One particular boy plagued me stubbornly. He waited outside my Spanish class, often making it difficult for me to get inside the door. When the bell rang he was still outside, and I was flustered about how to avoid him. The final confrontation occurred the last day of September. As I left Spanish to go to my locker, he grabbed my arm tightly. "Are you ready, baby? Know where we're going today?"

Mustering my little strength, I yanked my arm out of his grasp. "I ain't going nowhere with nobody!" I announced brusquely. The words echoed in my mind as I marched triumphantly down the hall, and I was a little stunned at my own audacity. But I realized I had taken a first step toward forging my own way in this new world.

October

CHAPTER 3

I stepped onto the improvised wooden platform serving as stage, and the hot spotlight enveloped me. I couldn't see any faces, but I heard the restless shifting of the black audience. The Institute gym was filled to capacity with West Side residents of all ages, gathered for a community celebration. Emma Lee, a respected Fifth City leader, had just recited a poem about the beauty of the Negro, and it was my turn to entertain. I swallowed and adjusted the tiny microphone around my neck.

The opening notes of my piano introduction were barely audible above the hum of conversation and loose chatter gradually rising around me. This is it, Sue, I thought. Now or never. I closed my eyes and began to sing. "Lorna, Lorna and Joe . . ." My voice was unsteady and I fought to control it. "Somehow it sounds so right! Somehow you feel what I feel too . . ." All right, *now*, I told myself. "I wanna be with you! I wanna be with you, I wanna be with you!"

From somewhere on the right I heard a shout that resembled, "Yeah, baby!" But I wasn't completely certain, for the noise in the gym had reached a fever pitch, and I wondered if anyone was listening at all. Suddenly, however, I wasn't alone on the stage. Emma Lee, that huge black woman with blazing eyes, was standing next to me, her arm raised. My voice dropped. Music from the piano faded as Emma's powerful form commanded attention.

"We have gone to a lot of trouble to get this entertainment for you!" Her eyes rolled from right to left over the audience, and I felt her anger and strength quiet them. "Now you be quiet and listen!" she glared. "Give this girl a chance." Her last words were a tense whisper.

She touched my shoulder, nodded for me to begin again, and disappeared into a dark corner of the gym. I stood there under the light, a hand on my hip, sizing up the mood of the audience. "Are we ready now, people?" I whispered to myself. "Okay, here we go. . . ."

The silence that accompanied my beginning notes was almost frightening. But Emma's sudden intrusion had given me time to gather courage, and when I began to sing it was with new confidence. "I wanna be with you! I wanna be with you! Honey, life could be so great for us. Here's our chance, it's not too late for us. Grab it fast or life won't wait for us! I wanna be with you! I wanna be. . . with you!" The immediate whistles and thunderous applause made me smile. They liked it. I was beginning to belong.

Some days at school I wondered how anyone could learn anything. One Tuesday I went to Division, Marshall's term for homeroom, and Miss Crane never arrived. Since she brought the key in the morning, none of us could get into the room. We spent ten minutes standing against lockers in the hall. At the beginning of second period Mr. Wagner was not in class and again the door was locked. We weren't upset about missing algebra, but my feet were beginning to ache, and my arms hurt from holding books. After twenty minutes, however, Mr. Wagner appeared, grinning with a story about getting caught in a morning traffic jam. We had fifteen minutes of class.

Third period we were all dressed for gym inspection and lined up on the floor in rows. But again the teachers were late, and one was a substitute. They called roll all period—there are one hundred girls in the class—and the bell rang while we were still sitting in our suits on the floor. We had to rush to change clothes, write out our own late admittance slips, and have them signed by the gym teachers.

I did not arrive late enough fourth period to miss an exam in English. But I didn't have enough time to finish all the questions, and in my panic, was tardy for chorus. It didn't matter, though. As I walked into 237, Elijah, the senior president of chorus, was making an announcement: "Miss Ellis says that all those who have paid their chorus fees can go to lunch. She won't be in class today." I sighed, picked up my books, and followed a small group of students downstairs to the main floor.

I had two periods of lunch that day.

Because the city schools worked in shifts, I was through with classes at 1:18 and walked home by myself. One afternoon as I was heading for my locker, preparing to leave, I passed a group of boys who had congregated in a corner of the second floor.

"Hey, are you a teacher?"

Was he talking to me? Did he think because there were no other white students I must be on the faculty? And was he confused by my youthful appearance? Puzzled but still wary, I decided not to answer.

"Girl, are you a teacher?" My eyes focused straight ahead,

and my arms tightened around my books. Just keep going, Sue, I thought. I was about to turn the corner, when I heard muffled laughter. "Bitch," a low voice muttered.

I turned the corner, opened my locker, and put on my jacket. Perhaps I was foolish to leave school by retracing my steps down that same hall. But I did, probably from habit. Two of the boys from the group stopped me.

"How long you been attending Marshall?"

"Since September."

"How you like it here?"

"It's okay."

"Say, I'm awful sorry about what my friend said." One of the boys pointed to a dude in a yellow shirt sitting in a hall guard chair. The word "bitch" formulated in my mind.

"That's all right," I answered. A third boy had moved over toward the wall.

"Don't blame me," he said. "I didn't say it." His grin warmed me. And a fourth boy came up behind him. "You a senior?"

"Yes." The two were playing with each other. "Go away," one boy shoved the other. They both wanted my attention. "Do you know many people here?"

"I know some. I'd sure like to know more."

"Well, I might take you out sometime," he said. I was beginning to enjoy the feel of this game. "Don't bet on it," I teased back.

"Oh, he's nothin'," the fourth boy butted in, and I laughed.

"Well, this is James, and I'm Cornelius." James was wearing shades and a black shirt. "My name's Sue Gregory," I smiled.

"My *last* name is Hemingway."

"Oh, famous last name, huh?"

"Yeah. . . . What is it, Ernest Hemingway?"

"That's right."

"Well, we don't have any Ernest in our family." Pointing to Cornelius, James said, "He's my brother."

Within five minutes a touchy confrontation had turned into a pleasant episode, and I was laughing inwardly as I turned and headed for the stairway.

"I'll see you, Sue!"
I waved to them and left the building.

Marshall was five blocks from the Institute, and my journey
home was seldom uneventful. Each day I began the walk by
passing through the groups of boys in baskin caps and black
leather jackets who hung out on the sidewalk along Adams
Street. Perhaps they were cutting class or were free on their
lunch period. In any case, Adams was always alive with
activity. I often caught the wail of a "boss jam," a hip soul
record from someone's transistor, as I ran through the light
traffic and crossed the empty lot in front of school, absently
knocking glass and paper several feet as I went. Rusted cars,
long ago abandoned on the lot's weedy gravel, provided excellent resting places for boy and girl couples who sat on car
hoods, dangling their legs in the afternoon sun, or leaned
against side doors, teasin' and jivin' the hours away. Sometimes
a dude called to me as I approached. "Hey, baby! What's
happenin', sugar?" And I returned the greeting with a smile,
or perhaps ignored the words if I didn't like the grease in the
dude's "process" (the method by which his kinky hair had
been straightened and lay slick and flat on his head), or the cut
of his clothes, which suggested he was a "pimp" and not to be
trusted.

Beyond the lot I continued down Fifth Avenue, glancing
into the open doorways of dilapidated buildings, reading the
scrawled words and phrases—"VICELORDS," the name of a
well-known West Side gang; "Ruby loves Otis," someone's
declaration of loyalty. Once I noticed a large crowd assembled
on the corner of Spaulding and Fifth. Police cars were parked
along the sidewalk, and several officers in blue uniforms stood
on the sidewalk. I was curious, but I walked past the crowd
and went home.

When I turned on the radio in the apartment, WVON was
broadcasting the news: "Two Marshall students were shot in
the legs at the J&L Food Mart on Fifth Avenue this afternoon.
They were stopped by a man who demanded they give him

their transistor radio. When the students refused, the man pulled a gun. . . ." I had walked through the crowd minutes after the shooting.

Farther down Fifth Avenue another afternoon, the wind blew the upper-story window of a tenement onto the sidewalk. I was following several girls down the street when we heard a tremendous shattering. Someone screamed. Splinters of glass rained down onto the street in front of us as we turned and ran backward several feet. Fortunately, no one was hit. I don't think the building was occupied. It appeared as though it was scheduled for the wrecking crew.

Down by Vienna's, a hot dog place across from a gas station, I usually waited for the light to change. On the other side of Jackson and Fifth several men often sat out on the stoop of the local laundromat, next to a Negro-owned barbershop, and a lot away from the Certified Grocery where Ann and I shopped for Mom. This particular intersection was the hub of Fifth City's community activity, and crossing Jackson, I sometimes overheard the conversations of dudes talking on the corner.

"Hey, man, where'd you get the bread for them rags, man?"

"Got me a gig, jim, working over at Sears."

"For real, jim?"

"No jive, man."

"Hey, man, you seen Ronnie anywhere?"

"Ain't seen him. Where's he cribbin' at now?"

"Over on Monroe. Do-jim, you should see this babe he got. She is *fine.* . . ."

"Yeah? Well, dig here—I got me a rap, and I'll lay it on her one time."

"Well, look here, man. I got to make this run, check out the scene over on Congress. Handle it, now. . . ."

When the light changed on Homan I walked by the corner cleaners and several residential buildings. Sam's Cut-Rate Liquors was on this block. Once I glanced into the little alcove between two buildings and saw a black man standing there alone. He wore a shirt and hat tilted back on his head, and his hands held the sides of his pants which were pulled down onto his thighs. The sight of bare legs was blurred, for I turned my head quickly and kept on walking, trying to erase the strange picture from my mind.

Often I peered into the dirty front window of the deserted tavern on the corner of Fifth and Trumbull and then outlined in my mind the large yellow End Slums sign painted on the side of the brick building. Several afternoons on Trumbull I noticed a truck from the Chicago Sanitation Department parked along the curb. Its red leters spelled something about insect and rodent control. I recalled the tragic death of thirteen dogs killed on Trumbull in one week. Daddy and I had passed a dead animal one morning on the way to school. We knew it hadn't been struck by a car, for there was no sign of blood on its fur as it lay completely still on the sidewalk. The poison put out for rats by the Sanitation Department had meant the loss of the dogs, several of which belonged to members of the Order. I shook my head one afternoon, upon seeing the truck again, and looked down just in time to avoid stepping on a dead mouse with a thin gray tail.

Trumbull was the last block of my walk. It was normally a quiet street, lined with homes painted brightly by Fifth City residents. On the left corner of Trumbull and Van Buren a chain-wire fence closed off a parking lot used by employees of the Bethany Hospital directly across from the Institute. An aging cop, hired by the hospital, always sat on the corner next to the mailbox, waiting for some action. I couldn't help wondering how he would handle an emergency, however, should one arise. He was so old and had been injured one night when some young boys jumped him.

Most of the time I jay-walked across Van Buren, resting my books on my head like an African woman. I said hello to any members of the Order who were out on the street, pausing to talk for a moment, and stopped finally at the side door of the Institute's administration building to ring the bell. Upstairs the person on phone duty pressed a buzzer in response to my call, unlocking the latch on the door. I opened it, went upstairs to the main hall, checked the mail, and walked up another flight of stairs to the apartment, where I collapsed.

I braced the heavy tray against my shoulder and left the side door of the kitchen, crossed the Institute courtyard, and entered the chapel. It was the first weekend course of the fall quarter, and I was assigned to serve the students who had gathered on the campus from various universities and colleges in the area. Because of the great numbers of participants on such weekends, the chapel basement was often utilized as a classroom and dining room. But the kitchen was located in the administration building about a hundred feet from the chapel basement. This meant the trays had to be carried from one building to the other.

I had made several trips through the cool night air before I noticed a group of five neighborhood girls, all about nine or ten years old. One of them was wearing thick glasses and a pair of tan slacks.

"Can we go in the kitchen?" she asked, one hand on her hip, her closely cropped hair framing a head tilted to one side as she looked up at me.

"No, you can't go in there right now," I told her. Children from the neighborhood were not allowed inside Institute buildings, especially the kitchen, when the courses were in session.

But as I turned to re-enter the kitchen and load another tray of food, I heard her voice mockingly repeat, "No, you cain't go in there right now." I paid no attention and completed another trip to the chapel.

The girls were not going to give up on me, however, and outside the kitchen door I felt a sharp stab of pain. One of them had savagely pulled my hair. "Bitch," I said under my breath, smarting from the sudden small attack and wishing they would go away. But there was more food to be served, and again I walked across the Institute campus with a steaming hot tray.

The girls followed me. The one with the thick glasses stood out as the leader, and the other four took their cues from her. Their hopes for entering the kitchen were forgotten, and the girls asked if they could play in the chapel. I had been using the back entrance—cement stairs leading down into a dark cement hall with a door on the left—and all five girls began to run up and down the stairs.

"They're having seminars down there now, and you can't come in," I said as politely as I still could. The leader began mimicking me again in a squeaky voice, and ended up by asking, "Why are you so mean?"

I didn't answer, and she seized a fistful of my hair. I struggled to break away from her and managed to squeeze inside the chapel door with my tray still intact. I was breathing excitedly in the seminar room as I distributed the bowls, one for every eight people. The students were laughing and talking noisily, enjoying themselves inside, while I struggled outside to deliver their food.

Once again outside the chapel door, I stood for a minute in the dark, summoning my courage. I knew the girls were waiting for me. Five figures, one to a stair, leaned against the brick wall of the chapel, their faces lost in the shadows. Determined to face the situation, I began to mount the stairs slowly. The journey to the top was one of the longest I can remember. The girls began to push me around, tearing at my clothes and trying to trip me.

"Leave her alone!" I heard one of them say. By that time, my wrap-around skirt was half torn off. I held it around my waist, facing the leader standing on the top step. For a moment all was quiet as we stared at each other. I was prepared to walk right by her. "Why you treat us so mean? Why can't we come in?" she challenged.

I tried to retain my composure and not to fight back. But my first step forward triggered the final attack. The girls jumped on me all at one time, clawing at my clothes and my hair. I couldn't fend off five at once, and in the end I was knocked to the sidewalk. My head hit the cement, and I scraped my elbow badly. My skirt was thrown into the bushes when the buckles were finally ripped off.

The sight of me in my blouse and slip scared the girls, and they ran screaming out the front gate onto Van Buren. I picked myself up, found my skirt, and hurriedly wrapped it around my waist. One of the Order children was leaving the kitchen at the same time as David Norris came out of the chapel. I was shaken and they wanted to know what had happened. I shook my head, feeling hot tears in my eyes, and took refuge in the apartment. The four rooms were deserted because each member of the family was on weekend assignment like myself. Alone, I dressed my arm, put on a fresh skirt, and started out again. The food still had to be served. The job had been assigned to me.

As I began to walk down the stairs to the chapel back entrance—the same stairs the girls had held in seige a few minutes before—I slipped, turning my ankle severely. Tears stung my eyes again. I could barely walk. A member of the Order was leaving the chapel and saw me. He helped me up the stairs, and I managed to limp back to the apartment. There the frustration of the evening erupted, and I gave in to the release of a good cry. The story of the fight reached Al Langley, an Order member considered particularly wise and experienced in West Side community relations. He knocked on my door and came into my room.

While we talked, my ankle swelled and turned a bluish green. Al wanted me to go back outside, find the girls, and give them hell. He said it was the only way to handle what had happened and not to worry about being attacked again. It was my responsibility, he said, to let them know they had better not mess with me again. I had to stand up for myself. It was outrageous to let them treat me as they did. It was outrageous that I had not felt free enough to scream, "Don't step on me!" I should go out on the street, he urged, and set them straight with brutal love. I should show them I was a human being with dignity, thus revealing to them their own dignity as persons.

But I hadn't wanted to fight them. I hadn't wanted to hurt them. I didn't hate anyone. What Al said confused me. The whole evening had been a confusion. Possibly, next time, I would be more aggressive. But to go back out to face them again, that same night?

Al talked to me about Shirley, too. He said I should keep one step ahead of her and not let her feel she was getting the better of me. But why did I have to play these games, I asked? Confused, my face streaked with tears, I sat on my bed, feeling my ankle become tight. Al finally realized that I couldn't try to find the girls because of my ankle injury. Nonetheless, he assured me it was the right approach.

After Al had gone, I turned on the radio. I tried to relax, but the wheels of my mind spun about in confusion. Maybe I had been wrong. Maybe the language of the city is violence, and the next time I got into a fight, maybe I should be as vicious as my adversaries. But wouldn't love do more good? And why not love? Love *is* the most powerful social force. But would it help me on a dark street, when I was all alone?

But I don't hate! Must I meet the West Side on the West Side's terms? Could I survive any other way? Uncertain and bewildered, I lay down and closed my eyes.

The doctor at the Emergency Ward of Presbyterian St. Luke's Hospital, where Mom took me the following day, wrapped my ankle in an ace bandage and told me to soak my foot in cold water. He said I should wear the bandage for three weeks, but I ought to be able to go to school.

Just being white made anyone conspicuous at Marshall, but a sprained ankle added even more to the condition. My own shoes were too small to fit over the bandage so I wore one of Daddy's leather slippers on my right foot. I had to clump around the halls while everyone stared at me.

I was not allowed to participate in gym, so I sat and watched the other girls exercise. The instructors were understanding. Miss Fitch, the head of the gym department, asked me how I

felt. Miss Johns, my own gym teacher, allowed me to keep my
slipper on during the class, although I changed into my gym
outfit. A number of students asked me how I injured myself,
but no one seemed to believe the story. The girls all teased me
in the locker room.

"You got into a fight!"

"Well, yes, but that's not how I sprained my ankle."

"Aw, come on."

"I fell down the stairs. Honest!"

"Your boy friend pushed you—"

"No, he didn't! I *fell*."

Shirley rolled her eyes and I knew she wasn't convinced.
Why did they insist it was a fight? Spraining my ankle was an
accident, but I gave up trying to make them believe me, although I appreciated their concern.

Al Langley invited me to listen to four Fifth City junior
high school girls sing. He wanted to present them at the Fifth
City meeting as proof of the talent in the neighborhood. I
listened to the girls in the upstairs of the chapel. We had a
record player, and the girls sang the Marvelettes' "Don't Mess
with Bill," as the record played.

They were extremely shy, very withdrawn, and nervous.
Cookie, the tallest girl, stared at her feet, and little Brenda kept
giggling. Al and I did our best to open them up. After the
run-through, I advised the girls to *feel* the music, to loosen up,
and just let the sound pour out. "Be yourselves—that's the
most important thing," I assured them.

Several days later Al asked me to take charge of the girls'
rehearsal. I directed them through two numbers, gradually
gaining their confidence. At first they insisted on having the
volume of the record player turned up as high as it could go.
That forced them to sing louder. Slowly I turned it down
and, with encouragement, they weren't afraid.

They began to ask me questions about their routine. "Sue,
what about this? Did you like the way I turned . . . and
Cookie snapped her fingers?" I grinned and pointed out weak

spots in their footwork and their general stage presence. We worked on putting together a smooth, well-coördinated performance. By the end of the rehearsal the girls asked me if I'd be their manager. They wanted to make sure I would be at the meeting the following evening. Flattered, I assured them I'd be there.

The next evening, just before they went onstage, we practiced for the last time. The girls trusted me, and I was amazed at the transformation I had witnessed within four days. They had begun to sing with freedom and a sense of authority. They hardly needed the record. They were spirited and confident.

I laughed as we packed up the record player and prepared to go downstairs to face the meeting. "Do you see what's happened?" I asked. "Do you realize? When you first came here to sing you were shy and hesitant and unsure. You looked at your feet, and you were scared of your own voices. *Now*," I shook my head, disbelieving; they awaited my words eagerly, ". . . well, you're great!"

"Oh, Sue!" Kitty said. "You will be with us tonight, won't you?"

"Why, of course! Now you wait here. I have to find Al."

While Al introduced them to the audience in the basement of the chapel, they whispered to me, nervously. The number of people scared them. I squeezed their hands as they walked past me, sensing their sudden fright and praying they wouldn't withdraw completely. The record player gave me trouble, and the girls had to wait in their places on the stage, fidgeting and looking at the floor. When the machine finally worked, the girls had lost much of the spirit they had displayed during rehearsal. But I was proud of them anyway. We had a relationship of trust, and that was the most important element of the whole event.

Questions about my ankle injury came from both friends and strangers.

"Hey, girl, where'd you get that new suede shoe?" a boy asked me as I crossed the empty lot in front of Marshall one afternoon on my way home.

"Hey, white girl, what are you doin' wearin' a man's shoe?" another dude called.

"I'm starting a fad," I called back, amused at the curiosity.

Two weeks after my fall, I removed the bandage from my ankle, and my foot was back to normal. Waiting another seven days as the doctor had recommended didn't seem necessary, particularly since I thought I could walk well enough without the bandage. It was funny to notice how students glanced at my feet as though expecting to see me hobbling around. I enjoyed their double takes. Finally, the "new suede shoe" was gone, the endless questions stopped, and I was able to participate in gym again.

Homecoming was held on a Friday. For the first time in the history of Marshall, a large parade preceded the afternoon game. The parade started at one o'clock, and Miss Novotny took our Spanish class out onto the street to watch. I was really excited! The school band played; pom-pom girls and majorettes pranced down Monroe. Rudy Harris, from my history class, marched with several boys representing M Club. The ROTC was in perfect formation. A small motorcade included one decorated convertible with the two Homecoming Queen contestants seated in the back, cheerfully waving to everyone. Students carried flags and sang the Marshall loyalty song. Everywhere there were beanies in the school colors, maroon and gold.

When the parade disappeared down the street, it was time to go home, and I went sadly to my locker. On the corner of Homan and Fifth, I could still hear the band and see police blocking off traffic. Because of a ticket complication my arrangements to attend the game had not worked out. Now I was sorry, I really wanted to go. The parade had nourished my school spirit, and I realized as I walked the last blocks to the Institute that Marshall was *my* school. For the first time I felt a part of it.

November

CHAPTER **4**

It snowed lightly early in November. I looked out the window of my bedroom one morning and each rung of the fire escape had a little white ridge.

Despite the cold, Marshall's heating system was not yet operating. The rooms were freezing, and we sat through classes thoroughly chilled. Mrs. Vashka told us that for two years she had been pressing for better heating facilities in 204. The room was like an icebox in winter even when the heat was supposed to be working. She advised us to wear sweaters to English.

No place in the whole school was colder than the girls' gym, however, particularly when we were in gym suits. I rubbed my bare arms and legs and sat on my number, waiting for roll to be taken, trying not to shiver from the effects of the wooden floor which felt like cool, polished marble.

In the midst of the cold spell the administration began campaigning to get students to morning Division on time. Mr. Dixon, the counselor who gave me my placement test the first day of school, entered our division one morning. Not many of the students liked him. He was condescending and his lack of compassion was known all over the school. While he was explaining a pledge he wanted us to sign—"I promise to be in Division at eight o'clock"—a girl opened the door and began to walk to her seat. Mr. Dixon ordered her to stand still.

"Why are you late? Don't you have an alarm clock?" he yelled at her.

I looked at the girl's hard, tired face. Mr. Dixon's biting question echoed in the silence of the room as her eyes slowly met his.

"Yes," she said tensely. She began to sit down.

"Don't sit down till I'm through talking to you! If you have an alarm, didn't you set it? Didn't it ring?" he flung at her.

I dared not glance at my fellow division students. Though their faces were masked in bland indifference, I sensed a deep, underlying bitterness toward Mr. Dixon.

"I slept through it," the girl replied, struggling to control the rise in her voice and contain the anger that would surely bring disaster if unleashed. Mr. Dixon continued his interrogation for several more minutes and then began to leave. He kept the girl standing all the time he talked.

"Deadbeat," he sneered at a boy in the room who was dozing. With a final few words of advice about tardiness, Mr. Dixon vanished behind a slammed door.

The minute his figure disappeared, the room came alive. The chatter was instantaneous. We were united in our feelings against Mr. Dixon, and for several seconds we sighed with relief that he was gone and mutually moaned over our dislike of his oration.

But Miss Crane's voice stopped the flow of conversation.

"He's right, you know," she stated simply. All eyes focused on her desk, and for one brief moment I thought several boys were going to rush her. They rose from their seats, but hands restrained them, and the bell signaling second period snapped the electric tension of that instant.

Sometimes it suddenly poured over me at Marshall: "Where am I? And who am I, to be here?"

I thought a great deal about what Al told me the night I was involved in my first fight. I thought too about Al's advice concerning Shirley. I couldn't accept either.

Four of the girls who attacked me later apologized. They knocked on the apartment door after school one afternoon. Al urged them to talk to me, but I couldn't help thinking if I had sought them out that October night, the road to apology might have been blocked forever. I would have made permanent enemies. As it turned out, we became friends, and I had nothing to fear when I encountered the girls on the street.

Shirley shouldn't be treated brutally either, I decided. I was convinced that she hated herself. Shirley was critical of everyone. We ate together regularly during sixth period. Shirley found fault with other people's appearance, mannerisms, and speech. She told me racial jokes and made unnecessary comments, comments I felt revealed her own insecurity and self-hatred. Was she intentionally demeaning herself and her race in order to win the friendship of a white person, I wondered? Or was her obsession with race part of her own deep, sick, self-loathing? I wasn't certain.

Al had suggested I play her own game with greater skill. But that wouldn't have helped solve her self-image problem. Shirley needed to know she was accepted. She needed affirmation and support. All the love and understanding I could give her would be necessary to aid her in formulating a positive self-image. Striking back would only further enhance Shirley's feelings of inferiority. I just couldn't buy Al's methods.

"Hey, Sue!" someone called out. I recognized the voice and saw the arm raised high in the air.

"Rudy!"

We were both attending a Human Relations Conference at Thornton High School in Harvey. I had missed the departure of the main body of Marshall students and arrived late in a car with a teacher and several other kids. With half the day already gone, Rudy and I had finally found each other out of the tremendous crowd of high school students from all over the Chicago area. Delighted, we ran to each other and squeezed hands. "Man, am I glad to see you," I laughed.

"Come on, Sue," Rudy pulled me across the hall. "Join our discussion group. Come on, girl. . . ." I was quickly and efficiently whisked into a room and took a seat along the wall. Other students drifted in. Our discussion leader was a man from the American Friends Service Committee.

Rudy really led the afternoon's debate, however. He waged a verbal battle with two white boys from Gage Park High School. The three of them argued about Mayor Daley, the Democratic machine in Chicago, white backlash, and the Robert Taylor Homes—a two-mile-long housing project on the South Side. I kept waiting for an opening to enter the conversation and assist Rudy. I admired his beautifully controlled performance in the face of sometimes flippant, snide comments. Rudy was considerate, powerful, and sincere in his arguments. But I wanted to help him fend off the boys from Gage Park, and I couldn't find a means to lend my support.

By the close of the discussion Rudy was tired and I felt badly. I had watched a fellow Marshalite put forth great effort, yet I had not said anything in sympathy. I wanted to apologize to Rudy, but it was time to go downstairs and see part of a play in the auditorium. Rudy disappeared into the crowd again, and I was alone, filled with great admriation and respect for him.

I hadn't really thought about what I would say. I had prepared no written speech or outline for the presentation. The only props I took along were several Marshall newspapers. The incidents, the images, the experiences were all in my mind.

Daddy finished with his slides and talk about the Institute and Fifth City. We were sitting in the basement of the Winnetka Congregational Church, in a North Shore suburb near our former home. Twenty white New Trier students who were members of the church's youth group had come to hear us speak about the city and our move to the West Side. And it was my turn to face the group. I wasn't scared. I was concerned that I would be able to say all I felt, that I would at least be able to convey an impression of my love for Marshall.

The faces before me reflected curiosity, indifference, anticipation, and excitement. I began with an explanation of why the Gregorys had moved and how I had felt about changing schools. I emphasized the value of experience in both a city and suburban setting. As I began describing Marshall, the words came easily, quickly, falling over one another in a jumble of vivid memories. I talked about my classes, pointing out small, subtle differences between Marshall and New Trier.

"Probably the first thing you notice about Marshall is the vitality. The halls are alive with noise and teasing and jivin' around. At New Trier everyone is in a hurry to get to class on time. But half of Marshall is still in the hall when the bell rings! People sing in the halls. They sing in the lunchroom. Five boys, a table away from me, jam every day during sixth period. I'm eating and all of a sudden I hear 'Ooooo—I'm losing you!', the Temptations latest hit record. The boys start to laugh, and nobody thinks anything of it. Marshall is bubbling with energy.

"In the lunchroom, you should see the food! There are three lines every day. One is a snack line, the second is hot food, and the third has hamburgers, french fries, and coleslaw, every day! You can buy pop, too—coke, RC, and an orange drink! You can't beat that anywhere!" My obvious enthusiasm warmed the audience.

I told them of my confrontations with boys—until I was laughing and they were laughing and we were all relaxed with each other. Daddy had to signal me, indicating his watch, and I cut it off with, "He's trying to tell me I'm talking too long!"

A short question-and-answer period followed. They asked about gangs and whether I thought I was receiving a second-rate education. "I haven't had any personal contact with gang members. Gang activity doesn't seem as predominant at Marshall as it used to be. Marshall has a reputation for being a 'gang-banger' school, but the problem is not nearly as crucial or as serious as it was several years ago. There may be gangs operating on the West Side—Marshall boys may belong to them, but I have not witnessed anything specifically labeled 'gang activity.'

"As far as education goes, Marshall's standards aren't anywhere near New Trier's, academically. City schools are definitely inferior to suburban schools. But on the other hand, I am in several honors classes at Marshall, and the challenges are similar to any four-level New Trier class. I don't think *I* am suffering, because of the background I have, but Marshall students *are* suffering from the lack of high standards, in a general sense."

Afterwards in the car, driving along the expressway, Daddy and I talked about our reception. I kept remembering all the things I hadn't said. But at least I had shared a taste of Marshall with New Trier, and I realized, leaning back into the front seat, watching the bright lights of the city, that the West Side was home. I was glad.

Rudy said something marvelous in history: "The Negro doesn't have to prove his freedom. The white man just has to accept it."

I had a difficult time in chorus. We were learning "The Hallelujah Chorus," and very few of the kids read music. Miss Ellis had to play all the notes on the piano, drilling us by ear. I could tell when we were flat, and it irritated me. I felt as though I was fighting the entire soprano section to sing the right notes.

Despite the tendency to be flat, however, chorus was a refreshing break in the day. Everyone loved to sing. The boys particularly were spirited and fifth period was often forty minutes of fun and laughter. Delbert Jackson liked the harmony so much he would stop Miss Ellis in the middle of a passage by slapping Rudy's hand and saying, "Oh, man, do it again! Yeah, *do it again!*"

A Negro spiritual entitled, "Sinner Please Don't Let This Harvest Pass" required a soprano solo, and after class Miss Ellis auditioned six girls. I was asked to sing twice and got the part! Although I was pleased, I also was concerned that the other chorus members might resent my solo. Being new to the school and to the choir, and then walking off with one of the first leads offered, could offend them. I expressed some hesitancy to Miss Ellis, but she scoffed. "You have the better voice. You get the part," she said.

I was walking into chorus fifth period when suddenly I felt a hand in mine. It was warm and squeezed my palm. I looked up to see Delbert Jackson smiling at me. Delbert's ears stuck out, and one of his front teeth was chipped so that when he grinned he was about the sweetest thing on earth. I adored his tenor voice. We stood, swinging hands for a second.

"How you doin'?" he asked softly. "Fine," I smiled. And we took our seats.

When Miss Ellis told us to take out "Harvest Pass" from our folders, she made no announcement about the choice of soloist. She simply nodded to me to begin. The entire first page belonged to the soprano soloist and was sung without accompaniment. Nervously, I found my beginning note and sang, "Sinner, please don't let this harvest pass. . . ." I struggled not to falter. "Sinner, please don't let this harvest pass . . . and die, and lose your soul . . . at last. . . ."

Every eye in the room searched for the owner of the voice they had never heard in solo before. I felt small and humble when the eyes discovered me.

During sixth period Rudy approached my lunch table. When

I said hi he took my hands. "Ooooo, Sue . . . It was beautiful," he said.

"Did you really like it, Rudy? Did you really think it was
all right?" I didn't want him to tease me.

"Sue, you can sing, girl. . . . Ooooo!" His assurance made
me glow. It was all I needed.

Boarding the bus in front of Marshall I took a seat, hanging
my maroon robe on a pole above me. It was a Sunday afternoon, and the Advanced Mixed Chorus was to sing at a church
on South Ashland where Miss Ellis often played.

Looking out the window I watched another chorus member,
carrying a robe over his shoulder, walk past the empty lot
littered with huge logs. The West Side seemed desolate and
cold, wrapped in the gray haze of winter. I heard Miss Ellis's
voice from the front of the bus and some girls singing in the
rear.

It was way past the time Miss Ellis had told everyone to be
at the bus. Rudy hadn't arrived yet. I wondered if we would
leave without him. I didn't see Delbert either. And he and I
had a duet together! Somebody said hi to me. I returned the
greeting. The bus gave a rumble, and we pulled away from
the curb. I found myself listening to all the laughter and talk,
while I stared out the window.

I wondered how I could express my love for the people
around me, even though I still felt outside their chatter. My
silence isn't rejection, I wanted to say. I'm happy and where
I want to be. But please understand I'm not hip to everything
yet, and I need time to learn.

The bus turned a corner and the streets became dirtier and
more desolate. Whole houses were caved in between shabby
tenements, and bricks and wood lay tumbled forward, almost
reaching the sidewalk. Torn curtains blew from the broken
window of a house. A small girl in a ragged dress that barely
covered her thighs walked slowly down the sidewalk. "Black
Power" was scribbled on the side of a building. "Mighty Rangers" was painted on another. I tried to read a battered street

sign, but couldn't.

We turned onto South Ashland and arrived at the church. The bus parked on the corner, and we piled out. At almost the same time I heard Rudy calling, and from across the street, he, Delbert, and several other people got out of a car and joined us. My concern for them melted into relief that our group was complete.

It was fast growing dark. Inside the church we were led down a narrow hall to a room in the basement that had a piano sitting in front of rows of chairs. All the girls were combing their hair and putting on robes. We joked as we dressed.

The room looked as if it had been used for small services. There was a raised platform at the front with a podium on it. Pots of flowers and pictures of Jesus were scattered about the room along with wooden-handled fans.

We rehearsed without accompaniment and filed into the sanctuary to the choir loft on the right side of the church. Our seats were individual chairs covered with red velvet. There were too many of us for the loft, and we overflowed into the first pew on the main floor. Miss Ellis put all the basses there.

I sat on the end of the first row in the choir loft, looking out over the black faces. I was the only white present. There were several students from Marshall in the pews, but the majority of the small congregation were older men and women. They sat quietly listening to the women of their church, the leaders of the hour, read the Scripture and give announcements. Some of the women that spoke had to be called to the pulpit from their places in the sanctuary. Dressed in bright dresses and hats, they walked slowly, lifting their great weight with dignity.

Everyone rose to sing a hymn but no one had books. Everybody knew the song, including many of the Marshall choir. I had to fake my way through it, though I enjoyed listening and watching Rudy and Elijah sing. From his place in the first pew on the main floor, Rudy's sympathetic glances encouraged me.

When the offering was taken, collection plates were passed

around. A group of four women, in pastel dresses, came up to the front of the church where a table had been set up. Each in her own way made a plea for money. As the tray came to the end of my row, I realized I had no money with me. I was also unsure what I should do with the plate.

"Go on, Sue," Vera nodded to me. "Take the plate down." I rose from my seat and carried the plate to the ladies. They accepted it, and I returned to my seat, feeling my robe flowing around me as I walked.

The four women bowed their heads in prayer. One of them began to pray, and her words ran together, her phrases rising and falling as she knelt, clasping and reclasping her hands. When her words became frenzied, the second woman took up her cry, her voice reaching a fever pitch. During the prayers, the old men of the congregation contributed with "Amen!" and "Yes, Lord!" A woman kept repeating, "Don't you know," over and over. As the third woman began to pray, there was a moan from the back of the church. It became louder and was joined with another response from a different part of the sanctuary. Moaning and crying seemed to beget more moaning and crying. When the fourth woman had finished, there was a corporate prayer, and then all the voices faded into silence.

Several times during the service the Marshall Chorus was introduced. Vera and Elijah sang solos in "Waters Ripple and Flow," and Jasmine closed her eyes and sang the verses to "Fix Me, Jesus." The congregation responded with "Amen" and "Yes, Lord" and "My, my. . . ." Delbert and I sang "Sleep Little Tiny King," a calypso Christmas song, and I faced the church alone, trying to sing "Harvest Pass" with real sincerity, knowing the faces looking up at me saw and felt, as I did, my whiteness.

A women's gospel group had been expected to make an appearance and several references were made to them during the service. When they arrived, their director, a thin black woman, apologized for being late, explaining that she had been very ill with flu. She appeared to be weak and tired, but she told us she would try to perform anyway.

She grasped the sides of the pulpit, paused for a moment, then nodded to the accompanist at the piano. When she sang, her soprano was high and searing. She played with her voice, letting it out, and controlling it, revealing tremendous volume and amazing softness. The notes seemed to rip from her bowels, until her face contorted in pain, and tears streamed down her cheeks. She possessed incredible power and remarkable control. I was awed.

When it was over and I wondered where she found the energy to continue, she led her group in a rocking spiritual.

The Marshall chorus did one final number. Rudy, Elijah, and Delbert were called to the front and they led us in "Down By the Riverside." Although we had never practiced it, chorus members from previous years had sung it many times. I simply followed Miss Ellis, who was singing along. "Gonna lay my burden down!"

"Now where?" Elijah boomed.

"Down by the riverside! Down by the riverside!" we answered. Then Miss Ellis directed a special interlude, adding a layer of harmony with each verse. The sound we created was thrilling. "Down by the river . . . down by the river . . . down by the riverside!" The song seemed to last forever.

The service itself was interminable. Late in the afternoon, speakers continued to deliver meditations. Several chorus members had to leave.

Finally, when we were downstairs changing again, a little Negro girl came up to me. "You have a pretty voice," she said sweetly.

Back on the bus all the kids were keyed up, and I listened to gospels, pop songs, and Marshall cheers all the way home. En route, Miss Ellis suddenly called, "Is Susan here?" I stuck my head out from behind a robe. "I'm here. I'm here." She had missed me, but then, everything was all right.

Rudy wandered into history late and I said hello, but before he could get to his seat, Miss Wilson appeared in the doorway.

She was a huge, white teacher, with an iron face and short yellow hair.

"I want to see you," she bellowed, forcefully gripping Rudy's arms. He quickly wrote a note for the history teacher who was not yet in class, gave me a despairing look, shook his head, and as Miss Wilson dragged him into the hall, yelled, "*This* is why we march!"

I cracked up.

December

CHAPTER 5

In an attempt to improve my college board scores, arrangements were made for me to retake the exams at New Trier, where I had been tested in my junior year. On a Friday afternoon in early December I packed an overnight case, walked to the Kedzie-Homan El platform, and waited for a train.

The book I took along to read on the long trip remained unopened. I stared out the train window, watching the brick buildings of the city become well-kept suburban homes. Each stop brought me closer to Wilmette and nine years of childhood memories. Elbow on the window sill, fist clenched over my mouth, I settled deeper into my seat, trying to ignore the sight of familiar streets, as well as to control emotions at seeing them again.

When the train pulled into the end of the line, I picked up my overnight case and walked through the small station, pausing for a moment on the sidewalk. The four-way intersection was deserted. The clock over the drugstore across the street read a quarter to four. There was no sign of movement anywhere on the streets.

I began to walk past the stores in the snow, feeling the December wind bring color to my cheeks and watching the white cloud of my breath dissolve in the cold. Each step recalled the past, an image of another younger time when I had walked the same street, alone or with a friend. At the corner, I stopped, looking left toward the business section of the village and right toward the beach and Lake Michigan. The only sound was the soft slush of a car's wheels on wet pavement, several blocks away. Headlights glowed in the early evening. Was I the only person on Central Street, I wondered. Warm lights burned in the living rooms of the houses I passed, each wrapped in a thin blanket of white.

"Where is everybody?" I whispered to myself. The picture of a West Side street flashed in my mind—dudes in leather jackets talkin' jive on the corner, the sound of music from someone's transistor, a woman yelling from a second-story window at her husband on the sidewalk. Here, I was alone, with only the crunch of my boots in the snow to break the silence. Crossing the street, I saw two children, probably on their way home from school, walking down an alley.

The home of an old girl friend came into view, but I didn't want to linger. I felt driven to walk faster, to hurry through that life I had known, a life that had become strange and foreign and unreal.

I passed a street-corner mailbox. Ann and I had often walked to it on warm summer nights to mail letters. Across the street was the yellow corner house where I used to baby-sit two little girls. And at the end of the block was familiar, busy Lake Avenue, where the traffic flowed in a steady stream.

I deliberately stopped and looked for a long time at our gray home across the street. A second story light was shining through the bay window of what had been my room. At this time last year, I thought, I would have been in that room, tired after a day at New Trier and beginning a long night of studying. But the room belonged to another girl now. I could no longer walk up the sidewalk and enter the house.

Once, earlier in the fall, we had all gone back for a brief visit with the new owners. They were also family friends. They showed us their improvements—bathrooms brightly painted, new curtains in the den. The modern furniture appeared awkward somehow, lost in the vast space of that high-ceilinged Victorian living room. Red plastic-covered chairs in the kitchen seemed out of place, and I recalled the rustic air our battered picnic benches had given the family corner where we shared morning and noon meals.

Only the basement remained relatively untouched. While the rest of the family chatted upstairs, I wandered around the stacks of boxes and our stored belongings, smelling again the damp cement and remembering the long hours I had spent constructing miniature castles and towns. A mobile of birds, which Ann had made, still circled slowly from a string fastened to the ceiling. Weak light filtered through the dirt-crusted windows, adding a musty yellow coloring to the furniture and boxes.

I could hear the quiet of the countless afternoons when I had bent over a toothpick chair or stood back to admire a tiny pipe-cleaner character, newly completed. I recalled again the complex miniature metropolis Kathy and I had created on a ping-pong table, remembered the games we had shared together, the laughter and the music from a record player, while she carved a delicate soap pitcher for a bedroom and I glued the walls of a house together. We had toiled for hours. Time was such an abundant commodity then. Imagination was the key that unlocked our dreams and made dreams reality. We had lived a thousand adventures in the basement.

Gazing at the house I had patterned after a scene from *Ben Hur*, now covered with plastic and forgotten in a dark corner

of a bay in the basement, I felt great sadness. Some of the
rooms had been damaged, and it was as if someone had
wounded a deep part of me. Standing on tiptoes, I tried to
reach under the plastic to right a fallen table, put a hand-sewn
pillow back onto a clay couch. Why was it so hard to forget
young dreams? Why was it so hard to say goodbye to them?

At that moment our family visit was ending, and Daddy
came down the stairs to get me. He mentioned how unchanged
the basement appeared, as we walked past Ann's Beatle poster,
still taped to the wall, climbed the stairs, and closed the door.

Standing on the street corner that wintry December evening, I wondered if the basement had been cleaned since our
visit. But there was no time left now for childhood. I crossed
Lake Avenue and walked toward Janet's house. I rang the bell
and Janet answered the door. Best friends at New Trier, our
relationship was such that we could pick up wherever we left
off.

Janet and I had to wait outside New Trier's cafeteria in a
crush of students anxious to take their college boards. We were
jammed into the hall that Saturday morning. In all the pushing
and shoving I felt someone pull my hair. I turned around, irri-
tatedly, but no one was mischievously smiling at me. I
shrugged, and then winced as an elbow jabbed into my side.
The crowd was moving slowly forward to the registration
tables, but I couldn't understand why anyone had to be so
childish and impatient about waiting. At Marshall I had never
experienced such conduct.

The noise in the hall was unbearable, but through the up-
roar, I heard my name. "Sue! Hey, what are you doing here?"
I managed to move away from the shoving to see who it was.

"Peggy!" For a moment her red hair startled me. I had been
accustomed to black for so long. Peggy's eyes were sparkling
from behind tremendous, round prescription glasses, and I
laughed.

"Well, how *are* you?

"Fine," I responded.

"What's it like?" Another good friend had appeared at Peggy's side, and both stood looking at me eagerly. I knew what they expected to hear, that the Chicago public schools were as bad as everyone said. They wanted to learn about the violence, hoping I would confirm all the rumors, the myths, the newspaper stories. But how could I tell them my impressions in that stifling crowd? How could I give them the real flavor of Marshall and the culture of the city—a culture so different from anything they had ever known? What could I say that would be honest and would leave them with a clear impression of my experience?

We were moving toward the tables as I measured my reply. But, as I began to talk, I felt the girls slipping away from me. I knew that within a few moments they would be gone, content with whatever I had said and, busy with their own lives, their thoughts might never again touch the West Side. But I would be going back. I would re-enter the world of cool dudes, littered streets, and jive that was heavy and thick. Could anything I said reach them? Could I communicate anything meaningful before they disappeared into the cafeteria and were enveloped by New Trier and the North Shore again?

I could not think of anything equal to the task. Suddenly I felt an incredible barrier between myself and the two girls who had greeted me. They couldn't know what had happened to me. And they really didn't want to know. Another smiling face was beaming delightedly at me, and I said hi to Marilyn. "What's it like?" she asked.

"It's fun. I'm having a great time," I told her. I couldn't bring myself to elaborate. The barrier was overpowering, and frustration had won. I'm at New Trier again, I felt myself saying, I'm at New Trier. I felt empty.

"Hi, Sue." The tone of voice was light and surprised. But the face of a boy who had shared the 1965 Summer Seminar was a welcome sight.

"Hi, Bill," I greeted him.

"How's it going?"

"Great," I said, with conviction.

"Wonderful," he answered. I watched him disappear into the crowd to register. For a moment two people had communicated easily, naturally. Alone again in the crowd, I felt reassured and appreciated seeing Bill, who had offered me a note of hope and affirmation.

Almost the last one getting into the cafeteria, I had difficulty finding my seat. I hung my coat on the back of my chair and looked around the room. I could see the familiar faces of students I had known for three years. We were seated two or three to a lunch table, and no one spoke. I had changed, but they had not.

The proctor asked for identification. The only thing I had was my Marshall ID. When the answer sheets were passed out, the head of New Trier testing spoke to us, using a microphone. Both the new and old cafeterias were filled to capacity. The microphone and podium were set up midway between the two sections. Careful instructions were given to us on filling out the complex boxes on the sheets. If anyone had a question, he was told to raise his hand and a proctor would help him. I recalled Mr. Dixon and the placement tests I had taken my first day at Marshall. But I had been more comfortable in Marshall's library.

"You may break the seal of the test booklet with the eraser end of your pencil. Turn to Part One. You will be given thirty minutes. Read the directions carefully. You may begin. . . ." The image of pencils hitting table tops flashed across my mind as I tried to concentrate on the test before me.

But questions that weren't on the exam intruded to upset my efforts: Why must anyone be judged by a standardized test? Is such a result an intelligent criterion for college admission? What does it say about the human being?

The math section plagued me. After two hours I rebelled against the story problems, the endless riddles to be solved. I felt that I should stand up and shout that the test was meaningless, that it could not possibly evaluate me—my thoughts and feelings, the experiences that had shaped my personality. I glanced around the room. The faces appeared tired, but heads were still bent diligently over papers. Didn't anyone share my turmoil?

My palms were wet. My neck ached. I wished the proctor would call time for the last section. I wanted to leave—to run from the tension and pressure to achieve. I wanted to be out of that vast cafeteria where my humanness was being stifled by a proctor, a microphone, and a clock.

When the tests were finally collected, Janet and I waited on Winnetka Avenue for her father, who drove me to the El station for the return trip. I was so tired I almost fell asleep twice on the ride home. At Kedzie-Homan I got off the train and stood for a moment on the platform. Cars rushed by on the expressway and a lone black boy sat on a bench, his elbows resting on his knees, waiting for a train to the Loop. I could see the Sears and Roebuck home-office tower. It was the most predominant building of the skyline and seemed to rule like a monarch over the West Side. Rows of brick houses stretched along Congress Parkway, and someone with the symbolic black beret of Fifth City crossed the expressway bridge.

Walking up the ramp from the El I heard a voice call out, "Hey, baby!" I began to relax. I was back in the ghetto, my home.

The following Saturday I got up early, had breakfast, and dressed. Daddy drove me over to Crane, another over-crowded black West Side high school. It was eight o'clock on a cold, gray morning. A layer of snow and ice lay over the city, and it was still snowing lightly when I stepped from the car.

A white boy preceded me into the side entrance of the school, and two men directed us to the third floor lunchroom. The white boy told me he was from Tuley High School. We showed our admittance slips to the teachers at the door, and we chatted as we entered the cafeteria. We were at Crane to take the ACT's, the American College Tests required for all students seeking state scholarships.

Taking off my coat, I waved to a girl from my Marshall English class, to Cordell from my algebra class, and to two boys from Spanish. I didn't feel nervous or tight. There was no pushing or shoving this time, and the quiet in the room was relaxing. Some of the students appeared older, and were probably junior college level. The rest were from high schools. Most of them were black, and a few were Puerto Rican.

The boy from Tuley shared a table with me, and we talked. Students continued to enter the room, some carrying packages as if they had come from shopping, others were bundled in jackets, scarves, and gloves. Each person was directed to a seat. There was nothing formal about the testing procedure. I felt no pressure, no academic coldness. The proctors talked to us as if we were real people. "Are we all ready to go on to the next part? Have we completed part nine now? Okay. . . ." It was a contrast to the impersonal atmosphere of New Trier.

There was no microphone set up at Crane. It wasn't needed. There were fewer students for the ACT's, and the proctors simply talked to us as they circled the room, helping anyone in need. Even after the test had officially started, students were admitted and provided test materials—an unheard-of procedure at New Trier!

A policeman was present in the room during the entire morning. I wondered why he was needed. A quieter, more serious group of people I had never seen. The officer wandered around, gun on his hip, passing out and collecting papers at the appropriate times and occasionally falling asleep on a chair by the door.

I didn't finish all sections of the test, but I was neither upset nor frustrated by that fact, for I felt like a "person" in a school where the reality of unique personhood was recognized and respected.

When the ACT's were over, the boy from Tuley told me he had never had any geometry or algebra in his life. A great deal of the math section had required knowledge of both, and I was shocked. "How could you get by without taking either?" I puzzled out loud.

"I had four years of bookkeeping," he answered.

The proctors let us out, a group of tables at a time. I buttoned my coat, and the boy from Tuley said goodbye to me on the sidewalk, car keys in his hand. Alone, invigorated with a sense of independence, I walked to the El and rode two short stops home.

After three months at Marshall, some of the intricate problems besetting a ghetto school became apparent. I began to comprehend the cultural patterns and to discover the intricate and complex web in which the students were entangled. Behavior at school was often directly affected by what had taken place at home or on the street the night before. Understanding a student's actions in the classroom required a clear understanding of his family and community environment.

Marshall enabled me to put the pieces of a troubled ghetto area together. I watched teachers attempting to cope with problems too vast and overpowering to be solved by one person, no matter how well-intentioned that person might be. Marshall enabled me to feel the frustration of both teacher and student, to share the small but human incidents that were a part of a friend's life in the city, and gradually to appreciate the context out of which they had originated. Through daily encounters with Marshall teachers and students, I was brought face to face with the frightening realization of the complexity of black, urban problems.

The door to Miss Crane's room was locked early on Monday morning. Leaning against a locker waiting for the teacher to arrive, Brenda and I talked.

"I didn't get a chance to smoke a cigarette this morning," she complained. She went on to tell me she hadn't finished some of her homework because she had to work the night before.

"But this shorthand," she smirked, holding up the book, "it ain' learnin' me nothin'." I laughed. Brenda was a tiny girl, about my size, and we had become good friends.

"You know, Sue, my back's been killin' me."

"Have you gone to a doctor?"

"I did, but they don' never tell me the truth. The first doctor
I saw tole me I had kidney trouble. I had to go to the hospital.
Now I've got three sets of pills, and this other doctor, he tole
me I was anemic, real weak, you know—and I didn't eat the
proper food." She shrugged. "My mother says I should quit
work." Every day after school Brenda kept the books at a
clothing store. "But I'd rather drop out of school. I like
workin' there. It's fun, away from home. Besides, if I quit,
it'll have to be after Christmas. The money I'm makin' *is* our
Christmas presents. PERIOD."

"But you should consider your health," I cautioned.

"I just wish that old Miss Crane would get here," Brenda
grumbled, changing the subject. "She talks about signing
pledges to be on time. She ought to sign one herself!"

When Miss Crane did arrive, we had just enough time to
hear the bulletin before the bell rang. I waved to Brenda and
climbed the stairs to algebra.

Violet was sitting on a chair in the hall, bent over a paper,
as I approached. She seemed to be at least twenty-five years
old, wearing earrings, knit sweaters, and heels to school every
day. Perhaps she was that old—in experience.

"Sue," she greeted me, "did you finish your homework?"
I nodded, remembering the equations I had struggled with the
night before.

"Are you having some difficulty?"

She looked up at me, and I could see the dark shadows under
her eyes, even though she had tried to hide them with make-
up. "My boy friend was spitting blood last night. I spent the
whole night at the hospital with him. I didn't get a chance to
finish this," she pointed to the paper in front of her.

For a moment I didn't know what to say. Was homework
important in the face of hours spent worrying in a hospital
waiting room? How did algebraic equations speak to Violet's
life? How did they relate to her boy friend spitting blood?
If there had been time, I would have helped her, but the bell
rang, and we hurried into class.

Mr. Wagner handed back tests we had taken the week before. Sixty-five per cent was written in red ink at the top of mine. I shook my head, knowing that would mean a C at New Trier. But when Mr. Wagner put the grading scale on the blackboard, 65% was the highest mark in the class. Would that mean an A for me when 65 out of 100% was such a poor showing?

"I don't want to embarrass one student in this class," Mr. Wagner said, standing in front of his desk, "but on the last two tests, Susan Gregory has gotten the highest grade. She does not have the highest math aptitude in the class, but she does have something else, which she got in another school system—good study habits. Those of you who are college bound will have problems your first year if you don't have good study habits. You just won't make it."

I had always had difficulty with math. My high rank in Mr. Wagner's Algebra II had given me new confidence and initiative to tackle a subject that had always been my stumbling block. But if I was doing better than anyone else, what did that say about the skill of the others in the class? Obviously, measured by New Trier's performance level, a good many would fail. It was a stark thought to consider what little mathematical proficiency these students would graduate with or to weigh them against New Trier standards.

Cordell asked to see my paper. He sat across the aisle from me, always forgot a pencil, jumped up and down in his seat eagerly waving his arm when he wanted to answer a question, and was generally the loudest, funniest boy in algebra. I had become fond of him, supplying him paper and pencils. We often put our heads together over problems, while Mr. Wagner wrote on the board. When we thought we had the answer, Cordell would beg Mr. Wagner to call on him, and Cordell always winked at me when Mr. Wagner said he was correct.

Cordell had done poorly on the test. He fingered my paper, smiled, and handed it back to me with an awkward expression of praise. I considered asking him what mistakes he had made, thinking perhaps I could do something to help him. But he began beating his desk top lightly, with the palms of his hands, simulating an African rhythm. He played the drums in band and was known for his dexterity with bongos.

He had learned to shut out disquiet and was lost in the enjoyment of sound. For those few moments he was in his own world, untouched by low scores on algebra tests; untouched by Janis, to my left, who was talking to Denise; by Willie who sat in the back of the room reading a newspaper; by Anthony who was going over his paper carefully, trying to understand where he had been incorrect; by Gloria who sat sullenly staring out the window; by Joe, whose arms were folded in front of him and whose head was bent, eyes closed, exhausted from whatever had happened the night before. Remembering Violet's conversation, I wondered what *had* occurred in Joe's life last night.

I pulled my books, gym suit, and shoes into a pile. Mr. Wagner called out the next day's assignment, Cordell finished his creative rendition, and the bell rang.

The locker room was hot, and Shirley arrived as I was dressing for gym. "You cain't hurry love—no, you jus' have to wait. . . ." Shirley sang as she dumped her clothes inside the locker.

"Ooooo, Susie polished her shoes!" she teased me. I unfolded my gym suit carefully, trying to keep it as wrinkle free as possible. My shoes were a bright white. Maxine began to unwrap the plastic protecting her suit, and Ray Etta walked into the locker room with her uniform on a hanger, washed, ironed, and carefully covered with plastic.

Monday was inspection day, and this time I wasn't taking any chances. The week before, Mom had ironed my suit for me and, not realizing the high premium placed upon such details, had failed to remove all the wrinkles. When my row was called up to the front of the gym to be checked, Miss Johns was displeased with me. My shoes were polished, and my socks were properly rolled down at the ankle, but she objected to my suit. Failing inspection meant failing gym, but, more importantly, failing gym meant not graduating.

Surprised but resigned, I had returned to my place in line. As we were exercising Miss Johns stopped in front of me. "It does *look* clean," she commented, eyeing my gym suit critically.

"Oh, Miss Johns," I agreed, "I did wash it, my mother ironed it, and I folded it. It *is* a little wrinkled."

"All right, Gregory. Come with me." The whole class watched as I stepped out of my row and followed her into a side room with a large mirror. Seeing myself as she had, I had to admit I looked unkempt. She left me alone in the room, and a few minutes later, I heard her call my name. "Gregory!" Going to the door, I found that everyone else had left the gym.

"You can pass. I just wanted you to see how you looked. Do you understand?"

"Yes. I'm sorry it's so wrinkled."

Downstairs in the locker room, the girls all pressed around me, wanting to know why Miss Johns had taken me out of the gym. I sensed they would have been indignant and angry if I said Miss Johns picked on me unnecessarily. They would have fought for me. I told them it concerned my suit, and they accepted the truth. Still, their interest pleased me.

This week I was prepared for gym inspection. When Miss Johns called our row to the front, I passed without a comment. Inspection took almost the entire period to complete. This extreme emphasis on appearance seemed silly to me. Rarely did we do anything athletic in gym. We had had several days of soccer, three days of what the instructors called basketball, and some acrobatics. But there wasn't enough time for everyone to try a roll using the mat. Forty minute periods were too short for classes of a hundred girls. Consequently, the most important aspects of gym had become clean suits and simple exercise calls of "one-two-three-four."

Mrs. Vashka didn't come to English fourth period. Some of the boys left. The rest of the class worked quietly. I was reading when Odetta Thomas stopped by my desk and asked me if I was in the Honor Society. I told her I had not applied for membership.

Odetta said it didn't matter. She needed help planning a tea for the society and wanted ideas. It seemed no one was willing to take the responsibility for the entertainment. The tea was scheduled for the following week. The best skit anyone had suggested dealt with the Nativity.

"I really don't think that's appropriate," I told her. Odetta half smiled in agreement and resignation. I had confirmed her own misgivings. She had come to Chicago from Mississippi. When she walked, she carried herself proudly. Though only a senior in high school, the lines of her face spoke of her maturity, and I felt I was in the presence of an experienced black *woman*. I admired her strength, her toughness, her special wry humor. We began to talk about student apathy.

I mentioned examples of New Trier student indifference, and then explained what I had seen at Marshall. "Really, Odetta, I think every school has its own apathy problem. At New Trier we had rallies and posters and special meetings to promote an event. Here at Marshall we are limited to the use of newspapers and posters. There is definitely a publicity problem here. Students don't receive the news of programs soon enough, if at all.

"At New Trier we had intercoms that could be used every morning in advisor room—the equivalent of our Division. Any school organization could promote an event using the speaker system. New Trier had better facilities for publicity and less administrational red tape.

"In our Marshall classes, each teacher uses his own approach toward overcoming apathy. Mr. Wagner asks us each morning, 'Are you going to the game? You should go! Why aren't you going?' He even gives extra credit for attending a play or an athletic event! I've heard about an economics teacher who threatens her students with failing her course if they don't purchase tickets to school functions. Mr. Carlson emphasizes what you missed if you weren't there. My Division teacher simply shrugs and says, 'Well, it's your school. . . .' "

Odetta asked me what I thought was needed to make an organization interesting and how we could induce students to become contributing members. We brainstormed ideas, reaching the conclusion that, although we both were aware of apathy, neither of us knew any real way to deal with it.

By the time Odetta left my desk, I realized I had not given her any suggestions for the tea. But I felt reassured because of our shared interest and concern about Marshall school spirit.

"Hey, Suuuuue!" The arm was raised high and I knew that loud, open greeting belonged to only one person.

"Rudy!" I yelled. He was standing outside chorus and took my hand in his. We walked together into 237, taking our black folders off the piles on the piano. Miss Ellis played the opening chords of "Sleep Little Tiny King," but as she began to direct, she noticed that Sheila, an alto, didn't have her folder.

"Sheila, would you get your music, please."

"I can't find it."

"Look for it then."

Slowly Sheila rose from her seat. She meandered down to the piano, casually lifting absent students' folders and other objects from Miss Ellis's nearby desk. She finally located her music.

"Where did you find it?" Miss Ellis's question stopped Sheila on the way back to her place.

"Another girl had it." There was a tension in her voice. "She wasn't s'posed to be using it."

"You just didn't look for it," Miss Ellis clipped. Sheila's large round eyes were blank and staring. They rolled to the ceiling, and then focused on the folder she had in her hand. "I don' have all my music."

A girl at Miss Ellis's desk gave Sheila the missing song. An argument ensued. Suddenly we heard the slap of Sheila's folder hitting the floor.

"Why did you do that?" Miss Ellis was standing by the piano now, trying to contain herself.

"That girl threw the music at me." Sheila glared at Miss Ellis. No one in the room moved.

"Pick it up! Pick up that folder!" Miss Ellis's command was ignored. Sheila began to talk back. "You ought to be ashamed of yourself!" Miss Ellis suddenly stormed. "Now shut up or get out!"

Sheila slowly returned to her seat. We began to work on "The Hallelujah Chorus." Immersed in rehearsal, the discipline incident was forgotten. But Miss Ellis caught Delbert chewing gum, reached behind the piano to the blackboard, and let an eraser fly. He ducked, and it narrowly missed its target, streaking his hair white.

Near the end of the period when we were laboring hard and listening attentively to Miss Ellis's instructions for improving our technique, the basses sang the wrong words— "And he shall reign forever, forever!" It should have been "forever and ever." Miss Ellis's hands came down onto the piano keys in a rage. She pounded several dissonant chords, stamping her feet on the floor at the same time. "No, no, no, no!" Her eyes fixed on the guilty persons. A taut silence hung heavy in the room. I breathed with relief when the rehearsal finally continued.

Before I went to lunch, I stopped at the main floor washroom. Opening the door, I was immersed in smoke. Several girls stood talking in a dark corner, cigarettes in their hands. We never spoke, although we were almost always there at the same time every day. I went directly into the first stall, the one with the door I knew could be shut. All the latches were broken, but I wadded paper between the rusted latch and the side of the doorway. Whenever there was no paper and I didn't have extra Kleenex in my purse, I bent over and kept my head against the door.

There was one sink on the side wall, but rarely were there any soap or towels. The tendency was not to wash your hands. The two mirrors were never cleaned. Once in a while, when I'd forgotten my comb, I'd borrow one. I never could remember the pomade grease until I had the comb in my hand, but I used it anyway.

"Hi, Sue." Jerry slid into a chair next to me in the lunchroom and sank his head into his arms sprawled on the table.

"Hey, aren't you cutting class?"

"Yes," he grinned. He was one of Daddy's sixth period students, but sometimes he came to the lunchroom early, and we talked.

"What class are you cutting?" I teased.

"English," he whispered. I shook my head in disapproval. "Oh," he sighed, "I just can't make it to class every day. It's awful hard on a Monday."

"Uh huh," I answered, wondering how I could push him to go, but knowing it probably wouldn't work.

"Say," he said, touching my shoulder and pointing to a girl a table across from us. "That's my newest flame."

"Really?"

"Yeah. Her name's Cassandra. She's the one with the blue blouse on. She's really a cute dish." He winked, and I laughed.

"Does she know you? Have you talked to her?"

Jerry said no. He was always eyeing girls from a distance but never making any other overtures.

"Hey," he suddenly said, "I gotta go."

I wasn't alone long, however. Alvin sat down next to me, put a hand on my leg, and said, "When am I gonna teach you that thing called love?" I tried to ignore him, but I could hardly disregard his hands. "Don't want to love a *colored boy?*" he asked. "See how fast my hands move?" At that I pulled his hands off my thigh and shoulder, and flung them onto his lap. At the beginning of the year he had been preaching the "gospel," and had wanted to know if I had Jesus in my heart. Obviously, his interest had changed!

Eventually Alvin bounced off to another table and another girl. I was by myself again in the lunchroom when a little dude quietly joined me. "Susan, Susan," he said, and I looked up to find Hosea.

"How you doin'?" I spoke softly.

"Fine."

I remembered the day, not long before, when he had talked about himself during lunch. "My folks, you know . . . they don' get along too well. They act like everythin's all right, you know, but every night they fight and holler at each other. My Dad comes home from work, and he's late. He works the night shift, see, and Mom, she says, 'Where you been since you got off?' and he tells her, and she says, 'You're a liar,' and they really get into it.

"I was doin' real well in school when I was a freshman. Sophomore year I was on the baseball team, you know, but when my folks started carryin' on, I had trouble concentratin' on my studies. I started messin' up. By the time I was a junior I couldn't handle it anymore. Home was gettin' to me. I couldn't think about nothin' else. I started to cut class.

"When Mom and Dad would fight at night, I'd try to get in the conversation and help, but Mom always said, 'Shut up,' so I went into my room, got an attitude, became hostile, you know. . . . I jus' went in my room and listened. My older sister, she was married. She didn't really know what was happenin' at home. My younger brother was out on the street —he wasn't home as much as I was. I knew and they didn't.

"So when I was a junior, long 'bout in March, I dropped out of school. I was confused. Didn't nobody come to see me anymore after that. I didn't see anybody 'cause I wasn't in school. Only people that came over to my house were Rudy —my main dude, my runnin' buddy, my ace boon pahdner— and George, a counselor from Young Life. I was ashamed to show my face in school. I jus' couldn't go back to Marshall cause I had leff."

"What did you do every day?" I asked him. "How did you spend your time after you dropped out?"

Hosea paused and then looked at me sadly. "Oh, . . . I got up in the mornin', . . . and I walked downtown, . . . and then, . . . I walked back. . . . Then I'd go to a bench in Garfield Park and sit, . . . and think . . . about home . . .

and all the things that had been happenin' to me. . . . I'd try to figure out what to do, you know. . . ."

I nodded. "But finally Miss Ellis and Mr. O'Bara and George and another teacher all got together at my house. I asked them, and they came and they helped me get back in school. You know what I want to be? I want to be a Certified Public Accountant! I got a B on my geometry final. Yep! I worked real hard. I like workin' with figures, you know. And now I want to go to college. I don' want nobody to jive with me about my abilities. You know, I want them to come outta their bags and tell it straight. But I'll work hard as I have to. I want them to tell me what I'm not doin' right, where I have to work harder. You know, like, don' play with me, man. Come on!"

I had laughed with him, but I also felt a strong admiration for someone who had traveled from performance to total alienation and back again.

Now Hosea and I were close, trusting each other. "How were your classes today?" I asked him.

"They were okay. But I don' like them."

"Why not?"

"The teachers—they don' care. They act like it's jus' a job to do, you know. They have to do it, so they do. But they don' care."

"That's rough. But listen, Hosea. Don't let it stop you from learning. It's too bad that sometimes you have to learn almost *in spite* of the teacher, instead of with his help. But fight anyway. All right?" He could see the pleading in my eyes, and he smiled.

"Yeah, I'm gonna work anyway," he promised.

Mr. Warren wasn't in history seventh period. We wrote our names on an attendance sheet, but several boys signed in and left the room immediately afterwards. Those of us who stayed had a lively discussion. Rudy, Walter, Otis, Charlcie, and I gathered in our corner of the room and talked.

Ronald, as usual, was in his jazz bag alone at his desk. He

played the French horn in band and hoped to be a composer
some day. Often in history he would sit in his seat, wearing
shades and moving his arms up and down in the air as though
playing an imaginary bass. With his eyes closed under his
shades, he added a vocal "boom, boom" accompaniment to
his hand movements. Once Mr. Warren had concluded a sentence of his lecture with ". . . and all that jazz." Ronald had
looked up out of his daze. "Jazz?" he echoed, out of a reverie.

"Be cool, Ronald. It wasn't what you thought," Mr. Warren had assured him, and Ronald slipped back into doing his
thing.

I knew Ronald had no lunch period. When he left school
in the afternoon, he went straight to work at Sears and did
not get home until late at night. He was usually so tired he
didn't do any homework. He was very bright, but unprepared in class. I watched his rhythmic absorption until Rudy
caught my attention.

"Hey, d'you know, coming home from a party in Chi it's
safer to walk down the street at three in the morning than
at six o'clock at night? Now in the suburbs at six," Rudy was
saying, "boy, it's quiet, man." Walter mentioned Mayor
Daley's bond issue to light the alleys, and everyone laughed.

"Yeah, I been waitin'," Walter said, "and there ain't no
lights yet!"

"But hang on, man," Otis pounded the table. "They're
gonna fix it so we can *see* the rats when they come out to
git us!"

The subject changed to college tests. Rudy joked about
how he and Elijah had guessed their way through the ACT's.
"You should have seen Elijah! He say, my boy say, 'Now
there's gotta be a system, man. If the answer to that was
number two, then this has gotta be four, see?'" Oh man, it was
thick!" Rudy waved his arms in the air, and I cried with
laughter.

Charlcie interrupted Rudy. "Y'all better face it. Those tests
were made for white, middle-class kids."

How could Marshall students be expected to score well

without basic grammar skills and exceptional vocabulary? How could they be expected to answer questions completely foreign to their own lives, which had nothing to do with their own culture? The tests were geared for the white, middle class, and yet Marshall students were being judged by *those* standards.

It was disturbing to see Rudy worried about tests. As Rudy, Charlcie, and I walked down the hall after class, I reassured him that not all colleges base their admissions qualifications on board scores. "Look, man," I said, "grades aren't everything. Some schools pick for the person. That's where your recommendations come in. Rudy, you've got more personality than anyone I've ever met! Colleges want variety, not a lot of brainy bookworms." But how could I make him understand?

He walked beside me with his head down, briefcase half slung over his shoulder, listening carefully, seriously. Since our first meeting over a year ago I had observed Rudy in a variety of demanding situations. In all of them he had given evidence of talent and intelligence, of charisma and leadership potential. How could any college refuse Rudy Harris? The idea was unthinkable! The thought of Rudy filled with anxiety because of test scores infuriated me.

"Rudy, you're *going* to get in college," I assured him.

"Sue, I'm gonna make you late for class. I'm fittin' to make a run." We were standing outside Spanish, and Rudy had my hand.

"Okay."

"Be cool." He turned and went down the hall. Charlcie and I made it inside the door just as Miss Novatny was beginning. "Clase—" She turned to me. "Cierra la puerta, por favor." I closed the door, and forty minutes of rapid-fire Spanish began. Miss Novatny never let us rest for one moment. Not until the very end of the period did we ever get release from relentless dialogues and drills.

Then one of Charlcie's friends turned to me. "Sue, you live around here, don't you?"

"Yes."

"How come I never see you on the street? Don't you even go to the laundromat?"

I laughed, explaining that the Institute had a laundry room where everyone washed his clothes. So I had no need to leave the campus for that. "But I *do* come out!" I added.

She slid down into her seat as Miss Novatny gave us an assignment. I noticed that Ronald was asleep at his desk. He probably didn't get home from work until very late last night.

When the bell rang, he woke up and joined us again as we moved out into the hall. I walked to my locker, selected the books I'd need for homework, put on my jacket, and left the building.

At the corner of Fifth and Spaulding, a car stopped as I was waiting to cross the street. A dude stuck his head out the window and yelled, "Hey, girl! Are you prejudiced?"

Had I heard correctly, I wondered. There I was, standing on the littered curb, books in my arms, tired—standing in what was now my home—standing there, as I did every day, alone, white. I began to laugh. I couldn't say anything. All I could do was laugh.

Surprised and puzzled, the dude pulled his head back into the car and drove away.

It was a long walk to the front of the Marshall stage. It was a long walk out to the apron of the auditorium where the one microphone stood, and I had to travel it all alone. I had the feeling of being in space, confronted with total blackness, knowing the audience for the Christmas Festival sat before me, but unable to distinguish faces.

I was nervous. I wanted to perform as well as I had in rehearsal, but my knees were shaking, and I knew my voice would quiver, too. I couldn't see Miss Ellis because I was facing the audience. In order to follow her direction, I had to turn slightly and glance over my shoulder toward her position in front of the chorus, which was standing on bleachers at the back of the stage. Waiting for her signal, I felt someone beside me.

"I think this is 'Harvest Pass,'" Delbert whispered through the side of his mouth.

"I know. It *is*," I whispered back. Realizing that I was supposed to be at the microphone alone, he grinned and returned to his place in the tenor section.

Miss Ellis's arm was raised and my muscles tightened. Her downbeat was my cue to begin. I established my own beat. "Sinner, please don't let this harvest pass. Sinner, please don't let this harvest pass . . . and die, and lose your soul at last. . . ." I wanted my voice to flow, but though I fought, I couldn't fully control it. Come on, Sue, I thought. This is for Marshall. I mustered all my courage.

"I know that my redeemer lives!" I had to be more sincere. "Salvation every man he gives. . . ." I sang, listening as Elijah came in on the bass. The stage lights were unbearably hot, and I could feel tiny beads of perspiration on my forehead and neck. My legs felt as though they were crumbling. I pulled my muscles into knots. You've got to belt it now, Sue, I told myself.

"My god is a mighty man of war . . . shows his sign by sun and moon and star. . . ." Miss Ellis was bringing the chorus to the end of the song. "Sinner, please don't let this harvest pass," I began to plead it. "Sinner, *please* . . . and die, and lose your soul at last. . . ." The song was over.

For a moment I didn't know what was happening. Then I heard the applause, and it was coming from the members of chorus as well as the audience. Miss Ellis and the entire choir were clapping. Several people shouted from the audience. I felt overwhelmed, humble. Miss Ellis was beckoning to me, and I took a bow.

Then Delbert was at my side again and the calypso beat for "Sleep Little Tiny King" sounded from the piano. I remembered how Delbert had taken my hand in 237 before we marched downstairs to the auditorium. "There's a big crowd," he had said, squeezing my palm. "We'll make it," I had replied, smiling, reassured by his warm hand.

Now modern dancers took their positions behind us and enacted the Nativity to our singing. Delbert did his solo. Then I sang, "To that stable from near and far; bearing gifts and prayers they came, until they knelt beneath that star which far and wide his birth proclaimed. . . ." The last page of the number included a soprano-tenor duet and a soprano descant above the choir. I could feel Delbert smiling as he sang. The audience was responsive and showed their enjoyment with loud applause.

As a mixed chorus we had one more song to perform. But a young stagehand, thinking our part of the concert was completed, walked on stage and gingerly lifted Miss Ellis's music stand, carrying it behind side curtains. Miss Ellis reached for her music only to discover it missing. Several chorus members pointed offstage, and the entire audience watched Miss Ellis motion to the boy who had taken the stand. Sheepishly he carried it back. Warm laughter broke out in the audience and the choir.

During a performance at New Trier, such an incident would not have been lightly dismissed. But Marshall responded with easy good humor, as if such "mistakes" were forgivable, were part of the natural flow of events. The people of the West Side knew how to cope with the unexpected, for so much of their ghetto existence demanded sudden adjustments and new directions. How well they knew disappointment and tragedy, and, when they had cause for it, how great was their experience of joy. A small mishap in a school performance was shared by everyone and was understood as only humanness could be understood in the black community.

"Hallelujah! Hallelujah!" Perspiration ran down my back, but I concentrated on Miss Ellis, becoming caught up in the celebration of Handel. "And he shall reign forever and ever. . . . King of Kings!" I gave it my best, hoping to hold the sopranos on key. Miss Ellis worked feverishly to bring everyone in. Page after page she turned, until we reached the climax, the final hallelujah. The sound of applause faded behind the curtains as they closed in front of us.

Someone sighed, "Oh, man. . . ."

"Shhhh . . ." Miss Ellis quieted us.

When the lights came on after the finale I was blinded by the sight of people on their feet, clapping, whistling, cheering. I tried to find Mom and Dad, but couldn't spot them in the departing crowd.

"They're over there," someone called to me. I turned to see a tall, strange, black man, smiling, as he pointed into the crowd. It hadn't been difficult for him to match the only white student on the stage with the middle-aged white couple in the audience.

"Thank you." I nodded to him and walked up the aisle to join Mom and Dad who were standing with Miss Ellis, talking and laughing.

The family drive to New Trier took almost an hour. We parked along the school tennis courts and walked into the gymnasium, which was decorated for the annual Christmas Concert. Chairs had been set up on the main floor for the audience, facing bleachers used by the one thousand members of the student choir. On a special platform, directly in front of the bleachers, sat members of the orchestra. The balconies on either side of the gym were filled with families eager to enjoy Christmas music on a Sunday afternoon. The Gregorys took their usual seats in the middle balcony, facing the bleachers and overlooking the main floor.

Watching row after row of students file to their seats on the bleachers, I reflected on the turn of events that made me a spectator and not a participant. I might have been singing in this festival for my fourth and final year. Members of the select Girls' Ensemble, dressed in long-sleeved white blouses and black velvet skirts, took their places. A year ago I had stood with them, between two sopranos, Melissa and Candy. Both of those girls were in their customary places in the Ensemble, while I sat in the audience. I had entered another school, another culture, another world. The Boy's Ensemble appeared, smart and clean in their white sweaters and dark pants.

Confronted by the white faces massed in a square of bleachers, I felt a strange emptiness. They rose on cue. They sat on cue. The one thousand students executed perfect timing during their entire performance. Their singing technique may have been flawless, but it was mechanical and without spirit. Musically, instead of a celebration of birth, I listened to a lifeless parroting of phrases. I recalled how hard we had worked in rehearsal for previous concerts, drilling for crisp pronunciation of words. For hours we had practiced entrances and endings of musical phrases, sharpening the holding of quarter notes until we were one voice, cutting off precisely on the fourth beat. Was this the effect we had achieved? I felt no emotion, listening to the festival. I expected to be touched, awed, or inspired. I wanted the music to bring me to my feet, to make me shout and whistle and applaud. The Marshall concert and the heady response of the audience were fresh in my mind. At New Trier such spontaneous expression would have been unnatural, improper, and undignified. I hungered for Marshall's honest embracing of life, that understanding acceptance of error, that wonderful passion for the freshness and feeling of the moment.

Again I realized the difference between Marshall and New Trier. Marshall's concert was joy and agony, while New Trier's festival was impeccable technicality—a modern Christmas tree ornament, beautiful, shiny, and diverting, but somehow without real substance, hollow, and lacking in import. Disappointed, I was silent leaving the gym. Indeed, no one in the family spoke. They too were contrasting this scene to the altogether wild and enthusiastic finale of Marshall's performance. New Trier lacked soul, I thought.

"Okay. . . ." Mr. Wagner was swinging his arms at his sides and then balling one fist into the palm of his other hand, like

Ed Sullivan. "Okay. . . ." He was signaling for us to be quiet
and class to begin. We had already had our daily argument
about the window. Every morning Mr. Wagner walked into
the room, took off his suit coat, and opened the window near-
est his desk. It didn't matter how cold it was outside. Even if it
were snowing, his routine did not change. And Janis always
complained. "Mr. Wagner . . . please. . . ."

"Oh?"

"It's cold out there," Janis groaned, rubbing her arms.

"Naw . . . it's good for you," he teased. "Oh, man!" Somebody in the back of the room expressed the class's exasperation.
Mr. Wagner simply grinned, enjoying the ten minute warm-up
for class work.

On this day, however, in an attempt to interest students in
extracurricular activities, he wanted to discuss the Christmas
festival. He began by asking which of us had gone. Several
people raised their hands.

"How many members were there in the boys' drill team? In
the girls'? What colors were the dancers wearing? Who was
in the first row of girls' chorus banging a tamborine?" That
brought a giggle from Pearlie, because she was the performer
in question. Mr. Wagner's pink face grew rosier as he laughed,
listening to the rapid-fire responses to his questions. Some
answers were simply guesses. Cordell kept jumping up and
down, shouting, "I know . . . Oh, Mr. Wagner! I know!"

"Who did the solos?" Mr. Wagner yelled over the din.
Several girls paused to consult one another. Janis beamed at
me, and Willie and Joe couldn't make up their minds. They
shouted the names of people they knew.

"No, no, no!" Mr. Wagner shook his head, calming everyone down. "No. It was our own—Sue Gregory. . . ."

"Who's she?" I heard faintly from the back of the room.

". . . who always has such a soft voice in class," Mr.
Wagner continued. "She was up there belting out those songs."

Cordell looked at me. "Susan . . . ?" he said softly. "You
soloed?" I nodded assent. He shook his head in a kind of happy
admiration.

"Hey, Susie, what did you do to your hair?" Charlcie bounded into the locker room and I turned around while putting on a pair of borrowed socks.

"What do you mean, what did I do? I haven't done anything to it! I've simply got to wash it, but I haven't had time. It looks awful."

"Awful?" Charlcie's sidekick, Jo Ann, was leaning against a locker. "It isn't awful. Did you put grease in it? It's cool."

The idea of putting grease in my hair sounded ridiculous. "I don't need to *put* grease on it. Grease forms naturally in my hair and makes it look dirty. The fact is, I try my best to get the grease out of it!"

Charlcie and Jo Ann appeared puzzled. For a moment, I almost laughed. How ignorant we were of each other's customs. Black people were busy trying to take out the curl in their hair and used grease to help, while white people were struggling to put *in* the curl and get rid of the grease. Yet neither race really knew of the other's preoccupation.

The last day of school before Christmas vacation was also my seventeenth birthday. Miss Ellis was late to chorus so Rudy, Elijah, and Delbert clowned. They demonstrated various "pimps," different ways of walking into 237. There were slow walks with eyes big and one hand over the mouth. There were low leans with arms hanging at the sides. There were quick struts with little cocky movements of the head. But the best entrances were the wild ballet executions Rudy and Delbert created.

Rudy would go out the door and, on a cue from Delbert, run headlong into the room, jumping into Delbert's arms and inevitably landing on the floor in a heap. I sat in my seat in the soprano section, exploding with laughter.

When the show finally ended, Rudy came over to my seat, took my hand and sang, "How are you, Suuuuuue?"

"Rudy, I'll tell you a secret."

"What?" He bent down so he wouldn't miss a word.

"It's my birthday," I whispered.

"Oh, I won't tell a soul," he promised. But before I knew what was happening, Rudy, Elijah, and Delbert were standing behind my chair, singing "Happy Birthday" in three-part harmony. They sang it a second time, with fast finger-popping and a little Tempts routine on the side. I didn't know what to say, but I knew it was one of the most beautiful birthday gifts I'd ever received.

January

CHAPTER 6

Through Rudy's friendship, I became involved in two Marshall activity groups. I joined Guidance Class, which met ninth period under the supervision of Mr. Best, a chemistry teacher, and Student Council, which followed during tenth period. Being a member of these groups meant remaining in school two extra periods each afternoon.

Guidance Class was held in the third floor chemistry lab. A number of seniors, many from my Honors classes or academically in the top ten per cent of their classes, gathered in front of Mr. Best's long lab desk. We sat on round stools and talked about subjects of particular significance to the group.

Little Dorothy Foster, Rudy's girl friend, was there with her best friend, Paulette; so was six-foot-tall Reginald Ferguson, who was rumored to have the biggest feet in school. Odetta came too; and James Jones, the top-ranking boy in the senior class, sometimes dropped by. James was known for his silent aloofness, biting sarcasm, and quick mind. Vera and Abbie were regular members of the class. Mella arrived after Spanish, and Andrez could usually be found leaning against the window ledge that stretched along the side of the room. From the third floor lab you could look directly down on Adams Street and the sidewalk in front of Marshall. Andrez often watched the street activity from that point, and sometimes I chose a place of my own on the ledge to take in the afternoon scene.

The class had no formal structure. The members themselves chose what they did and talked about. The first day I attended Guidance Class, Mr. Best was leading a discussion in an attempt to decide on a project we'd pursue. Several students suggested psychological experiments with rats. The idea appealed to us as a new and challenging experience. Mr. Best passed around a number of psychology books for us to examine.

I enjoyed the informal, experimental atmosphere of Guidance. Mr. Best commented on the closeness of the group. With the exception of Mella and me, both new, the others had been members before and a certain cohesiveness had been established. Each person was given an opportunity to express his opinion on the suggestion under discussion, and because I was a newcomer and my ideas were not known, mine was sought particularly. I agreed that I would be interested in the rat experimentation. Mr. Best assured us the Biology Department would supply us with the animals.

"Who wants to volunteer? Come on. Somebody has to help me bring up the rats." Dorothy and I raised our hands, and, in excited anticipation, we followed Mr. Best downstairs to a small room tucked away in the old building. I had never seen that part of Marshall. It seemed so secluded, isolated as it was from the pulse of the main halls.

A biology class was in session when we entered the room. Freshmen eyed us curiously as we approached the white teacher in the back, passing shelves with cages of rabbits, snakes, jars of pickled frogs, tanks of fish, skeletons, charts, and plants.

I had the preconceived idea the rats would be tiny, fuzzy, white creatures, and that for our experiment we would be placing them in labyrinths and mazes, learning about their behavior in various controlled situations. When the biology teacher showed us the cage, my illusions were broken. Three rats, at least nine or ten inches long, prowled their quarters, sniffing the air and crawling over one another unmercifully. Two were a dirty white and the third was murky gray. Their long pointed snouts, fanglike teeth, and rubbery tails were far different from what I had expected.

"They might bite," the biology teacher said, "but they shouldn't have rabies." Dorothy shuddered, and Mr. Best half-heartedly picked up the cage. I followed them with a jar of food. On the way upstairs Mr. Best discovered the ultimate disenchantment—a repulsive odor emanated from the cage.

Vera ran behind Mr. Best's sink when he plopped the rat cage down on the lab table. She refused to come any closer and stood watching from a safe distance. "I hate rats," she whimpered. Our efforts to assure her failed, and in a matter of minutes tears began streaming down her cheeks. Her face was flushed from excitement and fear.

The smell from the cage seemed to permeate every corner of the room. "My lab will reek from the smell of rats," Mr. Best lamented, concerned about the need to keep them in his classroom.

"Oooo, are they ugly," Andrez said.

"Well, we've got to be able to handle them if we're going to perform experiments," Mr. Best finally declared. He located a pair of rubber gloves and opened the lid of the cage. He was unable to grab hold of a rat, however, and he recoiled from the smell, squinting hard as he turned his face away.

Andrez, Reginald, and Sherwin, the senior class vice-president, were anxious to try their luck. They dared each other to pick up one of the rats. Dorothy stood several feet away, glaring at the cage. Mella shook her head. "My sister was accidentally locked in the bathroom with a rat once, and she ain't never been the same since." I realized the reactions I was witnessing now were based on past experiences with rats, which had ranged anywhere from mildly unpleasant to terrifying.

Reginald opened the cage and Sherwin reached for a tail. He pulled the rat up into the air. Instantly it became rigid, its legs sticking out grotesquely, its tiny claws like bony fingers suspended in time. Vera screamed, Andrez burst out laughing, and Sherwin dropped the rat back into the cage. The lid flapped closed with a resolute slap.

Mr. Best was bewildered. He tried again to lift a rat from the cage, but the squirming and final rigidity were too much even for him. The three rats were left to prowl their cage undisturbed. It was obvious we hadn't known what we were getting into. The experiments were not going to work.

Vera calmed down. She apologized for her loss of control and Mr. Best reassured her. We all eyed the cage as the bell rang. Our first project had not been a resounding success, but, although it had taught us little about rats, we had learned something about our own behavioral reaction to stimuli. We had seen fear expressed, and we had become sensitive to the conditions responsible for it.

On the day I joined Student Council the meeting was held in the lunchroom. Representatives from all Marshall Divisions sat around the tables. Rudy, as president, presided. The topic for discussion was Student Council action in relation to a pending teachers' strike. The teachers were demanding higher wages, and Rudy wanted the Council to join their Monday morning picket line as evidence of student support. The point was raised as to whether such action should be taken as a body or should be left to the individual Council member's conscience.

The debate was lengthy. Several Council representatives thought the best response to the strike would be to stay home from school. Others expressed a desire to join the picketing but not as representatives of Council. Most, however, agreed to take a vote, and the majority voiced support for the strike.

"How we gonna witness now? How we gonna show our agreement with the teachers?" Rudy asked. I felt an answer formulating in my mind, and, heart pounding nervously, I raised my hand. Rudy recognized me, and I stood up, my hands resting on the table in front of me. The room was quiet.

"We've already decided that the Council supports the strike. Why not allow each member to decide for himself how he will demonstrate that support. Give him the option either to stay home or to join the picket line. Then it will be a matter of individual choice between two modes of action." Several heads nodded. Rudy grinned. The bell rang as I took my seat. Rudy loudly adjourned the meeting.

Later he stopped me in the hall. "You're really cookin'," he said, pleased that I had jumped into my new membership in a school organization. I was relieved and encouraged by his response.

Student Council was dismissed at 2:45, much later than my usual afternoon departure time. I was quite tired and walked slowly upstairs to my locker on the second floor of the old building.

I noticed a group of boys talking in an alcove near the stairway. One dude in particular, whose hair was cut to a sharp triangular point in the front and whose lips played cooly with a toothpick, eyed me. I ignored his attention and stopped at my locker, putting on my jacket and exchanging several books.

When I started back down the hall, however, the alcove was empty. The boys had spread out along the hall. One stood at every classroom door and several more were spaced at regular intervals where the classrooms ended. What is happening, I wondered. They're all looking at me.

I was determined to keep on walking. The hall was completely silent except for the sound of my shoes touching the wooden floor. As I passed them one by one, the boys remained in their spaced positions, none of them speaking. Only their eyes followed my movements, and the dude with the toothpick twirled it in his fingers absently and stuck it back into his mouth. I was beginning to think no one meant any harm. I reasoned that I would be safe if I could only reach the stairway at the end of the hall.

As I approached the glass doors leading to the stairs I descended every day to the Adams exit, two boys turned from their positions at the top of the steps. I could see their faces, anxious and eager. Suddenly I realized this had been their plan all along—to trap me on this staircase! The boys in the hall were acting to bar any retreat.

Quickly, I considered, if that was their game I would play it too. Struggling not to panic, I opened the door, but, instead of walking downstairs as they expected, I swerved to the right and ran up to the third floor, as fast as I could. I heard the footsteps behind me. "Hey, girl! Hey, white girl!" The chase was quick and soon over.

I hurried down another passageway, and in a matter of seconds I was outside the front door of the building. The sight of Officer Wolfe, Marshall's only black policeman, was more than comforting as he patrolled the entrance. Breathing heavily, I calmed myself from the scare and went home.

We discussed the teachers' strike again in Student Council before the week end. It was scheduled to begin the following Monday. Rudy suggested that all interested Council members meet in front of Marshall to help the teachers picket.

All during tenth period, however, messages from faculty members kept arriving for him. Miss Ellis, sponsor of Council, and Dr. Bronski, Marshall's white principal, were not pleased with the steps Student Council, under Rudy's guidance, was taking in support of the strike. Their messages both advised and warned Rudy. By the end of the meeting the pressure from faculty and administration became too much for Rudy. He looked at us despairingly, threw up his hands, and said, "Do whatever you think is best Monday."

After school I told Mom about the strike. She shook her head. "I don't think you should go to classes in a school with few teachers, little supervision or discipline. Anything could happen." She instructed me to stay home.

"How would you like to go to the show?"

House Church, the Institute's Sunday evening meal, had just concluded, and Roosevelt Garrison beckoned me over to a couch in the lounge. He was a black student at Marshall, living at the Institute as part of the High School House, a small experimental project designed to help students prepare for college. I had met him at a New Year's Eve party.

"I'd love to, but I gotta ask my parents." I found Mom in conversation with other members of the Order. Since the teachers' strike was to begin the following day and I would not be in school, she gave her approval. "I'll meet you here in ten minutes," I told Roosevelt and floated upstairs, feeling light-hearted.

Ann was lying on the top bunk listening to the radio when I reached our bedroom. She sensed my excitement. "Where you goin'?" she asked, as I stood in the closet choosing a skirt to go with my bulky pink sweater.

"I'm going OUT!" I told her, humming as I changed.

"With who?"

"With Roosevelt!"

Back downstairs, bundled up warmly, I met Roosevelt in the lounge. He was leaning against the wall, cigarette in hand, wearing a black coat and a smart-looking black-and-white checked hat. I had a clipping from the movie section of the newspaper, and Roosevelt suggested seeing something funny. We decided on a Peter Sellers film.

As we stood on the Kedzie-Homan El platform in the clear, brisk January night, I told Roosevelt how long it had been since I had gone out. "You should be getting around," he said sincerely. I liked his manner. It wasn't phony. He didn't jive with me or play a game by making superficial conversation. Roosevelt seemed kind and considerate.

Downtown, we sat in the back row of a darkened movie theater. Peter Sellers had escaped from jail and was trying to devise a plan to seize a shipment of gold. I didn't particularly like the film, but being with Roosevelt made it worthwhile. His arm around my shoulder was gentle and warm, and when his lips touched my cheek, his kiss was sweet and tender.

At midnight, after the movie, we were holding hands on a Chicago street, laughing. It all seemed so natural, so right.

On our way home, I looked out the window of the Congress El and panicked to discover that, instead of being level with the expressway, the train was several feet above ground. "Roosevelt, we're on a B train! Ann and I made the same mistake once. We're heading South instead of West! We've got to get off right away!"

The train rushed past Presbyterian-St. Luke's Hospital and came to a stop. We got off quickly onto the wooden platform. "I know where we are," Roosevelt said. The outskirts of the hospital complex were deserted, and we walked under El tracks to a sidewalk. "This next street is Western. Harrison has to come in around here somewhere," Roosevelt reasoned out loud. Instead of being upset with our mistake, we were enjoying it as an adventure together.

We found Harrison, and then a transit authority building where we could get an A train. But, as we neared the station, several black men and a woman approached us from the opposite direction. The laughter of the men was loud and arrogant. They were not the kind of people to ignore an interracial couple.

They followed us inside the station where they were intentionally audible. "Okay, man, you jump the cat and I take the broad. . . ." One of the men chuckled.

"Hey, baby!"

I kept my eyes looking straight ahead. Roosevelt walked beside me as I ran my hand lightly along the metal hand railing of the tunnel leading down to the train platform. His calm presence gave me added strength, although I felt my eyes smart and my muscles tighten.

"Hey, sugar, where do you live?" Two of the men walked beside us.

"Baby, why don't you come with us?" Their eyes inspected me eagerly.

"Sugar, you got any friends?"

Suddenly I felt defiant. "I got plenty," I threw back at them, "but they wouldn't be interested in you!"

"Whats'a matter? I'm not your type?"

I ignored the question. We had reached the end of the tunnel, and Roosevelt and I walked calmly ahead, down the open platform. I felt the men slipping behind. Roosevelt and I ducked behind a support post, peeking around to watch the men jivin' with the woman who had been temporarily forgotten.

"If they lay a hand on you," Roosevelt said, "I'll get 'em!"

"I'll use my fingernails!" I declared, holding up my hand. We both laughed, feeling the tension of the moment dissolve into relief.

"Not until I'm down!" Roosevelt exclaimed, and I knew from the tone of his voice that he would fight for me. I felt secure in the belief of his courage.

"Hey. . . ." His voice was soft, and I looked at his smooth dark face, shadowed by the post he was leaning against. "You were wonderful. . . ."

I told Daddy about the boys who tried to jump me after school. He and Mom decided that Daddy should meet me after Student Council and walk with me to my locker. The arrangement worked, and I didn't see the same group of boys again.

One afternoon, however, as we were climbing the second floor stairs, Daddy and I ran into a ring of dudes. They had formed a circle, and in the center two boys were grappling. The outer circle acted as protection, as a means of insuring a fair fight. There was no rooting or shouting. A certain amount of discipline seemed to be maintained. But during a sudden lunge that threw one off balance, Daddy and I saw blood streaming down the face of a contestant.

For a moment Daddy was uncertain what to do. As a faculty member it was his responsibility to interfere. Yet it seemed that the situation was under control. The boys had organized the fight. It was their "thing," and they appeared to be managing it. As we walked away, the fight became overheated, and several dudes from the circle moved in to break it up. The solution had evolved without any intervention.

Frequently after Student Council meetings tenth period, Rudy lingered in the hall to talk. When Daddy came to pick me up, the three of us visited, often in wild hilarity, our voices ringing throughout the first floor. Usually the talk was casual and insignificant chatter. But more than once Rudy was seriously troubled and wanted advise. Daddy and I always listened and offered whatever help might be possible.

Invariably, when we waved goodbye to Rudy and left for home, Daddy and I commented on his energy, his passion for living, his incredible vitality. Rudy possessed enormous sensitivity and depth, and abundant qualities of leadership. Never before had either of us met anyone like him. Our moments together meant the formation of a bond of cherished friendship among the three of us.

One afternoon Daddy had a faculty meeting. I walked home alone, but as I was crossing the street near the Institute, a car pulled up. Inside were Carlos and Ken, two white members of the Order who taught at St. Mel High School on the West Side, and Juan Rabassa, a Puerto Rican student at St. Mel's who, like Roosevelt, lived in the Institute's High School House.

"We're going to the Marshall-St. Mel basketball game, Sue. Why don't you come?"

I was hesitant because of homework, but the three of them were persuasive. I climbed into the back seat with Juan, stashing my books beside me.

We parked behind Marshall, and I led Carlos, Ken, and Juan to the gym. They joined the spectators from St. Mel, and I sat

near the top of the Marshall bleachers. Scanning the stands
opposite me, I recognized several friends from my classes.
Rudy, wearing his maroon and gold M-Club beanie, was
patrolling in front of the stands, talking to students and keeping order. Soul jams were playing, and I sang along with the
music, waiting for the game to start.

When the Marshall Commandos ran out onto the gym floor,
I thrilled at their bright gold jackets. They formed lines on
either side of the basket, clapping their hands feverishly. The
first in line ran toward the basket, made a jump shot, and the
lead player from the other line caught the rebound and passed
it on. The ball moved with lightning speed and intensity.
When this drill was completed, the team members used a
number of balls to practice shooting freely from any vantage
point around the basket.

St. Mel's team, although predominantly white, was integrated. The boys from St. Mel came out onto the court wearing brilliant purple jackets and long pants. They, too, went
through several drills, each basket accompanied by a cheer
from their fans.

When the Commandos were introduced and took their
positions on the court, the Marshall cheerleaders did flips and
splits. A cheerleader had to be skilled in gymnastics. Cheer-
leading at any of the black Chicago high schools was an art.
It demanded the ability to perform intricate foot movements
and rhythms, to sing, and, at the same time, do acrobatics.

The buzzer sounded and a voice over the public address
system announced the beginning of the game. The referee
tossed the ball between the two boys poised for the jump,
and the action started. Marshall scored the first four baskets.

"Hey, Com—man—dos, Commandos! Hey, Com—man—
dos, Commandos!" we shouted, clapping with the beat. It was
fascinating to watch the speed of the dribbling and the sudden
attempts to shoot a basket.

The game was close. St. Mel caught up with Marshall
quickly and then took the lead. Every time we tied the score,
St. Mel made another basket, and we had to catch up.

"One—two—three, four, five! Marshall Commandos do not jive!" we shouted. When St. Mel intercepted, the cheerleaders screamed, "Take that ball—take that ball—take that—basketball!" A St. Mel team member fouled, and a tall, sleek Commando took position for a free throw. "E-A-S-Y, easy boys!" the cheerleaders called. We waited in tense silence, hoping to hear the swish of the ball through the net.

During the last period everyone in the stands jumped up and down. Several girls yelled hysterically, and I grinned at the girls next to me who were enjoying the excitement. I wished I had brought my beanie. "*Mighty*, mighty, mighty—*Mighty*, mighty, mighty—*Mighty*, mighty, mighty—OOOOOooooo!" That was my favorite cheer. It was simple with a rhythmic beat that ended in a free-wheeling exclamation. We were the Mighty Marshall Commandos.

Seconds ticked away, and the score was tied again. "Our team is vicious—our team is tough! Marshall Commandos don't take no stuff!" The cheerleaders clapped. "Hey, V-I-C-T-O-R-Y! Victory for Marshall High!"

"Come on! Aw, come on, man!" I cried, caught up in the frenzy of the final minutes, watching little Thompson dribble down the court. As the hand of the clock approached 0, he dashed toward the basket, and the ball sailed through. There was a burst of cheering and the buzzer sounded the end of the game. I rose to my feet, hugging the girl next to me whom I had never seen before the game. We were lost in ecstacy and relief. "Oh, man! We won!" The last basket made the score Marshall 74, St. Mel, 72.

Elated, I met Carlos, Ken, and Juan in the hall outside the gym. They were downcast. Juan moaned sadly, "I bet all my money on that game." I laughed as we walked out to the parking lot.

Carlos was smoking a cigar, and as he slid into the driver's seat, he passed it to Juan. "We oughta get high," he said, dejectedly.

"Oh, cheer up," I said.

"But I've lost almost ten dollars!" Juan complained.

When we arrived at the Institute, someone asked me, "Who won?"

"Marshall!" I announced, hearing in my tone the pride with which I spoke the name.

A certain restiveness began to take hold of me in the middle of January. I found it grew increasingly more difficult to stay in the apartment for hours at a time, studying. It became more and more difficult to be alone with a book. After completing an algebra assignment or reading a history chapter, I simply had to get up and walk around. I sometimes wandered downstairs in the evening, stopping at the end of the administration hall to stare out the window at the glittering ribbon of cars on the expressway. I had an urge to be with people, to stay up late, to bum the city. Something inside me cried out to "mess around."

One evening, in the midst of such a mood, I met Roosevelt on the way downstairs, and we stood together on the landing, leaning against a windowsill, looking out onto the street. By midnight, we were outside my apartment door; everyone else had gone to bed. Dark shadows played on the walls around us as we whispered good night.

For those few hours my loneliness had been dispelled and my restlessness had been soothed by Roosevelt's kindness. More and more I turned to him for understanding companionship.

In the middle of an eighth period Spanish class, the fire alarm sounded. Miss Novatny, upset because the drills always seemed to occur during our class, hustled us out the door and down the steps to the back entrance on Monroe Street. We joined the swarm of students at the exit and spilled out onto the parking lot and across the street. Some students had taken time to get coats from their lockers, but all of us from Spanish were freezing. We huddled together in small groups, rubbing arms, stamping feet, trying to keep warm. Delbert gave his jacket to a girl. Nearby doorways on Monroe and Kedzie provided shelter for other students waiting for the signal to re-enter the building. Some couples used parked cars as refuges. Curious passersby stopped on the sidewalk across the street to survey Marshall's student body, trapped outside at the mercy of the weather.

Suddenly we heard sirens and three tremendous, gleaming-red fire trucks raced onto Monroe, forcing the students in the street to dash for safety. The trucks turned the corner and screamed on. Was there really a fire, or was this simply another false alarm? No one on our side of the building actually knew. Our only concern was to get back inside. No one was anxious to return to class, but the biting cold was a far less desirable alternative.

For forty minutes we milled around the sidewalk and street, waiting, clinging to friends for warmth. Rudy, Delbert, and Elijah stood together on the curb, singing. They leaned into one another like the members of a barbershop quartet, invigorated by their own harmony. Ronald put his arm around me so that my back rested against his chest. When the doors to Marshall were finally opened, the crush of students moved slowly forward and inside. Teachers shouted to us as we entered the hall, "Everyone go to his ninth period class. . . . Go to your ninth period class. . . ."

An official bulletin, read before the end of school and sent downtown to the Board of Education, stated that a pipe had burst in a third floor washroom, creating a flood up and down the hall. Students had not been allowed back inside the building, the bulletin read, so that the water on the third and second floors could be mopped up.

I learned what actually happened when Daddy picked me up after school. Two fires had erupted at the same time. One had started behind a marble partition in a third floor girls' washroom and had set the ceiling sprinkler system off with immediate effect. The story of this fire was covered up in the official report sent to the downtown office.

The second fire began in a basement apartment on Fifth Avenue, a half block east of Marshall. When the fire trucks arrived, it was difficult for the firemen to decide which alarm should take priority. There was great confusion among the shouting, milling firemen. Finally, they rushed to connect hoses to the hydrant closest to the blazing apartment and stood poised in front of the flames. But the hydrant was frozen, and there was little water. The Fifth Avenue apartment was completely destroyed, and its four occupants, three children and one adult, died in the tragedy.

The students waiting on Adams Street had seen the giant flames leap up from the building's basement. Daddy and his class had watched the fire licking at the windows, unaware of the four people inside who lost their lives.

Daddy and I drove past the building on the way home. A crowd of neighborhood residents, talking quietly, stood on the sidewalk in front of the blackened debris and the remains of a mattress. Smoke still curled from a charred beam. Someone was already boarding up the front door and the gaping windows.

Miss Ellis didn't come to chorus one morning when we had an unexpected group of white visitors. Elijah acted as director. He chose to sing "Harvest Pass," and as I stood by the piano for my solo, I could see both the chorus and the visitors.

I wondered who the guests were and what they thought, watching and listening to the chorus of a ghetto school on the West Side of Chicago run through its paces. I wondered what the other choir members felt about the strange white people in their midst. At times, it seemed, visitors to Marshall regarded us as objects for study, specimens in a cage, rather than ordinary human beings. You sensed they had come to see a "real ghetto school"—to look at the "other half." You felt like exhibit A in a glass museum case. You were hurt and even a little defiant at their liberal naïvety. You knew they would not stay long enough to take in the problems of Marshall and life on the West Side. In a sense, they would understand only what they wanted to.

The visitors left chorus before the end of fifth period.

By sixth period I was starving. Before joining Guidance and

Student Council, I used to eat lunch when I returned to our apartment early in the afternoon. In so doing, I avoided the slow-moving lunch lines, which left only a small portion of the forty minute period for eating. What had seemed, at the beginning of the year, an ample amount of time had, in practice, turned out to be inadequate. I had spent many lunch periods studying, enviously eyeing the meals of students around me.

Now that my schedule would keep me in school until almost 3:00 PM, I had to consider other arrangements for eating lunch. Consequently, after chorus, I decided to buy the hamburger plate I liked so much. Shirley and I deposited our books at a table. I hoped she would accompany me through the line so that I would have someone to talk to. Perhaps, I reasoned, the tension that usually knotted my stomach when I stood there alone, confronted by so many faces, would not bother me.

But Shirley was not the type to wait in *any* line! She'd sweet-talk some boy near the front of the line to let her cut in. I never liked cheating anyone, even in so trivial an act as breaking in line.

Perhaps I was getting hip to Marshall when a dude offered Shirley and me a place in line near the food counter, and I accepted. Shirley's eyes and sugar-sweet voice were a "put on" which the dude understood and played along with.

"You're one of us now," Shirley said to me. "You'll be the only white Negro I know." I had given up one of my "lily-white" principles in exchange for time to relax and enjoy a meal.

Sitting in a chair by the living room window with the radio on low, I peered out onto the dark street. I was baby-sitting for the family in the apartment across the hall from us at the Institute. The only sound in the room was Herb Kent from WVON introducing "Beauty's Only Skin Deep" by the Temptations. "All right all you y-l's out there . . . I'd like to lay this one on you now . . . It's really ten-two-double-plus. . . ."

The wheels of a car screeched around the corner and its headlights flashed by. Otherwise the street was quiet. I turned away from the window and opened a book. "This is the cool gent, Herb Kent, playin' all the latest jams in Chicago. . . ." I snapped my fingers as Shorty Long came on with "The Function at the Junction."

There was a knock at the door. "Come in," I called, getting up and moving several steps toward the door before Roosevelt entered.

"Hi," he greeted me. He was wearing a maroon sweater, and he stood for a moment, simply smiling. We sat down on the small living room couch and began to talk. We recalled our first evening together and the many subsequent meetings when conversation often lasted long into the night. We shared the memories of an El ride we had taken the week before and the times we sat watching television in my apartment.

Then Roosevelt became serious. I was glad for the chance to express my thoughts and listen to him express his. On our first date I had sensed a genuine rightness about us—we seemed to belong together. Neither of us had to explain ourselves, to uncover reasons for who we were and why we acted as we did. There was no lack of communication. Instead, a deep affection began to develop. Because we both lived at the Institute, we shared many experiences—both the ordinary daily events of morning worship and breakfast, as well as the unique ones arising from our unusual situation as Order members.

Facing Roosevelt on the couch, I realized how rare our relationship was. His hand touched my shoulder. "I love you." His words were simple, direct, honest.

"I love you, too."

It was that open and sincere, and our emotions were not colored by sentimentality. The bond we were declaring was a vital, living force born out of a recognition of the ghetto world we were a part of and the strength we needed to endure the mistrust and suspicion our relationship would surely cause.

Roosevelt kissed me.

When the parents of my small charge returned, they greeted Roosevelt with warmth and friendship, and we said goodnight.

Record Day at Marshall was set aside for teachers to mark semester grades in the students' course books. No students went to school except those seniors who acted as teacher's aids. I had taken the opportunity to make an appointment with Mr. Pankowski, my counselor, for help in completing several college applications. Because of the unstructured informality of the day, it was filled with shifting scenes and moods.

. . . There was Mr. Pankowski, smoking continuously, and maintaining his "cool" in the face of incessant interruptions.

"Mr. Pankowski, please, . . . Can't you do anything about this D in Spanish?" It was Charlcie, distressed, her course book in her hand.

"Do you know anything about this student?" a teacher inquired. Mr. Pankowski checked his file cabinet. Moments later another student asked for program cards. The telephone rang. Mr. Pankowski ran out of matches, sent out for lunch, and through it all never once raised his voice or became upset.

. . . There was Rudy, slumping into a chair, letting his hands hang listlessly between his legs, and staring at the floor. "I'm gettin' two C's and two D's. . . ." he announced gloomily, only to bounce back, alive and energetic at the prospect of sharing a secret with a teacher down the hall.

. . . There was a conversation with Darlene. "Who's ring are you wearing?" I asked, noticing the chain around her neck.

"Tom Stern's."

"Really?" There was a note of surprise in my voice. During a class discussion in English Tom had accused me of being an atheist. I had been wary of him ever since.

"Do you think it's bad because he's mixed?" Darlene asked. (Tom was very light-skinned, half Spanish, half Negro.) "That's what everybody's been saying."

"Oh, no. That doesn't matter at all. I just didn't think Tom was your kind of person. But really, I'm in no position to judge. I do know when you really dig somebody, you see things in him that other people don't. I think it's wonderful." That brought a smile to Darlene's face.

. . . There was Rudy cavorting in the lunchroom. "Hey, did you see Adam Clayton Powell on TV last night? My boy —my boy was cool," Rudy said. "My boy Adam—he jus' walkin' around . . . and some other cat gets up there and he says. . . ." Rudy raised his hands in the air with a wild expression in his eyes. " 'We're gonna burn down the capital!' " Rudy puffed from his imaginary cigar and continued, "But Adam . . . my boy say, 'Keep the faith, baby, . . . keep the faith.' " Rudy pimped across the room imitating Powell, and everyone at the table roared approval. Several girls joined us, asking why we were making so much noise.

"Why don't you and Rudy get married?" Sandra asked me.

"Oh, Sandra! Me and *Rudy?*" I was both surprised and flattered. I felt I wasn't cool enough for him. "Rudy needs somebody really outta sight. I'm not his type."

Sandra seemed offended. "That was rank," she objected, using a term that implied thoughtless behavior, in poor taste.

"Rank? What's rank about that?" I was baffled, not immediately realizing she had misunderstood and added racial overtones to my remarks.

. . . And there was Daddy, joining us at lunch with a strange report. "You'll never guess what just happened!" "What?" we asked him.

"A bomb scare!" Daddy told us. He thought it was all very silly. "The announcement was made to all the faculty members. 'If you hear anything ticking, or see anything unusual, please let the administration know . . . or we may be blown sky high and end up in the street in the snow!' "

"Another average day at Marshall High School," I joked.

When Daddy and I left the school, the storm that had swept over Chicago the night before was still working havoc. We braved the wind, trudging through deep mounds of snow toward the parking lot. All around us were people in distress

—teachers in cars that would not start, others who were caught in mounting drifts. A man with a thick brown mustache and wool hat was assisting anyone that needed help. A city truck was pushing motorists whose cars threatened to obstruct the flow of traffic. I felt a growing excitement as the snow turned my black Fifth City beret white.

Daddy's passengers, two other teachers and myself, used all our energy to get our VW moving on the difficult journey to the Institute. All around us cars were either stalled or crawling along painfully slowly. Once out of Marshall's parking lot, we encountered no other difficulty until we ran aground near the Institute campus. There was no plow in sight and again the three passengers climbed out to push. I could feel melted snow dripping down my hair and back, and, although I was shivering, this was a most unusual adventure, and I was enjoying it.

Carlos came out the side door of the Institute. "We need help!" we shouted above the wind. With Carlos's assistance we pushed the car to a parking space along the curb. The snow whirled around us like a blizzard.

Inside the apartment I hung up my wet coat, put my mittens over the radiator to dry, and speculated about the effects the storm would have on the days ahead.

The next day Chicago schools were closed. The snowstorm had paralyzed the entire city. Huge drifts of snow blocked even the main thoroughfares. It was virtually impossible for people to travel. Food in stores was scarce because supply trucks weren't able to make deliveries. Power lines were damaged. All normal activity in the city came to a halt.

Institute men were up early in the morning to shovel a path to the gym where morning worship was held. We bundled up and walked single file along the narrow passageway they had dug through the middle of the campus.

After breakfast, listening to the radio, I began to realize the full extent of the crisis. People had been trapped inside stalled buses throughout the city. Looting was reported on the West and South sides due to the food shortage and the absence of effective police operation. The snow was still falling.

After lunch, Roosevelt and I decided to explore. I wore my heaviest coat, a scarf, and boots. Roosevelt dressed in a winter coat and his checked hat, and we went out onto the street.

Several men in the Order were trying to dig out cars that were completely hidden under the snow. The cars resembled white humps, regularly spaced on the street, until you rubbed the side of one and a window glass appeared. Children ran over the sidewalks that had been shoveled. Few of the streets were cleared. Everyone on the West Side knew from experience that snowplows arrived in the ghetto last. The Loop would be plowed immediately, but Chicago's black people would wait a long time before plows came to their streets.

Roosevelt took my mittened hand, and we trudged down Van Buren. Neighborhood residents were cleaning snow off their cars. We climbed over the ridges of heavy drifts and stopped at Albany Street by a huge Catholic church with twin towers. It was strangely quiet. Cars were hidden under snowy blankets, and we were the only persons outside. The usually bustling intersection was one endless patch of white, cold and silent. As we stood in the middle of it, hardly daring to break the silence, I whispered, "Roosevelt, remember this when it is summer and the July heat is baking the sidewalks. Remember how we stood here, knee-deep in snow." Roosevelt nodded, awed by the incredible sight.

We walked on, past the gas station near Marshall, and stopped in front of the school. A tremendous five-foot deep drift blocked the front door. Roosevelt, in a running frenzy, charged through the drift and landed in a gasping heap on the other side. Farther down Kedzie we found one snowplow in operation. Several big black men with yellow helmets were working to clear a single lane through the middle of the street. Roosevelt decided he should check in at his home to see if things were all right there.

His family lived on Fifth Avenue, next to a car dealer. Inside the tiny doorway of the Garrison's building, a mail box dangled from the wall, the metal scarred and rusted. Without asking me to join him, Roosevelt climbed up the dilapidated stairs, and I stayed at the bottom, looking at the bare, gray walls. A dog was barking nearby.

When Roosevelt appeared again, his two small brothers were with him. Roosevelt introduced us. We went outside to a basement entrance at the back of the building. His brothers were going to play outside, and they needed some equipment kept in the basement. Roosevelt cleared away a large chunk of icicles frozen above the doorway and climbed down the steep stairs.

Later, Roosevelt apologized for the way the property looked. I wished he had not felt it necessary to make excuses. People all over Chicago lived in buildings that were equally as bad, and I had come to know such people and to admire them. I had come to accept the buildings and the streets, but most of all, to identify with human beings struggling to survive in them.

Roosevelt led me back to Kedzie. We passed a woman and a child. The mother pulled the little girl away as we approached, but I heard her utter in surprise and disapproval, "Ooooo, white girl, colored boy. . . ."

There were several dozen people on West Madison Street trying to buy food. Some young girls slipped and slid over the icy sidewalk. An old man walked cautiously with shuffling steps. Roosevelt and I stopped at a small grill to eat. The waitress who served us was tired and indifferent. A juke box rattled a James Brown record from the corner, and the man near us at the counter had a process and very few teeth. Roosevelt and I each ordered a hamburger and a cup of hot chocolate. Looking out the grill window into Madison, we saw a policeman with a sawed-off shotgun rush by. We speculated that he was chasing looters. Roosevelt paid for the food, and we returned to the street, rested and refreshed.

At the edge of Garfield Park we stopped. The park was one tremendous expanse of snow. No one had set foot in the park, and the snow was fresh and unbroken. "Let's go all the way out to those two benches," I challenged. We could just see their green backs projecting from a field of white near the frozen pond in the center of the park. The snow was almost hip-deep and our progress was slow. We clung to each other as if we were the only two people alive. When we arrived at the benches, I climbed on top of the seat, weak and exhausted.

The walk back was even more difficult, until we found a section of the park which had been plowed. We stopped to draw pictures in the snow. I made Fifth City symbols and Roosevelt wrote names. When we left the park, my legs ached and my face was stiff from the cold. Roosevelt took my hand, and we ran. I laughed and protested as we dodged people walking along narrow paths in the snow drifts. "Stop, Roosevelt! . . . I'll die! Stop! I'll fall!" I yelled, gasping for breath.

As we neared the Institute, he stopped running. There in the street was an abandoned 7-Up truck. It was stuck in the snow. Neighborhood children had climbed into the back and stolen bottles of pop. Men from the Order were hauling cartons of 7-Up into the gym for safe-keeping. We joined the team they had organized, carrying the wooden cases inside. Several Fifth City residents pitched in to help. By afternoon the front hall of the gym was overflowing with stacks of 7-Up cases.

Finally Roosevelt and I went into the lounge and thawed out. I realized that the experience of roaming the West Side would not have been mine without Roosevelt. Because I was a young white girl, I could not move freely in the neighborhood without the presence of another person. Roosevelt's friendship, his masculine protection, and his familiarity with his community gave me valuable mobility and access to wider experiences.

February

CHAPTER 7

At the start of second semester my position at Marshall was decidedly different than it had been in September. I was familiar with the physical layout of the building—the halls and stairways, the classrooms and administration offices. I knew the academic demands to expect from the teachers, and I had a circle of friends in which I felt secure and accepted.

In the community outside the school, the streets had become my own turf. The buildings were welcome guideposts to the territory I called home base. I knew the places to avoid as well as the havens where friendly assistance could be found.

I belonged.

An incident in Guidance proved to me how totally my

"difference" had been forgotten. We decided to write a play. I suggested we create a story about ourselves as high school students and, by delving into the character of various authority figures in our lives, we might better understand them and gain insight into our own reactions to them. Odetta and Mella voiced their agreement. Mr. Best began a list of the necessary components for the play.

"Uh . . . first we'll need an integrated cast," he said, turning to the blackboard and making a large number one with the chalk. But shouts of disagreement interrupted him.

"No!"

"We don' need that, Mr. Best!"

"Whoa, man!"

His face flushing with confusion and embarrassment, he turned around to confront us. I was sitting on a stool by his front lab table. Slowly understanding the reason for Mr. Best's remark, every eye in the room turned to me.

"Susan ain't white." Rudy made the statement casually, as if it was widely understood. "She ain't white," he repeated, walking over and putting his arm around my shoulder. "She's a *sister!*"

For a moment no one spoke. Then I heard Andrez say, "Yeah, to be white, you gotta *think* white."

"Do you think white, Sue?" Rudy asked.

"No," I shook my head. "I think in green. . . ."

"Uh huh, and purple," Rudy continued, and the silence of the room was broken by laughter. With my position as a member of the group clarified, I was no longer the center of attention. Mr. Best turned back to the board and called out the remaining items for his list. Conversation once again became relaxed and free. The incident, which had occurred within a matter of seconds, represented a significant breakthrough for me.

There were still moments, however, when uncertainty taunted me. At times, when I was alone in the hall or sitting by myself at a lunchtable, I felt a tightness taking hold of me. It was like claustrophobia. The walls around me would close in and the faces would whirl into one strange, threatening mass. If I tried to relax, I only succeeded in becoming more uncomfortable.

In those instances the power of the Institute community helped sustain me. I remembered that I was not alone and when I caught sight of an Order teacher in the halls, we exchanged glances of mutual encouragement. I recalled the depth of conviction that flowed through the words we spoke in worship each morning. I realized that the other members of my family, although not physically with me, were each in his own activity in the community, working for a common purpose. Then I'd swallow hard and fight to maintain control.

As though sensing my need for constant reminders of our "spirit" relationship, Rudy seized a moment in Guidance to ritualize the bond we had formed. He announced that it was time for me to be initiated into the Soul Brothers and Soul Sisters of America. Standing in front of Mr. Best's lab table, Rudy stuck his right hand into the air, leaned back on to his left foot, and widened his eyes. "Now this is what you gotta do," he said. I imitated his stance. "Now, lean back and say 'Look heah!' "

"Look heah!" I said, feeling my face breaking into a smile as Rudy pounded the table in excitement. He asked for a piece of paper, and I pulled one from my folder. Quickly he scribbled "Application" in red ink. At the top of the "official" form was a place for my full name and address. In the center was the request for membership in the Soul Brothers and Soul Sisters of America, with a place for my signature. And at the bottom, with a flare, Rudy affixed his own name. I completed the form, aware that this little ceremony indicated I had earned a place in Marshall's world.

Still, I realized I could never completely belong. During an afternoon in which there was no Student Council business needing our attention, Rudy, Dorothy, Mella, Paulette, and I were sitting around a table. I listened while the four of them discussed a camp they had attended together in Colorado. Hearing them relate adventures and reminisce about their experiences, I realized how close they were and how well they knew each other. In the midst of the transient West Side community, it amazed me to find people who had shared so many experiences over a number of years.

I felt separated that day. The barriers built by our social system, the differences in our skin color, our divergent backgrounds could never be completely bridged. I belonged, yet I could never belong. I shared the groping struggle of my closest friends, and yet I would, ultimately, always be apart and alone.

Facing this final separation, I determined that my role among my Marshall friends, like my presence among them, must be a unique one. I was grateful to be included in their group at all, and I considered it an honor. If I could be one white person they could trust and confide in, the entire year at Marshall would be worthwhile.

Mrs. Vashka was upset fourth period. She received a message from the administration that faculty members were to refurbish their bulletin boards before the next week when CBS television officials would visit Marshall to film James Jones. We had heard through the grapevine that James had been chosen one of a number of high school students to be featured in a CBS special.

Only because people from outside Marshall were coming to visit the school had teachers been instructed to tidy up their rooms. Mrs. Vashka was told that the torn and dirty shade hanging in her classroom window for two years was finally to be replaced. All of us in English felt cynical. We thought the administration and the Board of Education were afraid to risk exposing a Chicago public school. They didn't want Marshall to be seen as it normally appeared.

Mrs. Vashka spent an entire morning putting up new displays on the bulletin boards in our classroom. Two other girls and I stood on chairs, taking down faded colored paper and stapling bright yellow and orange in its place. Mrs. Vashka had some difficulty locating enough paper and had to send a messenger to the art department. Several boys came to class and stood in the doorway long enough to survey our activity. Realizing that nothing would be taught there fourth period, they disappeared. Tom Stern, the only boy who stayed, sat quietly with a book.

Mrs. Vashka spent the rest of the day completing black lettering to grace the yellow and orange paper. She enlisted the help of other students in her later classes. For the sake of appearances, another day of learning was lost.

The week end brought news of a death in the Order of the Ecumenical Institute. Six-year-old Wendy Hollis had been suffering from a brain tumor for some time. Although everyone at the Institute had been aware of her illness, Wendy's death was still a shock. Late in the afternoon all members of the Order were called to assemble in a basement meeting area. We had been told to wear our black berets.

We formed a single line and walked silently out into the winter night, crossing Van Buren and progressing down Trumbull Avenue in the snow. Several residents of Fifth City stopped on the sidewalk to watch the solemn procession. The row of figures—men, women, and children—entered an Institute building on Trumbull and climbed several flights to the Hollis's apartment. Each person patiently filed past Wendy, pale and still, in a tiny wooden four-poster bed. A child's black beret hung on one of the posts near her head.

I had never seen a child in death. I remembered viewing my grandfather in an open casket, but Wendy was so small and so young. Her parents, brother, and relatives sat quietly nearby, accepting this expression of sympathy and tribute. The apartment and stairway became crowded with members of the Order as each one retraced his steps back to the campus.

The procession was a symbol of the way life was affirmed and celebrated within the Institute community. Because death was a part of life, it was embraced and confronted in the same manner as a birth would be. No effort was made to cover up the face of death—to hide or distort it, especially for the children in the Order. Instead, it was accepted as natural and upheld as part of the totality of life.

Roosevelt called for me at six o'clock. I was dressing in my bedroom when I glanced out the window into the dark, snow-covered courtyard below and saw him enter the side door of our building. We walked hand in hand to the El, but Wendy's death had deeply moved us both and our conversation was restrained and somber until we reached the downtown area.

We went to a steakhouse, and at a side table in the carpeted upstairs dining room, Roosevelt talked about his childhood. He had been born in Utica, Mississippi. He recalled the farmhouse of his grandfather and the afternoons he had spent riding bare-back in an open field.

"I'll teach you to ride someday," he promised when I said horses frightened me. "Oh, you jus' grab a hold of that mane, and you'll be off like the wind. . . ." His family had moved to Mobile, Alabama, then New Orleans, Louisiana, before traveling north to Chicago.

A small building on West Madison had been their first Chicago address. Then the Garrisons moved to Fifth Avenue near Marshall. "My old man runs a laundromat," Roosevelt said. "Sometimes I go over and help him clean or paint the place. We don' get along too well, though. I think he never really liked me. Maybe he was disappointed in me. I was the first born but I was always small. People would say, 'That your boy?' and my old man'd nod. 'Didn't grow no bigger than that,' he'd shake his head.

"But I could still outrun my brothers," Roosevelt explained, brightening. "And whenever they needed me, whenever they got in a fight, I never let 'em down. I was always there to defend 'em." He lit a cigarette and sat quietly at the table. I touched his hand, and he looked up quickly and playfully blew a smoke ring into my face.

The following weekend Roosevelt was steward for the train-ing courses at the Institute. The steward's job involved serving hot food to all the course participants at mealtimes and preparing snacks for seminars in between. Since I was not assigned any particular job, I helped him. Together we loaded trays and carried them to the course rooms. We made dozens of trips to the kitchen carrying tubs of dirty dishes. We sponged tables clean and poured coffee.

By Saturday evening Roosevelt had become impatient and clumsy. He spilled food on his shirt. He dropped a tray of vanilla ice cream servings in the entryway. He knocked over a coffee pot and began to cuss. I tried to give him moral support, wiping the stain from his clothes, cleaning up the ice cream, and righting the coffee pot. I tried to cool his temper, to soothe his anger, to keep everything running smoothly. I tried to help him when the responsibility of steward became particularly aggravating, to encourage him when he wanted to quit.

Our relationship was becoming one of real equality. Neither of us dominated. We gave to one another, naturally, whenever a need was present. We were keenly sensitive to each other's moods and feelings, and we met each other's needs with whatever help we could offer.

Sunday afternoon I was doing a family wash. Relieved to be through with stewarding, Roosevelt joined me in the laundry room. The basement was deserted except for the two of us. While the washing machines vibrated, Roosevelt and I clowned. I found an old straw hat abandoned on the floor, and we took turns putting it on and making faces in the glass of the largest dryer. Roosevelt punched a hole through the top of the hat and paraded the room, a shipwrecked king.

Sitting on the top of a washing machine, I dangled my legs as we talked. Roosevelt caught me unaware, picked me up off the machine, swung me around, laughing, and dropped me onto a nearby chair. Then he bent down and kissed me.

Whenever Rudy was part of a group, its whole character changed. Rudy's very presence was forceful, and his mood was infectuous. Realizing this influence, he used it to instill a spirit of hope and possibility, and sometimes a comic relief, to most situations. Rudy had many facets. But a penetrating and sensitive person could find, beneath his facade, admirable personal struggles.

As president of Student Council, Rudy was our "Moses." He called us his "chillen," and it was clear that wherever he chose to lead us, we would follow. Some afternoons Rudy would be extremely tired. Standing at the front of 129, he would rub his eyes and face with his hands and then wave at us to pay no attention. "Y'all have to forgive me, now," he would say, " 'cause I ain't together today."

Once during tenth period he was in an exuberant mood. We were discussing where to go for a May picnic, and Rudy called for suggestions.

"The island!" was one student's choice. This was an isolated circle of land set in the middle of a small lake behind the Museum of Science and Industry.

"Grant Park!"

"No, Garfield Park!"

"How about Lincoln Park? We could go horseback riding!"

"Washington Park!"

"If we go to Washington Park, we might have to mess with the Disciples." Next to the Blackstone Rangers, the Disciples was one of the largest gangs in the city, living and fighting exclusively on the South Side.

"You gonna get intimidated wherever you go," Rudy remarked. "Now if we go to Lincoln Park, round trip bus fare would be fifty cent." Then he continued, "Y'all should never talk 'bout anything where you got to bring money!" Everyone laughed.

A girl raised her hand and Rudy gave her the floor. "How 'bout if the girls ask boys to the picnic and fix the food?"

"If they yo' pahdner," Rudy nodded. "Now, some of the boys—they *cool*, but they ain't too *ready!*"

In the back of the room several freshmen were teasing each other. One dude was moving in on a girl, and she kept giggling. Noting the disturbance, Rudy suddenly sat completely still. Then his eyes widened, and his hand pointed directly at the guilty persons. "Today must be—'I ain't seen you in a long time, so let me look in yo' eyes!' " A howl of laughter erupted in the room, and the freshman girl "hit the dude upside his head." The conversation turned back to food for the picnic.

"Now we love to grub," Rudy said, "but colored people—they eyes is bigger than they gut!" Again the room exploded.

It was time to vote on a final location for the picnic. "Vote," Rudy advised us, " 'cause you got the right. You know, like, I don't *have* to look ugly, but I do 'cause it's my right!" The vote was taken and the majority chose Washington Park.

I often met Rudy in the hall after Spanish. He, Dorothy, and Hosea had adjacent lockers, and we would converge there as we changed books for ninth period.

"I jus' thought up a new thing, y'all," Rudy announced one day as we were getting our books from our lockers. "We gonna put *ar* after our names. Okay?" Abbie was walking toward us and Rudy grabbed her. "*Abbar!*" he yelled.

"*Rudar!*" she replied, as Rudy wildly swung her around in the hall. As we stood there laughing at Rudy's floor show, Hosea suddenly pointed at my feet. "Sue!"

"What?"

"Sue—look at yo' feet, girl! Look at them! Sue," and Hosea did a lean to the side as he pointed again, "you pigeon-toed!" I blushed as Hosea grinned. Then we all walked in a wild, noisy group to the lab for Guidance.

Rudy always wanted to share the things he enjoyed. When Mella came into the lab for Guidance one afternoon Rudy offered to teach us a Four Tops number. Elijah, Delbert, and Rudy sang the first couple of bars and then broke up the parts. I sang the high tenor and Rudy gave Mella the bass. "Loving you . . . sweeter than ever . . ." we jammed. Rudy sang the verse while we did an "oooo" background in sweet harmony. Then we came in with the chorus, "Because loving you . . . sweeter than ever! Who-o-o-w!"

"Oh, y'all! We jammin'! Do it again!" Delbert said as we finished. We repeated the chorus, and Rudy did the dance steps

that completed the routine. The song was simple to memorize,
but I couldn't master the turns and kicks and leans all at one
time. Rudy left Mella and me far behind. Still, it was wonderful fun, and I was exhausted by the time the bell rang, and we
paraded downstairs for Council.

Sensitive to my moods, Rudy approached me one afternoon
when I was tired and sitting quietly, resting my hands on the
table, listening to the jumble of sound around me. "Sue!" he
shouted, flailing his arms in my direction. "Stop sittin' there
lookin' collected! Look distorted! Woooooo!"

Rudy's capacity for leadership was best revealed one afternoon late in February. As soon as he walked into Council, I
knew something was wrong. He didn't say "what's happenin' "
to anyone as he usually did. He didn't laugh; he didn't wave or
do a little boogaloo or sing a line or two from the latest jam.
He was very quiet. He sat on the edge of the stage absently
rubbing his eye and watching Council members take their
seats. He appeared very old, very tired and spent. He was like
a great leader, caught in the terrible demands of responsible
leadership, admitting he possessed weaknesses to those who
were accustomed to seeing only his strength.

As Council president, he stood at the podium. I noticed Miss
Ellis was present, sitting behind the group. She sponsored
Council, but only on rare occasions did she attend meetings.

Rudy looked down at his hands for a moment. Then he began to speak. He said he had gone to hear Stokely Carmichael
at the Senate Theater on West Madison the night before. "I
wanted to hear what the man had to say," Rudy explained.
Everyone in the room was silent. ". . . And I have to tell you
'bout what I heard, 'bout what I been thinkin'. . . ."

Rudy's expression was deeply serious. Few people had ever
seen him so earnest and sincere. "I heard 'bout what it means to
be *black* . . . 'bout how we are beautiful . . . how we should
stand up . . . and walk *tall*. . . ." Rudy's eyes widened, and
each word was tearing itself from inside him. His big hands
gripped the podium, and you could almost feel the power coming out of him. The strength of his words, rising out of his

own visible struggle, was electrifying. He didn't stop talking for the entire period, and he was preachin', tellin' his "chillen" how they could be black and proud and beautiful. He was eloquent.

When the bell rang, we were too stunned to move. Slowly the room came back to life. There was a sprinkle of chatter as people rose to leave, but it was restrained and subdued. I wondered if Rudy realized what power he possessed.

Turning in my seat, I saw Miss Ellis. Her face, like mine, was streaked with tears, and when our eyes met, I knew she too had appreciated Rudy's compelling strength. But Rudy's speech had significance beyond inspiring Council that day. What we had witnessed was the budding of black power consciousness at Marshall.

March

CHAPTER 8

Daddy, Roosevelt, and I stood with the crowd of students on Adams Street, waiting for Marshall's front doors to open. Only students with first period classes were allowed inside before eight o'clock.

"What's happenin', man?"

"Nothin' to it, man," two dudes greeted each other. The sound of the bell signaled the opening of the doors, and slowly we moved up the stairs.

"Hi, Sue," a girl from my English class called. I returned her greeting, glancing down in time to avoid stepping on a cockroach that crawled along the molding of the entrance.

"Take off that hat! Take off those shades! And get that

toothpick outta your mouth!" Mr. Jensen, one of several white assistant principals, yelled at a boy pimpin' down the hall. Mr. Jensen always stood inside the door watching for late-comers. He carried a packet of tardy slips and a rubber stamp with his name on it. A student entering the front door late to Division or second period inevitably went to class with a Jensen slip in his hand.

The object of Mr. Jensen's anger whipped off his hat and shades and pulled the toothpick from between his teeth. But behind Mr. Jensen's back, at the other end of the hall, the boy decked himself out again and continued to pimp coolly upstairs.

I turned to Daddy, who had helped me carry several of my books. "Gimme my jive," I said, grinning.

"Roosevelt, did you hear that?" Daddy's eyes twinkled. "What did she say?"

"Gimme my jive, man!" I repeated, hearing my voice transformed by a West Side accent. Roosevelt and Daddy chuckled as the books changed hands, and we separated to go to class.

Fourth period English did not meet because of a performance of a gospel group, the Marshall Madrigals. I sat in the balcony of the auditorium looking down onto the lighted apron of the stage. Dr. Bronski, Marshall's white principal, stood before a microphone, preparing to introduce the Madrigals. I always thought he was a kind man, but he was too bland and indecisive to handle Marshall's problems with tough, honest involvement. He didn't live in the reality of the West Side. He appeared in the halls occasionally and spoke at school functions, but he had no creative vision for Marshall. Dr. Bronski was not a strong leader. He was simply a competent administrator working his way up the ladder of the educational hierarchy. "Today the Madrigals are presenting 'The Legacy of the Negro'" he announced, "a performance I'm sure we'll all enjoy."

Four students sat at a table to my right on the stage. I recognized Sandra and a boy from my English class and Nick and Melvin, who played on the football team. They were the nar-

rators, passing a microphone from hand to hand as they shared
the reading.

On the left side of the stage in three rows, one sitting and
two standing, were the Madrigals. Rudy, Anthony White,
Elijah, and Ken, a Student Council member, were the only
boys in the fifteen-member group. They were smartly dressed
in suits. All the girls, including Shirley and Mella, wore black
skirts and blouses, accented with single strands of pearls.

Mr. Lionel O'Bara directed. I recalled talking to him in
Chorus one morning. Standing six feet tall, his black face shining under a beautiful natural, he had invited me to come to his
office after school to join the Madrigals. But two extra periods
at Marshall had proved so demanding I decided not to take on
another activity.

"Good news! Chariot's comin'! Good news! Chariot's comin'! And I don' wanna be left behind!" One narrator explained
the origin of the Negro spirituals and told how the Fisk Jubilee
Singers had traveled the country making them famous.

"Live a-humble, humble, humble yourselves! The bells done
rung!" the Madrigals sang. Anthony stepped out of his place
in line. "Now watch the sun! See how she run! Don't let her
catch you with your work undone!" His tenor was clear and
bright. His eyes widened and his arm stretched out over the
audience. "Now you see God—and you see God—and you see
God in the morning!"

Mella's high soprano introduced the song that followed.
"Get you ready!" she called. "There's a meeting here tonight!"
the Madrigals returned. "I know you by your daily walk!
There's a meeting here tonight!"

"There's fire in the East! There's fire in the West!" Rudy
jammed alone. Mr. O'Bara's hands directed furiously, but Rudy
was free to give his solo as much feeling and individual interpretation as he wished. When several verses were finished,
Rudy, too, stepped back into line and the narrators introduced
the next spiritual, "Rockin' Jerusalem." I leaned forward in my
seat, lost in the excellent quality of the sound. It spoke of
power and beauty. The voices were untrained, yet their blend

was rich and vital. Fifteen singers might have been a hundred. "Ain't gonna let nobody—turn me around!" The freedom song Daddy and I had chanted on the Selma-Montgomery March awoke vivid memories. Ken had a solo in "Great Day," and then the narrators made a final statement about the evolution of the spiritual. The performance thrilled me. Leaving the auditorium, I regretted not having accepted Mr. O'Bara's invitation to join the Madrigals.

Rudy walked into Chorus rehearsal fifth period and stopped at my seat. Taking my hand, he asked softly, "What did you think, Sue? Did you like it?"

"Like it?" I was unrestrained in genuine admiration. "Rudy, I was so proud! Rudy, I was proud, man! It was beautiful!"

"Oooo," he responded, at a loss for words, his face aglow with satisfaction.

Marshall teachers could be both frustrating and invigorating. As authority figures, it was their task to discipline students, and their methods ranged from mild disapproval to incredible harshness. As pedagogues they exhausted themselves explaining concepts, attempting to communicate with the black faces they confronted every day in the classroom. Some became apathetic and indifferent under the strain. Others rigidly stuck to their lesson plans while their students slept. Still other teachers worked with a relentless drive that somehow kept them fighting, unwilling to give in to futility and despair.

Classroom work was challenge enough for any teacher. Adding frustration, however, was the necessity for surviving and outwitting the Chicago school system. Hours of painful red tape were a part of each normal class day, often requiring attention during the class periods. Additional red tape stood between the teacher and any change he wished to bring about—any creativity he brought to his work. The Board of Education was a bureaucratic monster—impersonal, cold, unrelenting.

Ten minutes of second period had already passed. A shiver shook me, as the breeze from the window Mr. Wagner had opened reached my desk. We were discussing the latest sports

news, and I wondered when Mr. Wagner would pass out the
tests we were supposed to take. Two boys on the track team
finished talking about a recent meet in the city.

"Oh, Mr. Wagner, let's not have the test today."

"Yeah—can't we wait until tomorrow?"

"We ain't ready. . . ."

Mr. Wagner had the tests in his hand, and my desk was
cleared in preparation. Fingering my pencil, I watched him
grin and begin to waver in the face of so much protest. Several
girls pleaded for another day before the exam. "Mr. Wagner,
please. . . ."

Why doesn't he make up his mind, I wondered. Why does
he waste time arguing? The debate went on for another ten
minutes. I wished he would take a position one way or the
other.

By the time Mr. Wagner passed out the tests and hushed the
room, I was quite agitated. We had barely half the period left
to complete the questions. We had been cheated of time, and I
was disappointed by Mr. Wagner's behavior. If he had really
meant to postpone the test, he should have clearly declared
that, and then helped us review.

A fuller appreciation of New Trier's teaching standards developed during those final months in high school. The control
and decisive direction of teachers who were allowed a wide
degree of academic freedom and who felt the support and encouragement of their administration were obviously major factors in a quality school system.

Miss Ellis worked us hard fifth period. We had begun rehearsing numbers for the Spring Concert in May. The sopranos
consistently sang several wrong notes on one page of a song.
Our section had been making the same mistake for weeks, and
Miss Ellis did not correct it. Every time I raised my hand to
get her attention, she changed pages or exploded impatiently
over another irritation. She wouldn't recognize me or give me
a chance to state what was bothering me.

I was aware of the difficulties she had to contend with in
order to teach music. Most of the chorus members had no

musical training, and few could read notes. But I felt the music deserved an accurate rendering, and I hated to see the mistake pass unnoticed. Some balance between the precision and technical excellence of former groups I had sung with, and the exuberant, natural, but inexact artistry of Marshall's chorus should have been achieved.

The Institute staff, in developing a community plan for the black ghetto, based their Fifth City program heavily on one central thesis. Long before it became a familiar and popular concept, members of the Order stated that the black man's deep spirit problem was one of self-image. They contended that no solution to the political or economic poverty of the ghetto, in the areas of housing or employment, would be permanent or adequate if it did not also deal with how the black man saw himself—how he "imaged" himself.

Years of white suppression and exploitation had scarred the black man. Treated as less than human, he had begun to believe what the white man told him—that he *was* second-class, worthless, unwanted, unneeded by his society. Within the black community, the white man appeared in all positions of power. The white man controlled the black man's schools, his stores, and law enforcement agencies. In effect, the black man was unable to make any significant decisions directing his own life, for the white man consistently overruled them. The black man had, in effect, acquired a "nigger" image. His patterns of action reflected the white man's belief in his inferiority. Expected to lose and fail, the black man came to mistrust his own abilities and judgments. He became, as white society knew he would: apathetic and irresponsible. He saw himself as a victim.

The Institute staff recognized that unless the black man's self-image could become positive, reflecting feelings of self-worth and dignity, all community programs in black neighborhoods would inevitably end in failure.

With this knowledge of the importance of seeing oneself positively, I became conscious of the underlying self-images of black people with whom I came into contact. Two teachers,

one Negro and one white, evidenced in particular not only a
high degree of influence on the self-images of their students,
but a personal struggle concerned with their images of themselves.

Miss Johns was black. One day a week her gym class met in
a room on the second floor for health instruction. We had a
number of books I felt certain had been written for junior high
or younger students, and these we read out loud.

Miss Johns came to rely on me to run errands for her and to
read to the class. If she had forgotten something, she would
send me back to her office for it, and then she would ask me to
stand by her desk with a book. I hated the picture of myself in
front of that class, for I was white and I represented what was
always chosen, what was supposedly better. I felt trapped by
my own conscientiousness in always obeying the teacher and
thus perpetuating the white image of superior talent.

"Gregory, read chapter one."

I would begin, hearing my own impeccable pronunciation,
hearing the words and phrases about first aid and bleeding and
injuries, and knowing I was not meeting the needs of the girls
who faced me. I looked at those black faces—tired, hostile,
bored, and indifferent. Here we were, seniors in high school,
reading aloud from childish books.

When another girl was called on, she stumbled over the
words. She faltered in the middle of a sentence, and Miss Johns
corrected her mispronunciation with a flippant vengeance. It
hurt me to hear that voice, sharp and biting, stop a girl's reading with an impatient correction. Was Miss Johns ashamed of
her blackness? Was she ashamed of the girls in her class? Did
their own poor reading ability confront and embarrass her,
causing her manner to become cold and harsh?

Once, in health, when we had an open discussion about mar-
riage, I heard Miss Johns laugh. She delighted in talking and
listening to our opinions about going steady and dating. Her
genuine sympathy had surprised me, but also convinced me of
her humanity, of her capacity for warmth.

What caused her, at other times, to appear so harsh? Did she

really despise the role she played? Did she feel she was forced
to be a tough authoritarian figure because of the conditions of
the school in which she taught? Did she believe there was no
other way to maintain discipline? I did not know the answers
to my questions. I only sensed that Miss Johns had realized I
was trustworthy and had exhibited her confidence by asking
me to perform various tasks for her.

Miss Johns's eyes moved down the rows of girls before her,
observing the empty numbers on the gym floor and marking
her book with the absences. "Okay, girls, move up on the numbers. . . ." We slid forward on our seats, filling in all the va-
cant spaces.

"Legs extended, widestride position. Hands on hips, place.
On the count of one, bring your legs together, two—knees up
to your chest, three—back to the floor, four—extended.
Ready? Exercise, one, two, three, four . . . one, two, three,
four." We moved in rhythm, making arcs on the floor with the
heels of our gym shoes. I watched Miss Johns as she paraded
the room, completing the exercise with the command, "Last
call—three, four," and snapping orders for the next.

"Legs together. You're goin' to go toes, knees, waist, knees.
Hands on hips, place. Begin—one, two, three, four . . . toes,
knees, waist, knees. . . ." Several girls relaxed their arms when
Miss Johns wasn't looking. I wondered if she was aware of the
hostility her domineering figure elicited from the girls in the
gym. Was Miss Johns intentionally condescending? How did
the girls see themselves as a result of her strict discipline?

When the gruelling exercises were over, Miss Johns and the
two assistants responsible for our class of one hundred taught
gymnastics. We spent many periods using the mats, sitting in
rows in back of them, and waiting for a turn. Although I did
not like acrobatic activity, I was surprised at the number of
girls who were honestly afraid or highly reluctant to take part.
While the teachers were working at the mats, girls near the
front of the lines would slip back in the line so that they
would never have to perform. Some spent entire forty minute
periods sitting on the gym floor waiting, and when the bell

rang, left unnoticed.

I decided that I would have to face my own dislike for acrobatics and my limited physical ability. Although I was tempted to slip to the back of the line, everyone in the class knew me, and there was no way for me to be inconspicuous. When my turn came to perform, I took position at the mat for the backward roll. I could remember having trouble with it in grammar school, trying again and again to go over, but never gaining enough momentum.

I was scared. I sat there with my hands on the floor at my sides feeling every eye in the room watching. There was dead silence. Miss Johns stood directly above me, hands on her hips. Her towering presence cast a foreboding shadow over my body. I couldn't move. When I took a breath and started to push myself backwards, I didn't go over and had to sit up again. A second time my attempt failed. It was funny, and yet I was anxious and frustrated. Somehow I knew I had to succeed.

Miss Johns was impatient. I could hear several girls whispering. The story would be passed around that Sue Gregory was unable to do a silly backward roll in gym.

"Gregory, what are you afraid of?"

I looked up into Miss Johns's face. "I don't know," I said honestly. For a moment I seemed to have touched her, for she had no answer to such direct sincerity. She placed her hand firmly on my head. I closed my eyes and she pushed me off. My legs rolled over my head, and miraculously I found myself standing at the other end of the mat. There were cheers and handclapping. Then the next person took position at the mat.

Later, in the locker room, someone punched me jokingly in the arm and I laughed. "Hey, Sue!" Vera called to me, "I'm glad you made it!"

"Yeah," Paulette said. "I almost thought we'd lost you there!" I smiled. I wasn't perfect, and everyone knew that now. The pats on the back were reassuring, but I never wanted to do another backward roll for Miss Johns.

Miss Magda was white.

"Dum-dum, open the window. It's hot in here." Miss Magda jerked her head at a boy in the first row of seventh period economics, and he crawled out of his seat and hoisted the window. The flesh of her arms shook as she sat at her desk, dabbing on make-up. Miss Magda was a heavy woman, and when she entered the classroom each day after lunch, she always gasped for breath and complained about the long walk upstairs.

I tried to concentrate on my econ book, but I was tired of reading. Miss Magda had done some exciting teaching at the beginning of the semester. She had led spirited, rapid-fire discussions. Neither Rudy nor I could forget the afternoon she had fascinated us with stories about the Federal Food and Drug Administration, telling us what strawberry ice cream was really made of, warning us about our choices of meat, and advising us to check the bottom of a soft drink bottle before we drank from it. But those seventh periods had become memories. Now we came to class only to listen to her endless commands and try to keep up with her lengthy assignments.

Miss Magda's name-calling was the most debasing technique I had seen used against Marshall students. Everyone was "Dum-dum." Often we were all "Idiots!" and "Stupid people!" Miss Magda never hesitated to rip up a piece of homework in front of the entire class, calling out the person's name and openly chastising him for his errors. Miss Magda called Bobby King, also a member of Daddy's English class, "King Kong." Another senior boy was "Vacuum" because, according to Miss Magda, he had nothing in his head. A dude who sat near the back of the room she labeled "Germ." And Rudy was named "F" because his grades in economics were failing.

"Hey, you!" Someone had allowed himself to doze in her presence. Miss Magda reached behind her, grabbed an eraser from the blackboard ledge, and, squinting her eye to aim and pursing her lips, hit the boy on the head with it. The eraser bounced off into the corner and the boy sleepily looked up.

"Please bring my eraser back; that's a good little boy. . . ." Miss Magda smiled, and the acid of her tone made me shudder.

I looked around at the feet of my classmates. We all knew that wearing gym shoes in Miss Magda's room was a mortal sin and would be punished accordingly. She had threatened to stomp on any feet found in gym shoes. The thought of all that weight deliberately crushing down on someone's toes was far from inviting.

"Remember yesterday, class," Miss Magda began, fiddling with a paper on her desk, "when we were talking about the shooting at Waller High School?" (A student had brought a carbine to Waller and wildly fired six shots during an assembly in the auditorium.) "Remember? I said that if someone had shot off a gun at *Marshall*, the incident would have made front-page news, and the police would have been on the scene immediately. Like last year, when we tried to get publicity for our play, the newspapers said it wasn't newsworthy, but we should call them back if we had a riot. Well, I was discussing this injustice with another teacher, and he said, 'But, Miss Magda, why are *you* so upset? *You're* not a Negro.' Now class, you understand that my concern is for us as a school . . . Marshall . . . *us!*"

It seemed to me that Miss Magda, like Shirley, was troubled with her self-image. Did she feel uncomfortable as a white person in an all-black school? Did she unconsciously hate herself? Had she ever accepted her own whiteness and her uniqueness as a human being? In the process of degrading black students, was she attempting to put herself in a favorable light?

"We know, Miss Magda, that deep inside, you're Negro!" It was Rudy, answering her comments about Waller, speaking from his seat in the back of the room. Miss Magda's face turned a bright pink, but she was flattered and for a moment reassured about her own identity struggle.

There was a knock at the door. Miss Magda had established a rule that no one was permitted to enter her classroom without her permission. The entire student body was aware of her rigid enforcement of this rule. A boy stood outside, his head visible in the small pane of clear glass in the door. Miss Magda sent someone out to talk to him, and the messenger reported that the boy wanted to speak to Diane. Miss Magda gave her permission and Diane vanished behind the door into the hall. Soon another head appeared in the little window.

"King Kong," Miss Magda motioned to Bobby King, "go to the door and let Victor in, but not Diane." I looked up from my book, seeing Bobby's confusion and reluctance. "Don't ask questions, Dum-dum. Do it!" Miss Magda glared. Bobby left his seat and went to the door.

I found it hard to believe the events that followed. Bobby took hold of the doorhandle, pushing the door open carefully. With all his strength he fought Diane, who was trying to pull the door open wider from the other side. Victor slipped inside the room through the slight opening. Bobby grasped the handle tighter and managed to pull the door closed, while Diane remained outside in the hall pounding for recognition.

I stared at Miss Magda. As the noise increased in intensity, I wondered why Diane should want to come back into the room at all. Why didn't she just leave 206? Perhaps she wanted to retrieve her belongings, which were piled on her desk. As Diane continued to beat on the door, another face appeared in the glass.

"King Kong, go to the door and let him in, but not Diane."

Bobby shook his head. "I don't want to go," he stated.

"I'm giving you the responsibility."

"I don't *want* the responsibility," Bobby replied.

"King Kong, if you don't do it, you will *flunk*. You will get an *F*." The finality with which Miss Magda spoke was not to be laughed at. Bobby was a senior and a failing grade threatened his graduation.

He rose reluctantly and walked slowly to the door. The previous battle was repeated, except that Bobby had a more difficult time closing the door. Though he lost considerable footing on the slippery floor, he allowed the strange visitor to enter the room while continuing to exclude Diane. Bobby returned to his seat, shaking his head with fatigue.

I buried my face in my book, afraid of losing my composure in the face of the ridiculous game I was watching. I wanted to stand up and scream in Miss Magda's face. Instead, I reminded myself of what Rudy had told me once when I had expressed disgust at Miss Magda's attitude. "Sue," he had said, "sometimes you just gotta Tom. Sometimes . . . you just gotta Tom. . . ." In other words, he explained, you just gotta be an Uncle Tom —do whatever the "boss man" expects and tell him "yassah" even when you hate it, just to get by. But that didn't satisfy me. It only raised other questions. Why should anyone submit to such humiliation every day? Why must anyone Tom?

John, Miss Magda's "Vacuum," added to my frustration. "What are *you* mad about, Sue?" he asked me. "She hasn't hurt *you* any." But did she have to insult me directly to upset me? Wasn't watching her pick apart my fellow students enough to aggravate me? Weren't exasperation and anger justified when I saw Marshall students' self-images systematically destroyed by her cruel remarks?

Ignoring the need for permission to enter the room and the possible consequences for disobedience, Diane finally opened the door and began to walk quietly behind Miss Magda's desk in order to get to her seat.

"Well, Diane," Miss Magda's voice was sugar-sweet, "where have you been? What kept you? No one said you couldn't come into the room. *I* didn't say that!"

This farce had gone on long enough. How dared Miss Magda make such a statement? I had reached the limit of patience. My eyes glared into hers.

"You *did, too!*" I shot back.

She fixed her cold stare onto my face. "*You,* Miss Gregory, will get an F!" A hush fell over the room as Miss Magda took a pencil and wrote something in her gradebook.

The bell rang and Rudy followed me into the hall, his round eyes wide. "Sue got a F. Sue got a F," he kept repeating, incredulously, until we reached the lunchroom.

"Well, goddam, I don't care. I hate that woman," I blurted out, noting the shock on several faces. They had never heard me swear before.

"It was only in pencil, though," Rudy said, still reacting to Miss Magda's grade mark. It *was* only in pencil, I thought. She couldn't really flunk me. She couldn't write the grade in ink and make it legitimate. She couldn't even do that for me— because I was white. Carol had told me how Miss Magda talked about me in her other classes. "You'd better study for this test because Susan Gregory in my seventh period class is going to get a hundred." She had poisoned the possibility of my forming friendships by setting me up as an example. She had used my name as a whip over the other students. Now, however, her strategy had backfired, trapping her. She could not fail the student she had so publicly held up as an example of excellence.

Never before had I actually despised a teacher. But Miss Magda's deep sickness, which led her to destroy my fellow students, brought me close to contempt.

Seeing the self-images of my fellow Marshall students undermined daily only increased my appreciation of their gifts as members of a unique black culture. I was always amazed by their spontaneous, uninhibited behavior and the natural talent they displayed. Several events in March pointed up this impulsively free and inspirational conduct.

One afternoon after ninth period a Jamboree was held in the auditorium. "Jamboree" was a term for Talent Show, and several singing groups, a ventriloquist, a guitarist, and "go-go" girls demonstrated their creative ability. The Ivories, a three-girl group that had recently cut a record, jammed Aretha Franklin's "Respect." Several boys, who always sang across the table from me in the lunchroom, did the Tempts "Say You," with a routine that was fast-paced and wonderfully funny. Rudy, Elijah, Delbert, Hosea, and another boy, forming the Delections, came on before the finale, doing "Reach Out For Me." Hosea and Maxine, both seniors, were impressive in a dance routine. They faced each other at opposite ends of the stage and came forward when the music started, their fingers popping and hips swaying. The two were almost the same height, and they captivated the audience with their rhythmic movements.

Attending classes and viewing the activities of my Marshall friends when they were jivin' with on another and performing in such functions as a Jamboree, strengthened my belief that, because of educational background and cultural values, the black youth of the West Side expressed themselves better physically and verbally than through the written word. Reading and writing, seen as highly important skills by members of the white middle class, had little achievement and prestige value in the black community. Dancing and singing were more significant modes of expression on the West Side. Open physical and verbal aggression was more common and generally better understood.

"Let's yell hurrah for Abbie's house when we see it. Okay?"

Members of Mrs. Vashka's fourth period English class were returning home from a field trip. Having read Tennessee Williams' *Glass Menagerie* in class, we had attended a local performance and boarded a bus for the return to Marshall.

"All right!" Someone responded

"Wait!" It was Vera. "Hurrah for my church!" she shouted, as our bus passed the building so familiar to her.

"Hurrah for Vera's church!" everybody replied.

"Hurrah for grammar school!" a boy called, and the group echoed his words.

"Hurrah for the Vashkas!" someone offered, and we took up the cheer.

"Hurrah for the bus driver!" "Hurrah for that dude in the brown jacket!" "Hurrah for the Midwest Boy's Club!" "Hurrah for WVON!" The calls were inspired by the scenes observed through the bus windows. Each call was returned by the whole group. The number of imaginative expressions was endless. I began to laugh, unable to control my amazement at the way Marshall students could enjoy the spontaneity of the moment.

"Hurrah for the senior class!" a student shouted, and everyone broke up with laughter.

"Hey! Hurrah! Abbie's house—there it is!"

"Which one?"

"That one," somebody pointed, ". . . the one next to the house with the red doors!"

I envied this ability to throw oneself completely into the happening of the moment. Such alive, vital expression was a gift I remembered witnessing for the first time one evening in Knoxville, Tennessee, when the Gregorys worked in a study-skills program for high school students, most of whom were black. In the basement lounge of a college dormitory, a group of students had gathered for a jam session. Crowding around the piano, the sweat from the heat of a summer night trickled down the black faces of young SSSP participants caught up in a hand-clapping version of Ray Charles "What'd I Say?" When the recorded verses of the song were completed, different people made up their own, and everyone else joined in the chorus. There was complete freedom in the creation of new words and phrases, and anything said about another student was accepted with good-natured humor. Ann, Dougie, and I stayed in Room 301 in the dorm. When Marcus King wiped the perspiration from his brow, grinned at me, and sang, "If you wanna have some fun, come on up to 301! All right!" I laughed, enjoying his teasing and knowing it was his way of including me in the group.

"Hurrah for Mella!"

"Hurrah!"

"Hurrah for Stella!" Stella shouted, but when we were all supposed to reply, Stella's voice cried "Hurrah!" alone, and she blushed.

The bus turned down Kedzie, and the brick walls of Marshall appeared. "Hurrah for Marshall!"

"Hurrah!"

As quickly as the bus stopped on Adams Street, everyone was suddenly quiet. The moment had passed, and it was time to take up a new activity. I climbed off the bus, watching little clusters of students go off down the street. Several girls talked animatedly, already immersed in another "moment."

Mella and I waved goodbye to Vera and crossed Adams. We took the El to Pulaski-Keeler and walked the last two blocks to Mella's home on Harrison, stopping at a small store for some milk Mella's mother needed. The owner was Puerto Rican. He always greeted us with "Buenas tardes," and we returned his good afternoon with a smile, banging the battered screen door of the shop behind us as we continued down the sidewalk, past an abandoned warehouse and the corner cleaners.

"Hey, girl with the long hair—what's to it?"

A dude with a do-rag over his greased head called to me. I didn't answer him then, but when he had disappeared, I turned to Mella and mimicked, "Hey, cat with the process—what's happenin'?" She laughed.

Mella's home was one of three buildings on a dead-end street facing Congress Expressway. Standing on the porch, I could look into an empty lot and alley to the left. Just beyond was the cement ramp leading to a bridge that crossed over the expressway. Mella unlocked the front door of the red building and we entered the dark living room, hearing the television blaring from the corner where Mella's brother sat engrossed.

Mella led me to the bedroom she shared with her younger sister. I pulled the string that dangled from the one light bulb hanging from the ceiling and dumped my books on the double beds that were tightly squeezed into one end of the room, leaving only a rectangle of walking space at their foot.

Mella's mother was in the kitchen at the back of the apartment, and we went out to say hello. She was a tiny woman with small brown eyes that forever glowed, as if she were keeping a wonderful secret. Sitting at a table, cigarette in hand, she looked up from the newspaper and smiled. Mella put the milk in the refrigerator and went into the dining room to put soul music on the hi-fi. She tried to teach me to bop, and we danced a good part of the afternoon.

Suddenly, Mella vanished into the bathroom, calling out "Hey, I gotta wash my hair." I remained at the hi-fi, playing the stack of 45's that were always piled there. When Mella emerged, what had been straight black hair was a head of frizzy curls. She went into the kitchen and sat down in a chair pulled near the stove. Her mother turned up the flame, so that it leaped high from the cage of the left-hand burner. Standing over Mella in her housecoat, she parted Mella's hair and rubbed grease from a tiny jar onto the back of her hand. Then Mella's mother stuck the black comb into the flame and, wiping grease onto a lock of hair, ran the hot comb through it. Mella winced, and her hair emitted a sizzling, hissing sound. Her mother continued to moisten grease into each lock of hair she parted and to run the hot comb through it. The process was a long one, but gradually Mella's hair lay flat and hung straight down at the sides of her head.

"Aren't you glad you don't have to go through this?" Mella grinned at me as I shook my head, shuddering at the crackling of the hair and the heated comb. The danger of burning the scalp seemed great, but Mella's mother was experienced with hair straightening and was careful. When she finally turned down the flame on the stove, Mella got up and braided her straightened hair.

I marveled at the practices of black people so little known or understood by whites. Every day I came to know another unique aspect of the black man's world. Though I had learned a great deal, there was much more to discover.

April

CHAPTER 9

Roosevelt and I stood in the light of a street lamp on Jackson Boulevard, waiting for a bus. It was the Sunday after spring vacation, and my family had just returned from a week-long trip. Roosevelt and I were glad to see each other again and had left the Institute campus to spend an evening together in the city.

"Hey, man!" Out of the shadows came a tall youth in a black trenchcoat.

"Eugene!" Roosevelt and I greeted him in unison.

Eugene flashed a grin and stood before us, hands in his coat pockets. He had been Roosevelt's "running buddy" before Roosevelt moved to the Institute.

"Where y'all goin'?" Eugene asked.

"We're on our way downtown, man," Roosevelt answered.

Eugene nodded, turned, and waved us off. I wondered who he "hung with" now that Roosevelt was occupied with other friends. It seemed so easy for a sensitive boy like Eugene, smooth and shy, to become lost in the fast-paced demands of the city. It seemed so easy for him to be swallowed up and forgotten. Where is he wandering to now, I wondered. It was not a waning friendship that had separated Eugene and Roosevelt, it was a matter of circumstance. Roosevelt no longer lived on Fifth Avenue, several doors away from Eugene. They couldn't "make a run" together whenever they had the urge. When Eugene called at the Institute to find him, Roosevelt usually was involved in a meeting or week-end course.

The relationship of Eugene and Roosevelt was but one small result of the instability of ghetto life. The people of the West Side were accustomed to the constant mobility of others and the presence of new neighbors. In the transience of the community, it was almost impossible to keep up with the affairs of every friend.

"It's our bus!" Roosevelt helped me up the step and dropped change into the meter by the driver. We were jostled to a seat in the back where we talked, ignoring the eyes of other passengers.

We left the bus in the Loop and wandered down State Street, crossing to Michigan Avenue and into Grant Park. We walked under the trees until we reached the corner opposite the Field Museum, its pillars tall and majestic in the night. Running across the wide boulevard, normally heavy with traffic, we climbed up the dark overpass connecting the park to Soldier Field. Last summer I had marched from Soldier Field and crossed the same bridge with a hand-clapping, singing, and sign-carrying throng. Martin Luther King had been the speaker during that tremendous rally.

Now Roosevelt and I were completely alone on the bridge, and it seemed longer and wider. We leaned over the side. A solid row of cars, headlights beaming, approached the bridge like an army of giant insects coming to devour us. Roosevelt cocked an imaginary gun and shot the invaders one by one, as they disappeared underneath us.

Farther down the bridge Roosevelt picked a blossom from the branches of a tree that spilled down onto the overpass railing. I kept the little flower, and we left the bridge, traveling around the back of the Field Museum, past the Park District Building where I had once auditioned for a community chorus. The wind from the lake was chilly and I buttoned my sweater.

"The hawk sure is out tonight," Roosevelt said, putting his arm around me. We passed the peninsula that stretched out into the lake, cradling the Planetarium at its point. Retracing our steps through Grant Park we crossed another bridge that took us back to Michigan Avenue. There we strolled, arm in arm, window-shopping, reading signs, and laughing as we walked through a crowd of business men chatting on the sidewalk in front of their hotel.

"I should tell you about what happened while you were away on your trip. . . ." Roosevelt said as we found ourselves in the glaring neon of State Street again. "Somebody stole a woman's purse right outside the Institute. A police car happened to be going down the street. I jumped into the squad car, and we chased the man. But the bottom of the car picked up an old mattress abandoned in an alley. We must have dragged that thing several blocks before we found out what was slowin' us up. The mattress just hooked itself onto the car! We never found the dude who took the purse."

"Hey, my feet are aching. We've probably walked four miles tonight. Let's head for home," I suggested. We traveled to the LaSalle Street subway tunnel and waited for a train.

The evening may have exhausted my feet, but it enriched my love for the city. To be in the heart of the city was to be where life was happening. You didn't need money to appreciate the city. Its streets were for bumming. It was neon and traffic and the park late at night. It was that tired man on the corner with no place to go. It was somebody's radio blaring loud and the sound of the El overhead.

My freedom with Roosevelt had helped me discover the vitality of the city and all that it could offer. I didn't want to trade that freedom for anything in the world.

My adventures with Roosevelt were not always far-ranging. Sometimes we simply stayed at home, and one afternoon I found Roosevelt washing his father's car on Van Buren Street.

"Gimme two minutes, and I'll help you," I called to him, running upstairs to change into the jean shorts that were splattered with paint from the week we had decorated our apartment.

Roosevelt had a bucket and several rags. He threw me a cloth, and I bent over the side of the car. Roosevelt took out all the rubber mats from the floor and shook them on the side-walk. He skirted in and out of the Institute, getting cleansers and brushes. We turned on the car radio, attracting children with the music and our activity.

It was a beautiful spring afternoon. Members of the Order, outside running errands, stopped, smiled, and commended our efforts. I finished Windexing the windows and Roosevelt hoisted me onto the roof.

"Hey! Everything looks great from up here!" I called. A little girl giggled, pointing up at me as Roosevelt playfully pulled my legs. "Hey, man!" I cautioned, "Watch that or I'll slide right off!"

Several of Roosevelt's friends waved from across the street and shouted their critical judgment of our progress. A police car made its rounds, and the driver did a double-take, surprised at the unorthodox car-washing team.

Sitting on the front seat of the car, cleaning the upholstery, I overheard two women passing on the sidewalk. "You oughta be ashamed of yourself, trying to get a job working for those whites!" the taller woman scolded. She wore a long black dress, and her hair, plastered down and partially exposed by a scarf wrapped tightly around her head, gleamed in the after-noon sun. The other woman was stockier in build and seemed to be listening helplessly to this barage of hate.

"Don't you never try to get a job with them no more!" The

taller woman pointed an angry finger at the Institute campus. "You know we should never work for nobody but our own kind . . . !" This tirade halted all activity on the street for a moment, as everyone listened. But when the two women disappeared around the corner, children began chasing one another again, Roosevelt continued waxing the car, and the tempo picked up where it had been interrupted.

Later in the evening Roosevelt took me to the Chicago Public Library Branch on Pulaski Avenue. I needed some information for my English term paper about the black author, Richard Wright.

The library was old, built of brown brick. Its windows were as gray and bleak as the streets that surrounded them. Roosevelt and I seated ourselves at a table in one of the research rooms. There were two shelves of magazines, but I unearthed little information about Richard Wright. The books on Negro history were inadequate and outdated. I did find one helpful reference volume and took notes. When it got dark outside, the lights of the library cast a hazy yellow over the page I was reading.

We left at nine o'clock when the lights blinked, signaling closing time. Roosevelt and I stopped at a corner drugstore and sat on stools at a counter. We ordered hamburgers from an old black man, nearly toothless, who, despite his age and appearance, was bouncing with vitality and humor. He approached each customer with warm concern and, talking animatedly as he worked, transformed what is often considered a menial task into a meaningful personal service. A couple to our right also enjoyed his jokes, and a lone man holding a coffee cup with both hands smiled in amusement. All of us were drawn together by the joy which the old man radiated.

I wondered about the old man as he poured cokes and cooked hamburgers in his white apron. Did he have a family? Did he live alone? How many years had he worked in a drugstore on the West Side? No one would consider him of much importance. Yet, there Roosevelt and I sat, in the middle of the West Side, enriched by a man who had undoubtedly suf-

fered considerable pain in his life, and who surely could not
live much longer, but whose insight and simplicity and humanity was immediately communicated. I felt relaxed and at home
and left reluctantly for the walk back to the Institute.

Feeling elated, I stepped into the street without looking for
traffic. "Baby!" Roosevelt yelled, pushing me out of the path
of a CTA bus, its headlights looming out of a fog of darkness
as it rumbled toward me.

We came to the edge of Garfield Park, walking behind a
boy and his German shepherd. Roosevelt began to joke about
the dogs of his childhood in the South. "Hey, don't make so
much noise," he indicated to the animal. "It doesn't look
friendly. . . ."

"Roosevelt," I asked, as he put his arm around me, "what
was it like living in the South? Can you remember anything?
Did you know about the 'world,' living there on a farm?"

Roosevelt led me around the back of the elementary school
my brother Dougie attended, on a corner of Garfield Park. "I
remember once my brother and me hitched a ride with a white
man in a pick-up truck. He wanted directions to a person's
house, and we lied 'cause we wanted the ride, told him we
knew how to get there. We took him to the right street but
the wrong side of town and jumped off the back of the truck
before he could get at us. He was pretty mad!

"I remember another day when a white man spit on me.
That was the first time anyone called me 'nigger.' "

I stared hard at the ground, intent upon watching my step
in the dark, while listening to Roosevelt's words. "And I remember," he went on, "That I was never 'sposed to look
directly into the face of a white woman. . . ."

My cheeks flushed at his statement, and I angrily kicked a
rock across the sidewalk. So these were some of the childhood
memories of a black boy from the South. How difficult it
must have been for this boy to trust whites. How difficult it
must have been for Roosevelt to accept the love of a white
girl, when not so long ago he had been forbidden to look into
the face of one.

Traveling the final two blocks home in silence, I squeezed
Roosevelt's hand reassuringly.

I was no newcomer to interracial dating. During the year before our move to the West Side, the black boy I had met
through the New Trier Summer Seminar had become a
central figure in my life. Using public transportation, sitting
in theaters, and walking the streets of the city and suburb, our
relationship had made me aware of the reaction of people to
interracial couples.

Because of their social conditioning—resulting from the
white man's restrictions on the black community—black people have developed the ability to "tune in" rapidly on the
moods and attitudes expressed by overt glances, voice tones,
facial "sets," and body movements of white people. They are
adept at sensing acceptance and displeasure, quick to perceive
nuances of feeling that lie under the surface of outward appearances.

My black escorts helped me acquire this sensitivity, so that
I soon became aware of the curious glances and the expressions
of disapproval of people we encountered on our dates. I also
developed a number of responses to such reactions.

When it was a matter of verbal assault, I ignored the remarks. "What are you doing with that white girl?" a middle-
aged white man stopped his car and shouted from the driver's
seat. "Is that your nigger?" a white boy yelled on the street.
"Tom! Uncle Tom!" a black youth accused my escort.

When we were openly stared at, I returned the curiosity
or disbelief with a smile or a wave. People often gaped at our
car on the expressway and it was my habit to look out the
window and smile broadly into the face of the other person.
Being friendly seemed to embarrass the curious observer.

We were careful with our remarks and avoided any physically aggressive encounters. If anyone was offended enough to
threaten physical force, we left as quickly as possible.

An incident Roosevelt and I often recalled with amusement
occurred one night when we borrowed his father's car to go

to the library. We never reached that destination. Invigorated by being in possession of a car that could take us out of the West Side, that could remove us temporarily from responsibilities and worries, Roosevelt drove down to the Loop and parked near the Planetarium where it was quiet and Lake Michigan stretched before us. It was so good to get away, with no one knowing about it. Here there was no Marshall, no Institute. Just us! We laughed a little. Roosevelt turned on the radio.

In another minute he was kissing me. He dumped my books in the back seat and took off his glasses. His hand ran up my arm and touched my neck, giving me shivers. He gently lowered me onto the seat, until I was lying on my back, my head near the steering wheel. "Baby, baby . . ." he kissed my face, my lips. I clung to him as his hands groped over my body.

Then there was silence. His face was inches away from mine in the darkness, and when I looked up at him I couldn't believe the sensitivity and beauty I saw. He bent toward me. Suddenly, he stopped and looked out the glass of the car window.

We sat up as a huge bus passed—a huge, sight-seeing bus. We both saw an old white lady staring down at the cars, and we began to laugh.

"See the sights of Chicago!" I mimicked the guide. Neither Roosevelt nor I knew if the woman had actually noticed us, but if she had, we were sure she would have a vivid memory of an interracial couple in Chicago.

Rudy's birthday was in early April. I wanted to do something special for him. I wanted to tell him all the things I had seen in him during my months at Marshall, to express my own deep affection for him.

I wrote him a letter, telling him how much I valued our friendship and admired his leadership ability. I told him I hoped he would use his gifts for the world, because he had the power to move people and because respected leaders were always needed, especially in the black community. Several

days later Rudy approached me in chorus and thanked me for
the message.

That letter added another dimension to our relationship. One
afternoon, ninth period, I found Rudy depressed in the lunchroom. "I can't handle this action," he stated. "I'm getting a
D average. How can I ever get into college with that?" I
knew he was having problems with a paper for his English
class, but an attitude of defeat would not help.

While Rudy talked in Student Council, I scribbled a note
of encouragement. "I ain't gonna let you do it, man. I ain't
gonna let you give up," I wrote, hoping he wouldn't consider
dropping out so close to graduation. At the end of tenth period
when I slipped the paper into his hand, I said, "I ain't gonna let
you, man!" to his face. He laughed, half out of pleasure at my
concern and half out of amusement because my accent was so
heavy. Squeezing my arm, he nodded, took the note, and
disappeared down the hall to go to cross-country practice.

As Rudy's and my friendship deepened, I made new friends
with a girl from my gym class. Carol Howard, active in the
drama department, asked me to become a member of the
Madrigal Singers, the group that performed the program of
Negro spirituals I had so admired. The Madrigals were rehearsing *In White America*, a drama Mr. O'Bara wanted to
produce after school, dealing with the history of the black
man in the United States.

"I didn't think you'd be interested in joining a group that
sang songs about Negro history," Carol told me when she took
me to my first Madrigals rehearsal.

"I thought the other kids in the group might resent my
becoming a member," I told her honestly. "I didn't want to
cause any hard feelings."

The afternoon rehearsal in Mr. O'Bara's office brought a
spontaneous rendition of "I Shall Wear a Crown," a spiritual
I didn't know but quickly learned. I found myself caught up
in a circle of hand-clapping, foot-stomping, singing students.
"I said as soon as my feet strike Zion, I'm gonna lay down my

head—be burnin'! I'm gonna put on my robe and glory! Shout, tell 'em my story!"

At first I felt awkward and misplaced in this uninhibited show of emotion. I felt foreign and inferior in the midst of such natural expression and wondered if I could truly be a part of a group with such rich, beautiful talent. I determined to try.

The production of *In White America* was temporarily postponed when the Madrigals were asked to furnish background music in the drama department's production of *Green Pastures*. This drama, written by Marc Connelly, depicted a Negro interpretation of the Old Testament. It was written for an all-black cast and Shirley said Mr. Bergen, the director of the production, would not be pleased seeing my white face among the Madrigals. "If we sing in the orchestra pit for the show, we'll have to put you in the back," she said.

I didn't consider the remark until I was home in the apartment, going over the afternoon's events in my mind. Then I felt a sting of embarrassment. My pride had been wounded. I wondered what it would mean to be insulted like that daily. What did it mean for one's dignity to be injured constantly? I tried to imagine sometimes subtle, sometimes direct, incidents of ridicule multiplied and repeated over an individual's lifetime. I had come to know a bit of the experience of the black man.

That afternoon I again weighed my self-doubts about my role at Marshall and the image I presented. Carol had told me I should get rid of my "rank, Texas accent." I recalled Andrez asking me how long I had been at Marshall.

"Since September."

"Well, you sure picked yourself up a Southern accent!"

I had picked up the language because it was impossible to listen to it all day and not consciously or unconsciously incorporate it into one's own vocabulary. I had picked up the language because it was beautiful and natural and in so many ways more expressive than conventional English. Why not, "Where's it at?" rather than "Where is it?" Why not, "I'm fittin' to go," rather than "I'm getting ready to go." Why not,

"I be's fine," instead of "I am fine." But did other students think my radical change in pronunciation and my use of slang was a mockery of their life style? Did they think I was imitating them out of ridicule? I decided to consult my father.

"Daddy, do you think I should intentionally try to eliminate the accent I've acquired?" Daddy was sitting in the living room of the apartment, resting after a day that had begun at six o'clock with the ringing of the bell for morning worship. "No, Sue, I don't think you should. Just be who you are. Your speech should be as natural and as free as this experience has made it. Don't deliberately try to change your expression."

His assurance temporarily eased my mind, and I attended the remaining rehearsals for *Green Pastures* without worrying about my speech.

Two full days were set aside before the performance to coördinate the actors, singers, stagehands, make-up crews, costumers, and others involved in the production. The Madrigals sat in folding chairs in the orchestra pit in front of the stage, half facing the audience. During the first complete run-through of the play we made a note of each black-out and stage transition. We were to fill in during the scene changes, keeping the audience occupied with our singing.

Miss Kent, the Girls' Chorus teacher, assisted us in organizing our songs while Mr. Bergen raced around the auditorium, listening to the show, stopping the action, yelling directions, and making lighting changes.

Elijah played the angel Gabriel, and he followed "De Lawd" across the stage, answering all his summons with his best bass voice.

"What time is it?" De Lawd asked.

Gabriel squinted at the sun and said, "Exactly half past."

All the well-known biblical characters are portrayed in *Green Pastures*. Cain slays Abel, Noah builds his ark, Joshua runs to the wall of Jericho, and Moses performs his miracles for Pharaoh.

My favorite scene in our performance took place after De

Lawd had created the world and was walking the earth to survey what he had done. He saw a group of boys kneeling on the ground with their hands poised together in the air.

"Ain't it nice to see people prayin'," De Lawd observed. Then the boys moved and dice rolled across the stage. De Lawd was furious at the sight of gambling. He grabbed one young boy by the ear. "Where's your mother?" he demanded.

"If you know, you're doin' better than me!" the youth retorted.

"You've been drinkin' sonny-kick-mammy wine!" De Lawd exclaimed, horrified. That line never failed to get a roar of approval from the audience. The boys used in the scene had never acted before—they were Marshall's best crap-shooters!

When the Madrigals weren't needed, we went outside to the auditorium lobby and rehearsed. Rudy gravitated to the leadership position and helped us formulate a routine for "Shoes," our entrance song for Act II. We had footwork as well as hand clapping and a special ending to the number.

On the second day of straight rehearsal we added more songs to our repertoire for additional fill-ins. Rudy directed us in "Go Down, Moses" for a scene change during the Pharaoh sequence. "Didn't it rain, children—talkin' 'bout rain all night long!" we sang as Noah built his ark. Everyone knew "Joshua Fit the Battle of Jericho," and we added "Pass Me Not, O Gentle Savior" and "We Shall Not Be Moved" near the end of the show. In all, we had a repertoire of twenty-three songs.

Although the two days of hard practice drew us closer together as a group, they also brought out personal problems of some of the Madrigals. Shirley complained about almost anything, irritating other members. Under the stress of leadership Rudy became moody. Mella was quiet and withdrawn. I tried to keep the group together and bolster morale. The play was several hours long, and by midafternoon we were all tired and nervous.

Our feelings about Mr. O'Bara united us. He was the official director, yet he had given the brunt of the responsibility to Miss Kent, who, though well intentioned, lacked the authority and know-how to provide us the leadership we needed. Consequently, Rudy had become the person we looked to for instruction, and Mr. O'Bara was criticized within the group for his lack of participation.

Our first performance was on a Wednesday morning at 9:30 in Marshall's auditorium. The Madrigals were fitted in maroon Calvin robes and caps. Tense and excited, we waited outside the stage door for the entrance cue. When the door opened, we entered, singing, "Oh, when the saints go marching in! Oh, when the saints go marching in!" We clapped and moved to our places in the dark of the auditorium, knowing few people could see us and hoping that we could be heard in the balcony. The auditorium ceiling was so high, the sound seemed to fight its way upward against some invisible barrier.

Rudy seated us, and the first scene began. As the play progressed, Miss Kent attempted to bring us in on cue, but Rudy did most of the work. Occasionally he whispered to Mella about a change in song, and Mella would lean over and tell me. "Pass the word," she'd say, and I'd tap the shoulder of the person to my left, so that the message was carried to each Madrigal.

Mr. Bergen had told us not to watch the stage, but it was difficult to keep our eyes trained into the auditorium, and I gave up trying to stare above the heads of the audience. Besides, the costumes on stage were utterly striking. Elijah wore a white and gold embroidered robe and two elaborate white wings. De Lawd's beard and black tuxedo gave dignity to his plump, stocky figure. The other angels in the play carried staffs, and their robes were bright purples and yellows. Pharaoh's fez was stunningly bejeweled and his head magician had a conical cap covered with shining half-moons and stars. We did our best to sing at the appropriate time, but I was not aware of the strain on Rudy until we had exited at the end of the first act.

"Why didn't y'all sing?" Rudy asked the sopranos. "You haven't been coming in! I been try'n to bring you in, but I don't hear nothin'! Y'all have to help me now!" he said, exasperated.

Shirley took Rudy's accusations to heart, and her big eyes filled with tears. "It wasn't my fault," she replied. "It wasn't my fault. . . ." She leaned against the wall, the tears dropping onto her cheeks and streaking her face.

We were standing in the hall outside the stage door when Mr. Bergen appeared. "What happened?" he wanted to know. "You missed a cue. Why didn't you come in?" No one answered the question. There was too much confusion and concern about Rudy, and the disturbance did not go unnoticed by faculty and administration personnel who passed in the hall.

When Mr. O'Bara appeared, Rudy turned on him. "You!" Rudy pointed wildly at him. "You let us down, man! You let us down, and you done me wrong. . . ." He was referring to the way Mr. O'Bara had left Rudy with the entire responsibility for our performance. Rudy was cracking under the demands placed upon him.

I had never seen a man cry the way Rudy did that morning. "You done me wrong!" he sobbed, tears streaming down his contorted face. "You let us down!" he repeated, pacing the hall, unable to stop crying or moving or saying what had been building up in him since the first day of rehearsal.

Mr. O'Bara simply stood in the doorway, listening to Rudy, making no attempt to calm him. When a break occurred in Rudy's outburst, however, he spoke. "Rudy, you've got to stand on your own two feet now. I did this so you could learn. You've got to make it on your own now, man."

"Oh, no, man. . . !" Rudy shook his head, the tears still fresh.

"It's your thing now," Mr. O'Bara said, "you don't *need* a director. You can do it."

I was torn between Mr. O'Bara's reasoning and Rudy's turmoil, but no matter how I rationally accepted O'B's position, my heart was with Rudy. The power of his emotions had touched me again, and I was in awe of the beauty and abandon of his agony. I felt very small in the face of his torture, like a child wanting to soothe and calm the thunder and lightning of a terrifying storm.

Elijah appeared in the hall, wearing his robe and angel wings. He grabbed Rudy, muttering, "Pull yourself together, man," and, with his arm on Rudy's shoulder, took him to the end of the hall where they could be alone. When Elijah returned, he criticized us for letting Rudy assume leadership of the group. "Didn't I tell you not to let him be director!" He shook his head. Elijah spoke out of his long friendship with Rudy. He knew Rudy always took responsibility for any group in need of firm command, and such demands could prove overwhelming.

Mr. Bergen called Elijah backstage to prepare for Act II. For several minutes all was quiet. We were a stunned and tired group. Several members looked indifferently out the hall window or stared at the floor. Rudy had thrown off his robe during his outburst, and Mella picked it up and took it to him at the end of the hall. Carol followed her. When she said, "Rudy," softly, he began to cry again. But it was time to get into formation for Act II, and the Madrigals formed double lines at the stage door. Rudy was still sitting in a chair alone. Finally he got up and walked to the front of the group.

All the confusion and emotion had been very upsetting to me. Rudy's pain had become my own. As we began to step in time to "Shoes," tears welled up in my eyes. When I began to sob, Carol turned around. "Oh, no, not you, too!" she half scolded out of a loving and protective instinct. She handed me a Kleenex to wipe my face. Miss Wilson offered words of comfort, but one look at Rudy, who had taken charge again, his eyes red and swollen, only served to increase my crying. O'B patted my shoulder and spoke a last word of encouragement as the stage door opened, and we disappeared into the darkness of the auditorium. My eyes smarted, but I could hear Rudy singing, "Well, I got shoes—you got shoes—all God's children got shoes. . . ."

As the curtains opened, I looked out into the audience, thinking, "You have no idea what we have just gone through to perform for you."

The audience was largely unaware of our internal problems and received the show with enthusiasm. Two additional performances the following day found us a seasoned and cohesive troup. Black students, performing in a quality drama written for black actors, felt pride in their achievement. This I was pleased to share.

May

CHAPTER 10

I was in my room doing homework when the phone rang.

"It's Roosevelt," Ann said, giving me the receiver.

"Hello, how you doin'?" I greeted him.

"Not so good." His voice sounded deeper than normal, and tired.

"What's wrong?"

"It's serious." I listened as Roosevelt described a family crisis. "It all happened since I've been here at the Institute," he said. "Mom is getting on my ol' man's nerves. He told me he can't stand much more of her. He thinks she should be in a mental hospital. Anyway . . . they've separated . . . and they're supposed to get divorced sometime this summer. My two broth-

ers . . . well, they've dropped out of school and are headed
for reform school for sure. My ol' man asked me to come
home and help. . . ."

Roosevelt paused, and I braced myself for what was coming.
"I'm leaving the Institute . . . *for good.*"

I had known something like this could happen any time.
There was little to do but adjust and make the best of it. Yet
it was difficult to deal objectively with the news, when my
emotions were so deeply involved. "Maybe that's the best thing
you can do," I replied, trying to think of Roosevelt and what
his family meant to him. "If you think it would make a difference, then, of course, you should go home. But Roosevelt,
look, you've got to be realistic too. Do you believe anything
will really change by going home? I mean, do you honestly
think you can help the situation?"

"Yes, I do," he replied. "I could work and bring in some
extra money, and that would help. . . . Look, I'm in the
middle of a meeting now and just stepped out for a minute.
Can I see you in about an hour? I need to talk to you."

"Sure. Come up to the apartment when you're finished."

While I waited, I thought about my last visit to his home.
There again was that narrow hall with the mail box dangling
from the wall and the thirty-eight stairs leading to his apartment. Fallen plaster greeted us at the top landing, and a naked
light bulb, hanging on a cord outside the apartment door, shed
a yellow haze over a broken bicycle and empty pop bottle
lying on the floor. A huge collie barked a welcome as I stood
in the doorway, looking into a gray bedroom with no light
from the window. The sheets on the bed against the wall were
crumpled into a heap, as though the bed's occupant had slept
fitfully during the night. The torn curtains on the window
hung limply, and to one was fastened a large wooden crucifix.
It was that crucifix which caught my eye as I waited in the
doorway, hearing the television from the other room and the
sound of Roosevelt's mother's bedroom slippers sliding along
the wooden floor. So that was home, I thought, that little
apartment with inadequate heat and no phone. So that was

home, and Roosevelt was planning to return there to repair the broken web of a family relationship.

Daddy knocked on my bedroom door, opened it, and grinned. "Roosevelt's here. Do you want to see him?" he teased.

"Yes, I want to see him. And don't laugh, 'cause this is serious. He's got a problem," I explained. "Maybe you can stay and help us."

When Roosevelt entered the room, his face indicated his exhaustion and despair and, at the same time, a kind of stoic control. Daddy, sober and sympathetic, sat down on the rug and crossed his legs. Roosevelt leaned back into an arm chair.

"Now what's this about a serious problem?" Daddy asked. His presence was reassuring. I was grateful for the calm and deliberate manner in which he opened the conversation.

Roosevelt explained the circumstances, slowly and almost listlessly. "My father and brothers came up to Chicago before my mother did. You know the area around Skid Row on Madison Street? Well, we lived there," he continued, naming the street and house number. He went over his family history, a history which was painful to him now and part of the struggle involved in his decision.

Daddy sensed Roosevelt's confusion. He felt the frustration of being confronted with another person's suffering, of reaching out to minister to it, of realizing how little he could do. Looking at Daddy, I thought of other times when we had listened to similar stories of struggle and pain, always wanting desperately to help, and trying to cope with that aching powerlessness when there is no certain way.

Roosevelt's struggle had become Daddy's. Slowly Daddy responded, searching for the thought or phrase that would help Roosevelt face his problem. "Roosevelt, why must people suffer so? My father died when I was eleven, and my mother became mentally ill soon afterward and never did recover for the rest of her life. . . .

"There is so much that separates people. Though you live

with somebody, at the same time you're very much alone. . . .

"Sometimes I want to take some of my friends by the shoulders and shake them. They don't see the beauty of other people—they *don't see*. Look at the man in China, or the Polynesian, the South American, the Latin American—they're all beautiful, real people."

Daddy was giving Roosevelt all anyone could give—the stark word about the way life was, the word that others faced similar problems, that all men shared a common humanity. He was reminding Roosevelt that he was a beautifully sensitive person, that he was intelligent, and that we understood the obligation he felt toward his family.

"But I'm helpless." Daddy shook his head. "I'm powerless . . . to make your decision. *You* have to make it."

"I've got to go," Daddy said, as he got up off the floor. "I'm sorry. I'm already late for a meeting." He touched Roosevelt's shoulder and walked out of the room, closing the door behind him.

For a moment I sat looking at Roosevelt, slumped there in the chair. Then I went to him, and, sitting on the edge of the chair, I cradled his head in my arms. When he felt my tears on his face, he pushed my head up. "Hey, it's going to be all right," he said, comforting me. Comforting me!

"Baby, I'm not worried about me," I said. "I'm worried about you."

"Don't." He wiped the tears from my cheeks. I rested my head against his shoulder, and he kissed me.

Later that evening Roosevelt conferred with several members of the Order about his decision. They decided to tell him he was being considered as one of the students to be sent to Africa during the summer. Since that prospect had been the chief reason for his joining the Institute Order, Roosevelt decided to reconsider his problem. With the help of the Institute staff, arrangements were made for him to help out at home without leaving the Order. He and they realized that a summer in Africa, bringing news of Fifth City's efforts at com-

munity reformulation to the black people there, could be in-
valuable to his personal growth and the understanding of his
heritage.

Because of the many demands on him, time with Roosevelt
became precious. The spring weather found us outside, delight-
ing in the campus trees in bud, reveling in the warmth of the
sun and the feeling of rebirth it brought to the West Side, long
entrenched in the hard, gray monotony of winter. On Sunday
afternoons Ann, Roosevelt, and I often played catch on the
little square of grass hugging one corner of the campus. Sometimes a child from the Order joined our game and often
children from the neighborhood wandered inside the open
gates to play with us. One small black boy, whom I nicknamed "little dude," eagerly retrieved the ball whenever it
went over the fence and bounced in the street. His smile, revealing even rows of shiny white teeth, was beautiful, and his
laughter was infectious.

Other children enjoyed the Institute's playlot, behind the
gym. Inside a fenced square were a sandbox and a small jungle
gym. Three huge brightly painted cement pipes were laid
on the ground, a perfect size for tunneling. In the center of
the lot stood a unique piece of play equipment—a huge jungle
gym in the shape of a rocket ship.

One afternoon, after a hard game of catch, Roosevelt and I
walked over to watch the children on the rocket. We sat on
the top of the smaller jungle gym where we were joined by
another high school boy living at the Institute. He was a
Marshall student and a member of chorus.

Tilting his head toward me, Jessie told Roosevelt, "I wish all
girls were like her." The remark took me by surprise. "She's
really the ideal girl," he said. I tried to detect a note of sarcasm,
but there was none. Coming as it did from a hip cat who had
a reputation for "checking out the girls," I felt highly flattered.
Even though I did not understand what prompted his remark,
I accepted the compliment as an honor and respected it.

Several young boys began chasing each other, scuffling and

shouting. "Let's get the hell out of here!" Roosevelt suggested. We left the playlot, found Ann and Doug, and took them down a narrow sidestreet to our favorite community food store. Jessie and Roosevelt bought pop. Ann, Doug, and I had ice cream. We were an odd crew, standing on the curb of Fifth Avenue, eating ice cream bars and drinking soda. When the street was clear of traffic, we crossed it in a scattered charge and returned to the Institute.

It was all part of a spring afternoon in Fifth City.

The Madrigals were scheduled to sing for a dinner at a Loop hotel, and Mr. O'Bara was anxious about being prompt. He wanted us to meet in his office at 6:30, but even though Daddy dropped me off at Marshall exactly on time, I was one of the first people to arrive.

I sat down on a couch and listened as Shirley and a friend strolled in, chattering. Conscious of my new black outfit, purchased the day before for the occasion, I asked Carol, the next arrival, "Are my pearls all right?" She nodded approval of the only necklace I owned.

Several boys appeared. Then Mr. O'Bara walked in the door, fifteen minutes late. "On C.P. time, huh, O'B?" Melvin cracked. C.P. was short for Colored People, and Colored People's time was a well-worn phrase satirizing the days of Uncle Tom. O'B stood there, tall and black and grinning.

"Hey, dig the man's pants!" Nobody seemed to approve of the way Mr. O'Bara dressed, but the jokes were in good fun, and O'B teased right back. Relaxing on the piano bench, he jived with us as we waited for the rest of the Madrigals.

"Hey, man!" Melvin greeted Rudy, who entered the room.

"Why are you always so late?" Mr. O'Bara demanded.

"You're a fine one to complain, O'B. You're on C.P. time yourself!" Melvin reminded him.

At the second mention of Colored People's time, O'B sat up straight. "It's Afro-American, baby," he said, his eyes dancing.

Carol looked at me. "What kind of American are you?"

I shook my head, playing along with the game. "I don't

know," I answered in an affected, sad voice.

"She's *white*," O'B answered, exaggerating the pronunciation, and then laughing. It was not a derisive remark, and I laughed with him.

When the narrators arrived, O'B took them through a quick rehearsal of their part in the program, and then we left the building, a noisy group of students excited about the evening's prospects.

I was the last one to climb into one of the cars that provided our transportation to the Loop. Because there were seven of us, I sat on Nick's lap in the back seat. (Nick was one of the narrators, and, as Moses in *Green Pastures,* had performed miracles before Pharaoh.) I bent my head slightly to keep from touching the roof as we drove down Warren Boulevard. Melvin told a joke about "white folks" and everyone turned to look at me. I had been preoccupied with the music on the car radio. "I'm sorry. I didn't hear it," I apologized, asking Melvin to repeat the joke for me. But he refused.

I sensed a tenseness on Melvin's part when I was around, and I wished he could relax. He didn't know how to react to me, how to accept me. He was wary of my being in Madrigals, perhaps even wary of my attending Marshall. The only way to reassure him, I was convinced, was to be myself. New acquaintances were often distrustful and suspicious. They found it hard to believe I was for real, that my sincerity and honesty were not put on. In simply being myself, they soon realized my white skin did not mean I couldn't be trusted. How long it would take for Melvin to understand, I didn't know, but I was unwilling to give up.

We parked in a lot across from the Loop building where we were to perform and crossed the street into the carpeted lobby. The elevator dropped us off at the thirty-ninth floor, and Mr. O'Bara led us to the room where we would sing. Rows of tables were occupied by principals from all the Chicago public schools, and Senator Charles Percy of Illinois smiled at us as we entered.

When the narrators were settled in position, the Madrigals

were introduced. I was in the center of the front row and looked up into O'B's fiery face. He jived with us during rehearsals, but during a performance he demanded the utmost in concentration and perfection. Hardly daring to take my eyes from him, I worked feverishly to give my best and help our blend. O'B gave Shirley a withering stare for talking in between numbers.

Despite the tension, we sang with confidence, invigorated by the sound we knew we were producing. Here for the first time I was part of the origination of that sound, I was one with the beauty, spontaneity, and natural talent I had seen on Marshall's stage in early March.

The narrators introduced "Rockin' Jerusalem," in which I had a solo. "Church gettin' higher!" I sang.

"Rockin' Jerusalem . . ." the others replied.

"Church gettin' higher!"

I was aware of the mass of white faces watching us and wondered what they were thinking. Dr. Bronski's fixed smile reached me from across the room. These were students from his school. Does his face reflect his real thoughts, I questioned. And what about the other principals, smiling and applauding heartily? Would our music in any way affect their attitude toward the black man? Or was it only polite attention we were receiving, and a cordial reception prompted by courtesy?

Kenneth stepped forward for his part in "Great Day." Then Elijah led us in "Amen," and we filed out of the room, the program over. Everyone broke into loud chatter as we congregated in the hall, enjoying the relief of the end of a successful performance. My legs felt like rubber and perspiration dripped down my back, but I teased Shirley and joked with Elijah. I was a real part of the Madrigals and joined in the group's antics as we left the building.

Out on the sidewalk, Carol grabbed my hand. She, in turn, was holding hands with Nick, who had hold of Rudy, and they called to me to ride home with them. For a brief moment as we stood together, fighting the cold wind, I sensed a warmth of friendship which almost burst inside me. It was with reluctance that I left the three of them to ride home with Mr. O'Bara, who was going directly to the Institute.

Back in the apartment, I shared with Mom and Dad what I had seen and felt at my first public Madrigal performance.

Seventh period we handed in our economics notebooks, the culmination of a semester of work. Miss Madga called off our names one by one and watched us walk to her desk and add our folder to the stack before her. For weeks she had threatened us with failure in her course if we neglected to turn in a notebook.

"You may turn it in by the end of tenth period, if you want," she stated, flipping casually through the notebook on top of the pile. I was appalled when she began to grade them during the period, skimming through the pages indifferently, and jotting down a mark which would be a heavy percentage of the student's economics grade, and affect, often radically, his graduation. It looked as though she was judging the caliber of the work by the name on the notebook. She couldn't possibly have read what any student had written in the time she took to grade it. Consequently, the student's mark was completely subjective. It was the result of her own particular bias against that individual, and it represented her prejudgment of his ability. No one in the class was receiving a fair, objective analysis of what he had spent an entire semester preparing.

Ninth period I found Rudy groaning at a lunch table. He was surrounded by ten other students, all busily putting together his econ notebook.

"Rudy!" I exclaimed, as his head dropped into his hands on the table, and he let out a desperate sigh. Carol turned to me and told me the only part Rudy had contributed was his name on the title page. Because of his numerous activities, he had found little time to organize a notebook and each of the students, Rudy's best friends, had helped to write a section, completing it. Carol said the differences in handwriting *were* obvious, but handing in the work as it appeared was better than not handing in anything at all.

As Rudy checked the finished work, the last page leaped up at me. There was a one dollar bill glued to it!

"Rudy, no!" I objected. In class one day Miss Magda had reminded us when the notebooks were due. "Oh, and by the way," she added, "I'll accept fives and tens."

"How about ones?" someone had ventured from the back of the room.

"Oh, they're all right, too."

But Rudy couldn't resort to bribery to pass the course! "Oh, man, come on . . ." I pleaded. He only shrugged. How far could Miss Magda push us? How totally would she destroy our sense of worth?

Rudy refused to remove the bill from the notebook. I knew how much he wanted to pass and graduate, and I left him alone.

Several days later, when Miss Magda returned the folders, Rudy and I compared our grades. I received an A. Rudy's notebook, with the dollar bill still in place, was marked D.

Tenth period brought a long discussion with my English teacher, Mrs. Vashka. She told Carol and me she was leaving Marshall and would not even complete the last two weeks before graduation. She confided to us what had driven her to leave so suddenly. Her reasons had been building up all year and finally had come to a head.

First, there was our Honors Class. We weren't responding to her teaching, and she thought it wise for someone else to lead us. As I saw it, the fault did not lie with her methods but with her expectations of the students. Most of the seniors in the class had quick minds, but they were hesitant about expressing themselves verbally. Discussions were difficult to build and guide. The only exciting one had occurred in the fall when someone brought up the race question and angered the class to the point of chaos. That day Mrs. Vashka had been delighted, not knowing which raised hand to call on next.

During the weeks when we had studied great modern plays and read them aloud, a boy from Santo Domingo and I had acted out a scene, using Mrs. Vashka's desk top. We played a silly, romantic, young couple. The class was intent and attentive until it came time for my line, "Oh, but your hair!" The stage directions called for the girl to run her fingers through the boy's mussy hair. When my hands reached for his nappy natural, however, everyone broke up, and the dramatic development of the scene was lost. We never recaptured the mood of that day, and Mrs. Vashka had become very disheartened.

There were other reasons for her decision to leave Marshall. She had worked hard to start a creative arts magazine for the school. The initial difficulty had been acquiring the approval of the administration. Finally, along with permission, they had given her an unrealistic publication date, hindering her choice of material. Pressed for time, she had resorted to using stories written by our Honors Class for the first issue. To her surprise, almost all the stories were censored. One, written by Odetta, described a day in swimming class when her bathing suit had come off in the pool. This was labeled "too controversial." Another dealt with a family concerned about a boy in Viet Nam. That was stamped "too political." Objections of this kind were raised by members of the administration on the majority of stories. By the time they had been ruled out, there was little left of the magazine. Mrs. Vashka was understandably upset.

"Do you know about the yearbook?" she continued. We shook our heads. "Well, several students wanted to put the Commando on the opening page." (The Commando was Marshall's symbol—a soldier with a hand grenade in his left hand and a gun in his right, poised for action in his helmet and uniform. The Commando was printed on all Marshall book covers and folders and was familiar throughout the school. The Marshall Commandos identified the school's athletic teams throughout the city.) "The administration objected. 'It's too suggestive,' they decided. They replaced the Commando with an innocuous picture of a boy and girl carrying books, under our school motto, 'Friendly and Scholarly.' They arbitrarily imposed a symbol upon the students, a symbol that had no validity for them."

Mrs. Vashka made a face expressing her disgust. "You just don't know the wrangling that goes on between the administration and faculty," she told us. "You have no idea of the futility and frustration we teachers feel."

"But couldn't you at least wait for your seniors to graduate?" I asked. "Couldn't you hold out for two more weeks?"

Mrs. Vashka apologized but said she couldn't. In Honors English we would have a substitute for the last few weeks.

After school I went along with Carol to a doctor's appointment at Mt. Sinai Hospital. While we waited in the hospital lobby, we talked about my coming to Marshall. It was the first time anyone had spoken frankly to me about his initial reactions.

Carol laughed, recalling how the seniors had resented me those first few weeks. "I remember a friend telling me about this white girl, and then some of us peeked into a classroom where you were. 'That is what we have in our senior class!' we said, pointing to you. . . . Then, when you came to Marshall with your ankle all bandaged up, we felt sorry for you. We were sure somebody had beaten you up, being new in the neighborhood and all. We were convinced you had gotten into a fight."

"Oh, we fought you for a while," Carol went on, "but finally we realized you were a part of Marshall. And *you are!*" she said firmly.

The door to a small room opened, and a nurse called for Carol. She rose and disappeared behind the door. As I waited for her, I thought about her remarks. I was amazed that people had had such reactions to me throughout the year, and I had not known how they really felt. Now, finally, it was becoming clear, and I was glad Carol was so open and willing to explain.

When Carol returned, we boarded a bus that took us near her house on Arthington Avenue. We walked down California Avenue the last several blocks. I was appalled at the condition of the streets. Some of the houses were literally falling apart. Empty lots reeked with garbage, old inner tubes, and piles of rubbish, and children played in the dirt. I tripped over a piece of glass. Broken glass seemed everywhere, lodged in the cracks and holes of the cement sidewalk along with the weeds. Carol pointed out her boy friend's house. We continued down the block to her own home—a small brick building with a porch.

Carol introduced me to her younger sister and her nephew in diapers, little David, who waddled over to me and stood there, his eyes like marbles glowing in the dark. I greeted Carol's mother who was seated in the kitchen. Carol told her we were going to the Currency Exchange to cash the check Carol received for part-time employment from the Neighborhood Youth Corps.

At the crowded, one-room Exchange on California Avenue, Carol endorsed her check with a pen chained to the side shelves. "Fuck you" was scribbled on the wall above the shelves. Carol was handed a wad of money at the window. We said hello to a fellow Madrigal member waiting in line as we left the building.

"Are you hungry?" Carol asked me. Farther down the street was a hamburger stand, and, waiting outside, we ordered through a window. Carol paid for me. The waitress looked at me questioningly and Carol, to dispel her doubts, assured her, "She's with me." We hung out with several other kids, eating our hamburgers and drinking pop.

"Let's go to my place," I suggested. A half hour later Carol was looking down at me from Daddy's favorite chair, as I relaxed on the floor in the apartment. Carol talked about her childhood. "We used to live in Mississippi, but Daddy was caught operating an illegal still to make more money. To escape the white lynch mob chasing him, he put us on a ferry heading up the Mississippi River. We settled on the West Side of Chicago when it was still predominantly an Italian neighborhood." I remembered meeting Carol's father one night at Marshall—a hulk of a man who spoke rarely and wore a straw hat over his heavy face. He had driven me home from a *Green*

Pastures rehearsal.

"The neighborhood where we lived began to change gradually," Carol continued. "Black people moved in. Whites panicked and fled, until there was only one Italian man left on our block. He was not well liked by the other residents. One day some people provoked him, and angry, he stormed out onto the street with a shotgun. He started to shoot up anything he saw. I was standing in the doorway of my house. There was a five-year-old boy on the porch with me. As I stood there watching, the man shot the kid in the chest. Before the police could be called, people with butcher knives ran out of their houses and cut the Italian up before my eyes. When the police got there, there wasn't much left of him. Miraculously, he lived. And so did the boy, I think. . . .

"Our neighbors have the habit of setting the house on fire every time there is an argument," Carol went on. "The son goes around pouring kerosene on the couches, and the place blazes. The third time he did it, we didn't even react. It was becoming so routine. . . . You know, I was never allowed to go South for fear I'd get into trouble. When I was little my mother took me to Jackson, Mississippi. She caught me walking on the paved road when Negroes were supposed to use the dirt one. A state trooper cracked a bull whip in my face and asked me what I was doing. Mother grabbed me and wouldn't ever take me South again. . . ."

"Carol," I commented, "do you realize that the kind of incidents you're relating, which are so common to black people, white people seldom know? We white people are heavy on intellect, but we have had few gut experiences."

At first Carol didn't understand what I meant, but as she talked, I'd often add, "*That's* what I mean by experience!"

She told me briefly about her involvement with the civil rights movement, how she almost left home to join the freedom rides in Kentucky, and how she cried when her mother wouldn't let her go to Selma. "Oh, I did all kinds of things for the movement. I decorated cars for motorcades and ran off ditto sheets for meetings. When I was fifteen," Carol laughed, remembering, "I wanted a denim skirt so bad I could have died. It was the symbol of civil rights workers, and I just had to have one."

Carol got up and explained, "I have to call my mother," and dialed the phone. Her mother had always worked, leaving Carol to fend for herself. Then, she became ill and stayed at home more, ordering Carol about and intruding in her life in ways she had never done in the past.

They argued on the phone, and Carol sighed as she replaced the receiver. "I have to go home right away."

We walked across the Institute campus together, and I waved goodbye to her as she boarded the Harrison bus. Then I went looking for Mom, to tell her about the conversation and relate the strength and endurance and wisdom of one black girl. I marveled with her at the black experience—so unique and beautiful because it had produced a people of enduring spirit and courage.

One weekend a member of the Order asked me to spin records at a high school dance to be given in the chapel basement. Roosevelt and Tom, another boy in the High School House, agreed to help me and act as security guards while I played the music.

Standing on the chapel stage with a record player and a stack of 45's, I was grateful for WVON. By listening regularly to that station, I was familiar with each record in the pile. I knew whether it had a fast or a slow tempo. The mood of the entire dance was controlled with my choice of record. If I played Lou Rawls' "Love Is a Hurting Thing" or Ruby Andrews' "Casanova," a dude moved easily with his girl friend in the darkness, holding her close to him, oblivious to any other couple in the room. If I played the Supremes' "You Keep Me Hangin' On" or Carla Thomas' "B-A-B-Y," the beat was right for the latest bop. If I played the Bar-Kays' "Soul Finger" or James Brown's "Cold Sweat" the room went wild with the boogaloo.

"Oh, Sue, be sweet," a boy from the neighborhood pleaded.

"Play this . . ." and I put on his record. I tried to be sensitive
to the mood of the dancers and to keep the party from lagging.

"Like to get better acquainted?" A strange dude gave me
the eye.

"You around here much?" another inquired. But they re-
treated when Roosevelt put his arm around me.

Near the end of the dance, we were startled by a loud sound
and the noise of shattering glass. Two windows on the left side
of the chapel lay scattered across the floor. Several girls
screamed and ran to the opposite side of the room. Roosevelt
and Tom ran out the door after whoever had broken the windows. I anxiously watched them disappear, knowing it was up
to me to keep everything under control until they returned.
They could not find the window breakers and rejoined the
group after circling the chapel.

There were no other problems that evening, and we closed
the dance on schedule. Roosevelt, Tom, and I swept up paper
cups used for refreshments and turned off the chapel light.
But, before we left, I put on Little Anthony and the Imperials'
"Hurt So Bad," and danced with both Tom and Roosevelt, one
after the other, enjoying for myself a few moments of a sweet
soul jam.

Roosevelt and I drove around the West Side one afternoon
after school looking for Tom who hadn't returned to the Institute since early morning. We stopped at Darlene's house to see
if she knew where he might be. Standing on Darlene's porch,
we watched the curtains behind the dirty glass of the front
door part and her head appear. She opened the door and ush-
ered us into the living room where she sat down next to Roosevelt on a small couch covered with plastic.

The room gave me claustraphobia. It was incredibly dark.
The long, dingy curtains hanging over the front windows cut
out any light. Over against the opposite wall was another
couch and an end table. Darlene's father sat there. A sadder
man I had never seen. A little portable television on a stand was
tuned to some inane western, and his entire attention was

turned to that screen. He slumped into the couch, lifeless, tired, and somehow defeated. His eyes scared me. They were painfully red and he blinked only with effort.

Two little girls played about the room as he remained immobile, watching the television. The girls' clothes were soiled. One of them had a yellow and blue beach ball she begged Darlene to blow up. The only words Darlene's father spoke were directed at the frustrated child. "You be quiet and get that beach ball outta your mouth!"

An arm chair was sandwiched between the two couches, and a second end table held a large framed photograph of Darlene. On one side of the TV was a table with a long, metal record holder filled to capacity. Pieces of china and several photographs stood on wall shelves, and two color pictures of Jesus and a cross decorated the otherwise stark walls. As Darlene talked about Tom taking her to the prom, I wondered how anyone could study or read in a household such as that one.

Darlene didn't know where Tom was, but she decided to join the hunt. Roosevelt drove us to Fairfax House, a hangout on the West Side run by several adults for after-school studying, recreation, and parties. We found Marshall students playing ping-pong in the basement, but no one had seen Tom. On the sidewalk outside Fairfax House, however, I met Nick.

"How are you?" he asked with genuine concern. I told him I was depressed about school. "The administration and some of the teachers are really bothering me." I explained how Miss Magda manipulated students and how this upset me.

He smiled and responded to my complaints and frustrations with comments that implied "that's the way it is." "Teachers can be so friendly one day and then turn right around and slap you down the next. You've just got to be careful," he observed.

Again I realized how such behavior was taken for granted. Here was this beautiful boy being so nice, looking relaxed in a blue sweatshirt, sharing his thoughts with me, and never questioning the way the world treated him. He knew what to expect. He knew that Marshall was inhuman in many ways, and yet that was the way the world had always looked to him. "You'd better accept it," he seemed to be saying, " 'cause you won't last any other way." It hurt to know what he was really saying.

"Don't be upset by it," he said softly. Nick knew the system, and I was just coming up against it for the first time.

When we left Fairfax House, the discussion with Nick stayed with me. Roosevelt, not having found Tom, drove Darlene home and took me back to the Institute. Before we got out of the car we talked about Marshall, and I told Roosevelt of my recent reflections.

"There are many things I want to share with my friends at school about what this year has meant to me, what I have learned from them . . . about their knowledge of life and what they take for granted. I wonder if I will ever get a chance to really reach them. . . ."

Young Life, a student religious group to which many Marshall kids belonged, held a meeting in the Institute's chapel basement one spring evening. Roosevelt and I joined the gathering of students, enjoying the games and the slides of the camp in Colorado that Rudy, Elijah, Delbert, Dorothy, and Mella had attended one summer. The meeting's purpose was to interest more people in the camp. George, one of Young Life's white directors, gave a short speech about its activities.

In the middle of the proceedings, Linda, a white Young Life leader I had met through Mella, tapped me on the shoulder. "Sue, I can't find my purse. I think someone has taken it."

"Where did you have it last?"

"I left it with some papers in a box in the back hallway . . . only for a minute. I had to get something. When I came back, it was gone."

I called to Roosevelt and explained Linda's predicament. We went into the hall and checked the box, which sat on the floor covered by a white sweater.

"The purse was right there," Linda indicated.

"What color was it?" I asked.

"It's blue and has two big handles."

"What did you have in it?"

"Car keys, identification, about ten dollars, and a plane ticket. . . ."

"Well, we'll look for it. I'm really sorry. We'll do our best to find it."

She left us in the hall to ask other kids if they had noticed anything. Roosevelt and I stood facing each other. "Man, I feel responsible," I told him, "because it happened here."

He was looking toward the outside door that led to the same cement hallway where I had fallen and sprained my ankle so many months before. "Anyone could have wandered in, seen the purse, and run off with it," Roosevelt reasoned. "Damn. . . ."

"Well, let's scour the campus. They might have taken the money and thrown the purse in the bushes or something."

Once again, as when we had stewarded, Roosevelt and I were a team with a mission. The unexpected had occurred, and we were challenged to solve the problem. It was not a time for fun. Our task was serious.

Outside in the warm darkness of evening we searched under bushes, trees, and on window ledges. We covered every corner of the campus, parting branches, kicking grass, and keeping our eyes on the ground. The limbs of the trees rustled in the night breeze, making eerie shadows against the chapel where light from a street lamp splashed white against black.

As we stood together for a moment, Roosevelt glanced out at the street and said, "Sometimes they'll leave things in alleys. I'm going to check the trash cans." He started out the gate.

"Can I go with you?" I called.

"You better stay there. . . ."

"Don't take too long . . . and good luck!" I watched his form blend into the darkness. Then I resumed my trek, asking members of the Order who wandered outside if they had seen anyone strange around. No one had.

When Roosevelt returned, he was empty-handed. We had no choice but to go inside the chapel basement and tell Linda we had not found the purse.

"We looked everywhere," I said.

"That's all right," Linda replied in resignation. Still, I felt badly.

"Hey, Sue . . ." Rudy stepped out of the gathering for a moment and joined us at the back of the room. "I wrote this at Fairfax House. There's another part, but I forgot to bring it."

He handed me a folded piece of notebook paper and disappeared into the crowd. The serious proceedings had broken up, refreshments were being served, and a small party had begun. In a quiet corner of the room, I opened up the paper. The note was written in blue ink.

Dear Sue!
Well anyway I don't how to start this off but I know I have something to say. Ive known you but a short time but it has been one of the most streangthing time of my life. What I'm trying to say is that I will give it one more try. You I thank God for people like you. Because it is a blessing knowing you and have you for a friend. As I said before you have shoulders strong enough to cry, lean or maybe fall on. You are going to make some lucky man a good wife and I'm for real man, you've really got some. Every since that first letter for my birthday I don't know! All I know is I have been please, also help in a great way to know somebody really care what happen to me. You have an understanding you can't find in others.

It was Rudy speaking in a way that touched me deeply. He had never been so personal before. I was moved by his response to the note I had written him, asking him not to be defeated and to give school one more try.

I folded the paper and went over to the cooler for a pop. Delbert had his arm over the lid.

"I'm sorry, Sue," he grinned, "but there ain't no more."

"I don't believe you," I kidded, opening the cooler myself. Sure enough, the bottom was covered with ice-cold cans. We both laughed and began to talk.

Delbert was attentive to my feelings about Marshall, the West Side, the beauty of blackness, and the culture of the city. I told him how we had come to the Institute, what our move had been like, and how much I loved Marshall. I explained to him how deeply I wanted my fellow students to feel about themselves as *I* had come to feel about them—that they were great human beings, vital and alive and real.

He seemed to accept what I was telling him, and I was grateful to be able to express my thoughts to him.

Suddenly, I felt arms around me. Rudy and Nick were standing on either side of me, their huge forms covering me from sight. They began to move me stealthily across the floor.

"This is a kidnapping," Rudy whispered to me.

"A kidnapping?" I said, feigning surprise and fear.

"Yeah. We're going to steal you, Sue," Rudy said.

I moved carefully between the two boys, playing the moment, as they were, to the hilt.

"A kidnapping . . ." I repeated. "You know what's different about it?" I asked softly.

"What?" Nick and Rudy both bent down farther to hear.

"I *want* to go!!!!"

Instantly Rudy let go of me and ran across the room, howling in a fit of wild shouts and hysterics. "Booooyyy!" Nick was laughing too, and I stood smiling, enjoying my own joke.

"Oh, Suuuuuue!" Rudy yelled. "Girl! You gettin' rank!"

I was going upstairs to the apartment after school when Roosevelt appeared. "Hey, man, I've been looking for you," I said. He kind of smiled and waved as I stopped on the landing. "Where you been?"

"Up in my room."

I was going to ask him to come with me, but as he climbed several stairs to meet me, I sensed something was not right.

"Hey, what you been doin'?"

He shrugged in reply.

"Now, come on."

He shook his head.

"You been drinking, haven't you?"

He smiled, weakly. "Sue. . . ." I could smell the combination of liquor and tobacco.

"Oh, man, go on—get away from me," I teased him.

"Baby!" he protested.

"I think you should go down to the kitchen and get a cup of coffee." He was swaying slightly on the steps. "Now go on! Doctor's orders! Or you might fall down right here!"

He grinned sheepishly, waved again, and started downstairs. At a bend in the steps, he turned and smiled up at me.

Silly boy, I love you, I wanted to say. "Get going! I'll see you later," I yelled. He vanished down the stairs.

The Friday of Senior Week was "Wild Day" at Marshall. The administration had issued a statement calling it "Hobo Day" and warned that only eccentric ties and buttons would be considered acceptable variations on dress for the celebration.

But the student body had a mind of its own, and I saw some highly creative and ingenious outfits. Brenda walked into Division with her hair in pigtails. She wore a blouse and very short skirt and topped off her baby clothes with a pacifier which she sucked quietly. Jerry sported ragged jeans and an old sweatshirt. Several other dudes in Division wore torn hats that were stretched out of shape.

As we went to our second period classes we heard that Miss Antiss, the assistant superintendent, was disturbed by the appearance of several students and had sent them home to change clothes. "Stay away from first floor if you can," the word was passed. "If Miss Antiss catches you, you're done for."

A group of us were waiting outside our classroom for health when Elijah walked by. He had on a white bathrobe and a black derby hat. His hairy legs were bare except for bedroom slippers.

"If you think he's something, you oughtta see Rudy!" a girl's voice rang out. "You won't believe him!"

Rudy walked into chorus fourth period dressed as the "baddest" cowboy that ever lived. He wore a black hat with a large brim, a pair of round, "granny" glasses, a shirt of several bright pinks, greens, blues, and oranges that clashed brilliantly, and pants that were all torn at the cuffs, with one trouser leg longer than the other.

Miss Ellis called the members of her special ensemble to the front of the room and arranged us in two rows. We had been selected to sing two numbers for the Spring Concert and used part of the chorus period for rehearsal. We sang Mozart's "Grant Unto Me" and a prelude by Bach. We must have made a hilarious picture! I had braided my hair and put on a pink blouse, long dark tie, and dark skirt. I wanted to look like a little, old-fashioned school girl. Rudy stood there in his cowboy outfit, and one of the altos was wearing a Sherlock Holmes spy hat. Elijah stood at the front of the group, and, as he sang his deep bass, he put his hand on his chest over his white bathrobe, imitating George Washington crossing the Delaware. "Grant unto me the joy of Thy salvation," we sang, but it was difficult not to join in the giggling that came from the back of the room.

In sixth period economics, Larry, who sat in back of me, was sporting a Scottish tam, tattered pants, and a sign that read, "The Spoiler." One boy had a baseball hat on backwards. Miss Magda didn't appreciate the class's costume humor and made her usual disparaging comments about some of us. Rudy was the butt of several of her jokes. Despite the tone of her voice, everyone laughed with her, playing their roles to her liking— the only way to survive in her class.

"Susan, come here." Obediently I went to Miss Magda's desk, playing my role as the conscientious student who, because of her seriousness and coöperation, is picked as teacher's pet. I longed to break out of that image. But, as with Miss Johns, I continued to follow teacher's orders and went downstairs on an errand for Miss Magda.

When I returned to class, it was evident something had happened in my absence. Several of the kids were whispering in the back of the room.

"You missed the show, Susan," Miss Magda said, obviously

delighted with herself.

I sat down in my seat, puzzled. "What did she do?" I asked Larry.

He winced. "Stepped on our feet . . . you know . . . all the kids with gym shoes. Ooooo, that woman is heavy," he frowned, in silent anger. I watched as Larry nursed his injured foot.

So she had actually done it! My errand had been carefully timed to be sure I would not interfere with Miss Magda's latest self-indulgence.

By the time Student Council started, Rudy had changed out of his cowboy hat and shirt. The spirit of the day had not been lost, though. Someone suggested having an African day when all the seniors would come in African dress.

"Yeah, and we'll all wear our hair natural!" That meant that, after washing it, none of the girls would straighten their hair and the boys would allow theirs to grow longer.

"Hey, wait a minute—what about Sue?"

"How can she have a natural?"

"I know," Rudy proposed, "we'll get her a black wig!"

I stood up at my seat. "Look, ya'll, this is as natural as my hair ever gets! This is what happens after I wash it. *This is* my natural!" I held up a lock of my straight brown hair, and everyone laughed.

Marshall's Spring Concert was half over, and it was time for the special ensemble to sing. The small group of us hurried down the hall in our choir robes, trying to get to the auditorium as quickly as possible.

Suddenly Rudy was behind me, and he put his arm around me. "I know Delbert's been tryin' to cut in my play," he teased, "but I'm taking you away." I laughed, enjoying his big arm holding me.

"That's not true about Delbert," I told him.

"Oh, no? I *know*," Rudy answered.

"One thing, though. . . . I haven't written any notes to *him!*"

He nodded, relieved, and held my hand as we arrived downstairs and lined up in a tiny hallway just outside the stage door. Joe, a stagehand, was waiting to signal us to go on.

"Close the door!" he whispered urgently, motioning toward the door in back of us. "They shootin'. Be careful. Close the door!"

Who was shooting? What was going on, we asked, suddenly sobered. A teacher explained that someone had been shooting into the windows of the auditorium. Nobody knew why. But we were advised to keep our door closed for protection. At that moment members of the Boys Chorus were coming off the stage. As Elijah went to the door, he saw them in the hall, talking loudly, oblivious to what might happen. He stuck his head out the door. "They shootin'!" he warned them in a voice tense with excitement.

My feet ached. I was tired and leaned against the wall. Supposing a bullet came right through that door and hit me, I thought in my exhaustion. But wasn't that the reality of the ghetto? It really never left you. It was always there. There was no place to go to escape it. Here we were, waiting to sing for a performance, and someone with a gun was firing into the windows at Marshall. How incongruous it seemed—a Spring Concert and a stranger with a gun. Yet that was what life was all about in this part of the city.

"Time for you to go on," Joe said. We took our places in front of the curtain on the edge of the stage and tried to do justice to Mozart and Bach.

Janet wrote me from Wilmette that New Trier's drama department was producing Arthur Miller's *All My Sons*. Having read the play in English at Marshall, I suggested that some members of our class might like to see New Trier's production. Although several girls planned to go, only Mella and Wanda joined Daddy and me on the drive to New Trier the Friday evening of the performance.

We picked seats near the front of the auditorium and took off our coats. Surveying the audience, I felt strangely out of place. The faces were all white. Two girls I recognized looked so much older. They were heavily made up and seemed to have frosted or dyed their hair. The boys were sporting madras jackets and Beatle haircuts. Everyone looked so well-dressed. Who were all these people? I was ashamed because I couldn't remember their names.

"What's wrong, Sue?" Mella asked.

"Oh, nothing. I just saw somebody I used to know. . . . Gee, there's a girl I was close friends with." But I couldn't remember her wearing so much make-up. Who was she now? Did I know her anymore? She appeared so sophisticated and so distant. What had happened?

I tried to check my emotions at seeing all those old faces—faces with names I simply couldn't pull from the back of my mind. It's been a long time, I thought. I haven't been back here in a long time.

The play was excellent. We were impressed with the maturity of the acting. When the lights came up, I took Mella and Wanda into the hall to see a little of New Trier.

"Hi, Sue. . . . Hey, am I glad to see you!"

I turned around and recognized Mary, a girl who had worked on a modern dance with me in gym. She was Janet's closest friend, now that I had gone to the city. The three of us had shared many classes together.

I returned her greeting with enthusiasm. Mary, too, seemed changed. Her hair was carefully pulled back around her head and the make-up she wore gave her a grown-up appearance.

"Uh . . . are these the girls you brought from Marshall?" She asked the question hesitantly, and I sensed an air of awkwardness.

"Yes. This is Mella . . . and Wanda. This is Mary. . . ." Everyone nodded to each other.

"I'd like you to meet. . . ." I did not hear the name Mary used but smiled at the boy standing at her side. "Now, if you'll excuse us, Sue—nice meeting you. . . ." And she was gone. I felt disappointed and cut off. Had Mary spoken to me out of obligation? Had she felt she *ought to?* What was there behind the strained encounter?

"Let's go to the cafeteria and get some refreshments," Daddy suggested. Janet had written me about a new practice at New Trier. After plays, an "expresso" was held in the cafeteria. Music was played and people could stay, talk, and have something to eat.

We sipped a drink and munched on cookies. Three boys were twanging guitars on a wooden platform and singing Kingston Trio songs. No one really paid attention to them. Their voices were too weak.

"What I wouldn't give for Rudy and the boys right now!" I joked. Mella laughed and we slapped hands. "I know Rudy could make this place swing!"

When I had asked my English class at Marshall about coming to New Trier, I had hoped there might be a meaningful interchange between New Trier students and members of the class. Janet had said it was customary for a discussion to develop at the expresso. But nothing was happening, and I realized it would take a great deal of organization and planning, and a break-down of barriers, for a real exchange to take place. I had been foolish to think it would be simple.

A couple, both of whom Daddy and I knew, passed us without a word. The boy had played with me as a child. Daddy had taught the girl. Didn't they know us anymore? I reminded myself that I was from Marshall now. This was no longer my world. We finished our cookies and left the building.

All the way home on the expressway we sang soul and pop numbers. Daddy dropped the girls at their homes, and the two of us completed our journey to the Institute, somewhat sad, but wiser.

Around the middle of May Roosevelt and I were sitting on the stairway outside my apartment door. We could hear the television Mom was watching and the steam from the iron as she pressed the clothes I had washed.

"Hey, let's talk about the future," he said, and half-jokingly went on to describe an island in the sea where we could have everything. Listening, I knew I couldn't live in a happy haven

with no other people. The only "happiness" that was real for
me came from sharing in the joys and agonies of others. The
"happiness" of being safe and sound in an isolated part of the
world had no appeal.

"Roosevelt, what do you really want?" I asked, with some
hesitation.

"Security. . . ."

No, baby, I wanted to tell him. Don't want security, because
there is no such thing as absolute, complete security in the
twentieth century. The sooner you stop looking for it, the
sooner you'll begin to live, I wanted to say.

But how did you tell someone not to search for the material
things—the values that television and radio brought into your
home and advertised daily? Ghetto residents were bombarded
with white America's standards of beauty, of housekeeping, of
being financially successful.

Before Roosevelt returned to his room, he agreed to look
for some other goal besides material security. But the conversation had upset me, and I went into the living room to talk to
Mom.

"Mom, how can you ask someone who has had so little in his
life not to want what everyone wants? How can you expect
him not to want to escape? How can you talk to him about
life beyond the material world when all he knows is going
without, and fighting to survive. . . . Oh, Mom. . . ."

I ran my hand through my hair. She smiled sympathetically,
with no answers to my questions, but with reassurance about
my struggle.

The following day Roosevelt and I went for a walk after
school. Stopping in Garfield Park to rest on a bench, we caught
the eyes of two black boys who stared at us in disbelief.

"Yeah, we're for real." I nudged Roosevelt, amused.

We got up and walked down a dirt path. Roosevelt turned
to me. "You know the first thing boys ask me—the first thing
they want to know about a white girl when they see one
around here?"

"What?" I asked with genuine curiosity.

"They want to know where she lives, where she comes from. They want to know where *you* live."

"And when they find out I live on the West Side, right in the neighborhood?"

"They can't believe it!" Roosevelt grinned. "That tickle me, boy . . . !"

Later, as we walked along Fifth Avenue, making a zigzag pattern around girls playing jump rope, men talking in little groups, and tiny boys dashing across the street to catch the ice cream man in his white truck, the street was vibrant with life. Turning onto St. Louis Avenue, I balanced myself on the curb and swung around a streetlight. I was feeling gay. Looking up, I could see the head of an old man, passively watching the street activity from a tenement window. A dog barked viciously from behind a fence. Roosevelt kicked a beer can and made a playful stab at my side. Then we swung hands.

It was, as he called it, a "stolen moment," when freedom and the city were ours. Roosevelt had taught me how to bum the city, and there was nothing I liked better to do.

As we neared the Institute campus, a little boy shouted from his porch steps, "Hey, is that your girl?" Roosevelt nodded and I smiled.

"White girl, colored boy," we heard him say.

Directly in front of the gate to the campus, something hit my arm. Roosevelt spun around. The boy was standing in the street. He seemed so small, it was hard to believe he'd throw a rock. Roosevelt glared at him. For a moment the entire street went dead. Everyone on the sidewalk waited to see what would happen. The heart of the street—the source that rushes the blood to all its arteries and gives it life—had skipped a beat, and now it pounded furiously again, with a kind of throbbing tension, waiting.

Roosevelt began to walk toward the boy. I didn't dare turn around. I was afraid of what Roosevelt might do, and I prayed there wouldn't be a fight. When I heard footsteps returning to my side, I knew it was over.

"I'll get the son-of-a-bitch later," he swore under his breath. I was relieved. It was only a silly rock.

When the Madrigals performed at Farragut, another black high school on the West Side, Rudy again displayed his ability to move people. He stepped to the front of the stage at the close of our program to lead "Amen."

"See the little baby," he began, "wrapped in a manger! On Christmas mornin'!" Suddenly, something happened. We all sensed a change of mood. Rudy was alive with fire. His voice was tearing itself from inside him as it had in February. By the time all the verses had been sung, people were screaming in their seats. Mr. O'Bara, standing in the wings watching, shook his head in disbelief.

"Hallelujah!" Rudy couldn't stop. "He's my savior!"

"Amen, amen, amen . . ." the group backed him up.

The sound of Rudy's voice echoed in the room. Farragut students couldn't control their responses and several jumped up and down, visibly moved and excited. I had never heard anything like this demonstration of "soul" before. It was like witnessing a miracle. When the music finally faded, the applause thundered in our ears.

Mr. O'Bara came out onto the stage, grinning, and shook Rudy's hand. Rudy stood there, completely spent. Three or four Farragut students bounded up onto the stage and surrounded him. They shook his hand, congratulating and praising him. Someone asked for his autograph.

Nick put his arm around Rudy, and he turned and looked at me. Still stunned from the intense emotional excitement and physical exertion of the moment before, he took my hand and squeezed it. Our eyes met.

"Rudy, you got the power, man," I said softly, earnestly. "You got the power. . . ."

"Thanks, Sue." He held my hand tightly for a moment, then walked off the stage.

I cried at the Senior Prom.

My head rested on Roosevelt's shoulder as we moved slowly over the dance floor in the Gold Room of the Pick Congress Hotel in the Loop. All around us girls in formals and boys in tuxedos were in motion. The black band on stage filled the room with a dreamlike aura, for when they had finished playing numbers with a boogaloo beat, they soothed us with a slow, quiet song.

I realized the evening would soon be over, and Roosevelt would be leaving for Africa within a week and a half. The thought of the West Side without him was unbearable. At that moment I wanted him to hold me and never to leave me. The loneliness I anticipated began to haunt me. The feel of his arms, the music, the knowledge that he was going soon, overwhelmed me and my cheeks were wet with tears.

Roosevelt sensed my turmoil, stopped dancing, and gently turned my face toward his. I couldn't speak. He walked with me over to the side of the dance floor. As he wiped my face, Darlene saw us.

"What did you do to make her cry?" she asked, accusingly. I shook my head, trying to tell her he was not at fault.

"Why is Susie upset?" Charlcie wanted to know.

"It's from happiness," another girl suggested, and I nodded, appreciating their concern. Even when they had left us, it was hard for me to stop crying. I saw the entire year ending and wondered what would happen to all these new friends I had made. What would graduation mean? Would we ever see each other again?

Marshall's prom was the first formal dance I had ever attended. "I'm having a wonderful time, Miss Ellis," I told her later in the evening. "I didn't know a prom could be so nice. This is my first, Miss Ellis, and it's beautiful."

"God bless you, child," was all she could say to my enthusiasm.

June

CHAPTER II

During my final weeks at Marshall, a number of incidents occurred that revealed the self-images of some of the girls at the time of their graduation from high school.

Charlcie had nicknamed me "Susie Smart" early in the fall. She often asked me for the answers to questions in Spanish class. I was hesitant in offering such help. I didn't want her to become accustomed to relying on me. Also, it would only perpetuate her belief in the myth of white superiority. She had to know that she could do the work too.

One afternoon in class Miss Novatny left the room after giving us a series of questions to answer. The students bent over their desks, working diligently, but Charlcie whispered to me from her seat across the aisle, "What's the right answer to number five?"

"I don't know. I haven't gotten that far yet," I told her as I glanced down the page to see what was troubling her.

"Come on, Susie. You're smart."

"Look Charlcie, you've got ability. *Use it!* Who says I can do it better than you?"

"Oh, well, what do you *think* the answer is?"

I grudgingly told her. Then she looked into her book. "But that's not right!"

"See, I told you I'm not so smart. You knew the correct answer and I didn't!" Charlcie had helped me prove my point.

One of the girls in chorus began taking a new pride in her blackness. Jasmine, well-known for her beautiful gospel singing, walked into the rehearsal room one morning with her hair styled in a natural. She was probably the first girl at Marshall to take that step. Previously she had straightened her hair like most of the other girls.

A hush fell over the room when she entered. Jasmine was a born innovator. She knew all the chorus members were staring, but no one else's opinion had ever stopped her from doing what she wanted. To accommodate the curious spectators, she proudly stuck her nose in the air as she marched to her seat. Before she sat down, she turned around several times as though she were modeling.

I thought of Rudy's speech to Student Council in February. That seed of black power consciousness had grown into a small tree and was beginning to bear fruit. Jasmine was the first to affirm her heritage by changing her hair style, and it was clear that after her move, there would be many more such affirmations.

Along with signs of pride at the end of the year, there were defeats too. Miss Novatny turned back our tests in Spanish, and Jo Ann sadly shook her head.

"I'm tired of failin'," she said. "I don't want to fail no more. . . ."

Miss Novatny's tests were difficult, and Jo Ann had consistently been disappointed in her grade. She never received anything above a D or an F. Failure was a common occurrence in her life. I wondered how that affected her self-image, and, if she managed college, how she would fare. Would she believe herself incapable of any achievement? Would she lose what little motivation and initiative she had?

A symbol of defeat felt throughout Marshall was the final list of graduating seniors. Our class numbered six hundred at the beginning of the year. By June there were only about four hundred students remaining. What had happened to the two hundred others?

It was not unusual for students to disappear suddenly or to transfer unexpectedly. Daddy told me about a boy from his English class, of whom he was quite fond. One day he did not come to class. This in itself was not unusual or a cause for alarm. He might simply have cut.

A week went by with no word from him and Daddy became concerned. When he returned to class after twelve days, Daddy asked him the reason for his absence. The boy smiled and said he had been shot. He had been leaving the Sears YMCA one evening when several boys began to chase him. He was shot twice as he ran, once in the buttocks and once in the leg. Turning into a gas station for help, he tripped and broke his wrists in a fall against the curb. The gas station attendant found him bleeding on the ground and called for help. The boy spent the next eleven days in the hospital and then returned to school.

This kind of incident was not the normal reason for a sudden absence from school, and yet, Marshall students were not surprised when one of their peers told such a story. Living in the ghetto meant a familiarity with violence, and everyone was aware of the possibility of being shot or beaten up, even though it may not have happened to him. Marshall students were accustomed to an atmosphere of sudden change, of tragedy, of struggle. If Mattie was pregnant and Grandpa got drunk, if Leroy was out fighting, or "humbugging," and Floyd got busted by the police, that was the way of life.

Marshall students had grown up in a world where the un-expected was not unusual. Some of the two hundred seniors who didn't receive diplomas could be accounted for. They had failed and in turn been put back a year. Others' families had moved. But there were still other seniors on the list published periodically at Marshall, naming students who had not ap-peared in class, that represented forgotten faces. Nobody knew why they weren't in school. Nobody knew what had hap-pened to them.

"Sue?"

Helen, a top-ranking senior girl, turned to me in the library. We were helping Mr. Pankowski pass out tests.

"Sue, I'm afraid. I'm afraid of graduating and facing that white world out there. I've lived on the West Side all my life. I've never been out in the white world. I'm scared."

Her confession was so sudden, so open and frank, it caught me unprepared. It would have been simple to tell her every-thing was going to be all right, to reassure her with pat answers. But we both knew the white world was complex and inconsistent.

"Helen, it won't be easy," I told her, searching for a way to reassure her, "but the important thing is to be yourself and not to let anyone cut down your feeling of self-worth. Don't let anyone stop you because of any misconceptions they may have about you. After all, you're a unique and valuable person. Don't let anyone tell you different."

Giving the word about being able to live was all I could do. Trying to meet the needs of the moment was all I could hope for. A comment like Helen's revealed to me again the great barrier between black and white people—caused by ignorance, suspicion, and fear. If nothing else, my year at Marshall had shown me what a tremendous gap in understanding existed between the two races.

The Institute's June festival for the Fifth City community was a celebration of the Eastern Indian, or Tan Man. The entire campus was decorated with symbols of India. A combination of neighborhood and outside talent was enlisted for the entertainment.

Al Langley asked me to sing. Since instrumental accompaniment was difficult to find, I decided to do my number without any. Several acts were introduced before I went on stage, and Dick Gregory, who had taken an interest in Fifth City, did a comedy routine just before my appearance. Our schedule to perform after each other created an interesting play on names.

One of the MC's jokingly asked me, before the performance, if I was Dick Gregory's sister. When I laughed at the suggestion, he turned the joke into an introduction. "The one and only—Dick Gregory's sister—Sue!"

"The shadow of your smile . . . when you are gone. . . ." With no background beat to follow, I kept my own time, increasing the tempo or slowing it down as I felt motivated. It was just me, reaching out to the audience. It was my own "soul."

When I stepped from the stage, a little boy tugged my dress. "Are you really Dick Gregory's sister?"

"What do you think?" I asked.

"But Gregory's colored!" the boy blurted.

"Ah ha!" I exclaimed, amused by his honest puzzlement.

On the orange bulletin boards of our English classroom, the black lettering Mrs. Vashka put up for the CBS television reporters read, "A wise man is a rare gem," "Truth is beauty," and "Love opens hearts." The blackboard was scribbled with remnants from third period. The American flag hung conspicuously from the wall in front of the room.

Pieces of glass covered the floor to the left. Someone had broken a window over the weekend. I went over and peered out the hole, fingering the fragments of glass on the sill while waiting for the bell to ring.

Boys roamed in the courtyard around Marshall. A crap game was in progress below. A group of dudes stood in a tight knot, and one of them bent down and rolled a pair of dice over

the ground. Everyone in the group froze in position for a brief
moment. Then there was a shout, and the dude straightened up
again.

The row of tenements behind school was relatively quiet. A
man walked up his back porch stairs and stopped by a garbage
can. Hands on his hips, he surveyed the sun and the activities
around Marshall. Then he disappeared into the basement.

Several other students entered the classroom. James Jones
was "rapping" to a friend in the back of the room. Helen
walked in the door. Vera looked tired. I stepped carefully over
the glass as I returned to my seat. The bell rang.

"She's not here," someone said.

"She's not?" A broad smile spread over a boy's face.

"Who? Miss Morgan, our substitute?" Milton asked.

"Yeah. . . ."

Everyone was relieved until another substitute, the same art
teacher who had taken Mr. Wagner's place in algebra that
morning, walked into the room.

"Today we're going to read Act IV of the play you've been
studying. . . ." We settled down to a dull forty minutes of
reading aloud, with no discussion and no excitement. We
missed Mrs. Vashka.

One afternoon, after a wild bike ride around the block,
Roosevelt and I sat on the Institute's Chapel steps. We talked
about the past several weeks. I told him I was tired of boys
teasing me and giving me a line. "I'm sick of raps and words
that don't mean anything, that are part of a dude's cool. You
know, like, I've had it with all the bull guys hand out to
impress me. It's not real!"

Getting a girl in the city was an art. You made your play,
throwing your rap on her and hopefully beating out all the
competition. The dude with the heaviest rap was supposedly
the winner. But so much of rapping was sweet lies, whispered
in the girl's ear to make her feel nice, and having no basis of
truth. Roosevelt had never given me a line, and he understood
my complaint.

"I agree with you," he said.

Talking about Marshall brought Rudy to mind. I explained to Roosevelt what kind of relationship we had and how I'd been trying to keep Rudy going with little notes of encouragement. "Rudy needs support and I've been trying to do what I can for him," I said.

"I'm glad," Roosevelt replied, understanding my love and compassion for other people. "I used to stick up for people." He described a Puerto Rican girl he had known in grammar school. "She was poor and everyone picked on her. The boys took her pencils and lunch money. She dressed real raggedy, and she was tiny and frail . . . hardly able to defend herself. One day I overheard some dudes talkin' 'bout how they were going to gang up on her after school. They were going to jump her. Well, that day I went out into the yard, found her, and walked her home myself. The boys didn't come near. . . .

"I used to fight for my brothers, too . . . whenever they got beat up, I got the dude that attacked them. I never lost a fight for my brothers, even though sometimes I was really scared." Roosevelt stood on the steps, his fists poised in the air. He acted out one of his fights, describing the scene in the alley, his tension, the blows, and his final victory.

It became clear how much of a boy's childhood in the city was taken up with proving himself in his neighborhood through physical prowess. A mark of manhood at school and a mark of a boy's acceptance on his block was his ability to fight. In the suburbs, such a requirement was of minor importance. In the city it was a necessity for survival.

The senior luncheon was held at the Pick Congress Hotel on a Thursday. We were served turkey, potatoes, and beans. Rudy, Mella, and Carol were sitting at my table and complained about the food. Somebody else made a face and said we should have gotten better food for our money. Everyone expressed a lack of satisfaction about the entire meal and about the waiters who served our tables.

Andrez expressed his displeasure by instructing Alberta to

put a cream pitcher in her purse. "We're going to take it home!" he declared. This was his way of retaliation for what he considered unfair treatment. Alberta took the suggestion and the pitcher disappeared inside her purse.

I felt that stealing one pitcher would not accomplish anything positive. I was more concerned about Marshall's reputation. We had been labeled a "gang-banger" school and people were distrustful of us. Roosevelt had been asked to pay an extra $25 to rent a tuxedo for the prom because he told the clerk at the rental store he was from Marshall. The clerk said a tremendous number of tuxes were never returned by Marshall students the year before. Taking a pitcher at the senior luncheon was not going to help our image, and it would probably make life more difficult for future Marshall students. I couldn't stand by and let Andrez go through with it.

"Do you think it's all right?" I asked Carol, who was seated next to me. Then in a voice clearly audible to the whole table, I said, "Andrez, I don't think you should do that. You shouldn't take that pitcher because you're dissatisfied with the waiters and the food. Marshall has a bad enough reputation as it is." Andrez listened, but somehow my comments became twisted with racial overtones. Andrez angrily blurted something about "nigger treatment" and left the table. Alberta quietly removed the pitcher from her purse.

I was left with the sting of what I felt was an unfortunate misunderstanding. I wondered if Andrez had understood my point at all. At home I wrote a note to Carol explaining my attitude and feelings more fully. Carol had become a close friend, and I unburdened myself to her and then tried to forget about the luncheon.

The next day, Andrez confronted me in the lunchroom. Taking my arm, he said, "I want to talk to you." I knew Carol must have spoken to him.

We sat down at a table, facing one another. Andrez wanted to make clear his position at the luncheon. He said he realized what I had been trying to do.

"I felt badly about it," I replied.

That displeased him. Andrez argued that if I apologized for what I had said, the force of my position would be weakened. "It's a question of whether you're worried about being accepted, or whether you want to be respected," he explained. Certainly that was a valid point.

I told Andrez how I cared for Marshall, and how, as a caring person, I felt I had to assume responsibility for things. But Andrez protested.

"You'll drive yourself crazy caring about everything," he said. "You just can't."

"But I do. . . ."

"Look, take me," Andrez continued. "*I* don't care. You're going to drive yourself insane. Me—? I just clown around. I'm apathetic." Underneath the humor of his explanation there was bitterness. I felt I was seeing through the mask he wore every day in school. He was revealing to me in a moment of honesty why he joked and bounced from table to table in the lunchroom. He couldn't afford to care. He wouldn't survive if he allowed himself to be like me. He was playing a role out of necessity.

I respected him much more after our conversation. Within a matter of forty minutes we opened ourselves to one another and exposed our inner feelings. We came to understand what made the other react as he did. For Andrez this was a rare happening and I admired him for lifting his facade and showing himself.

Our final chorus performance was at Proviso East, a high school in suburban Maywood. We gave a full, Sunday afternoon concert in the heat of early summer and took our robes back to Marshall for the last time.

During our regular class period the next day, Miss Ellis told the chorus she thought they ought to give me a hand for singing all year and for becoming a part of the group. I thanked her, and, after acknowledging the applause, asked if I could say something. The eyes of the chorus were on me as I stood up in the soprano section.

"I was scared when I first came to Marshall. Many people told me stories about what would happen to me. But none of those stories came true. Instead, I met some of the most wonderful people I've ever known, and I experienced a warmth and acceptance I've never found anywhere else. I've experienced a vitality, too, that is unusual. Thank you for letting me sing. It's meant a lot to me. And I'm not saying any of these things to make you feel good. I mean every word."

Rudy and Delbert yelled "Yeah!" and everyone clapped as I sat down. My heart was pounding furiously. Miss Ellis had given me an opportunity to speak to Marshall in a way I had longed for.

After school I browsed through the latest *Marshall News*. Miss Wilson had interviewed me for the special Keyhole section reserved for seniors, and I wanted to see what had been printed. However, my picture and comments were not in the paper.

The interview with Miss Wilson was memorable because of the trouble the student photographer had in taking my picture. We were standing in Miss Wilson's classroom where several students, including Nick, Melvin, and the newspaper editor, were quietly taking a test. They could not ignore the other activity in the room, however, and they watched as the photographer backed me up against a bulletin board and asked me to smile. I was self-conscious, and the smile wouldn't come.

"Well, come on!" Melvin called out. "Act like you're happy in an all-Negro school!"

That brought the smile, as the irony of his comment cut through my tension. If only you knew how happy I am, I had the impulse to shout. Melvin refused to believe I could enjoy Marshall.

During a fire drill the next day, Miss Wilson apologized for the mistake in the newspaper. "I sent all the pictures and interviews downtown where they had to be checked," she explained, "and when I got them back one was missing. I was short according to my first count, so I called the downtown office and asked the man who handled it where the other picture was. The man was surprised. He said he was going through them when he saw that white girl. He just assumed it was a mistake, for no white girl was going to Marshall. So, he threw the picture out. I'm sorry," Miss Wilson explained.

"That's the way it goes," I told her and laughed at her incredible story.

As we sat in the auditorium waiting for graduation rehearsal to begin, Carol talked about my senior class rank. The confusion over my official academic position had reached a climax.

Daddy had told me about three administration meetings to discuss what should be done about me in relation to senior class standings. The decision at the first meeting was that I should not be included in the ranking. At the second meeting they decided to wait and see what position I achieved when I *was* ranked. The administration feared that I would knock the Valedictorian out of her number one spot with my grade point average. At the third meeting, when it was determined that my grades were second highest, Miss Antiss came up with a ruling that anyone who had not been a student at Marshall for two years could not be Valedictorian or Salutatorian.

It seemed like a fair and reasonable rule to me, and I accepted it. I had not been in the class four years and worked to acquire the positions the other top-ranking girls had.

Carol told me that the class rank list had been issued for the final time and that I was number two. "I saw the list in Mr. Pankowski's office," she told me. "You're number two on paper, Sue. Why not in reality? Why should Helen be on stage as Salutatorian in our graduation ceremony?"

People were moving about the auditorium, and I listened to Carol's comments, thinking about what my presence on that stage would do to Helen. Her rank meant a great deal to her. The prestige and honor were important. The only value for me in being Salutatorian was the opportunity to speak to the class at graduation. The Salutatorian would give a speech and there was so much I wanted to say to my class.

Carol continued to talk. "Kids have accepted you as a person, Sue. If they have, why can't the administration? You came here as Sue Gregory, not as a white girl from New Trier. Is there really such a rule as the one Miss Antiss quoted? Do you really have to be at Marshall for two years to be ranked number one or number two? I'm going to the top and find out if that rule is true. I think it was made up for you. I'm going to the top even if I have to see Dr. Bronski." That was Carol, my "hell-raiser." That was Carol, standing up for me as the friend she was. That was Carol, with guts and determination.

"Please, Carol, I don't want to hurt Helen," I pleaded with her. "Forget it. Please . . . I don't care."

Miss Ellis called girls to the piano to sing. We had been practicing "Climb Every Mountain" for the ceremony. Carol and I joined the other seniors and temporarily forgot the ranking problem.

After the singers had rehearsed, roll was called. Any senior not present was knocked off the graduation list, even if he had just gone out of the room for a moment. I thought of how long it had taken to reach this day and what it must feel like to be thrown off the list now, with graduation so close. The threat of being taken off the graduation list had hung over us for months. We had been warned at numerous assemblies about tardies and absences and our behavior. The punishment threatened was always removal from the list. Even at the rehearsal for the ceremony, students were not secure.

A printer's mistake resulted in a confusion of names in the Senior Yearbook. On the page showing pictures of the graduating class whose last names began with "G," three names were misplaced. Under Donnie Green's picture was printed "Susan Gregory." Under Carolyn Green's picture was the name "Donnie Green." And my picture was labeled "Carolyn Green."

As the Madrigals boarded the bus to sing at an art fair, I heard Carol shout to Rudy. "Rudy, we gotta do something

about Susan, man. They threw her picture out of the newspaper, messed her name up in the yearbook, and now they
won't let her be Salutatorian. Rudy, what we gonna do?"

As I climbed aboard and started down the aisle, Carol
stopped me and said in a tone of mock authority, "Susan! Get
to the back of the bus!!!" I shrugged and sheepishly took my
place in the back seat. Carol enjoyed her joke and when O'B
appeared, she said, "Look what we did to Susan!" He grinned
as I waved to him. Then he laughed from deep inside his tall
frame. There was applause as smiling faces turned toward the
rear of the bus.

The next day a determined Carol walked into the auditorium
where we were rehearsing. She gave a note to the teacher onstage and the teacher called out my name. I wondered what
was going on. We had marched once to the strains of "Pomp
and Circumstance," and were listening to directions. Carol
beckoned to me. I left my seat and followed her out of the
auditorium.

"Mr. Pankowski wants to see you," she explained.

We went down Marshall's main hall, but we did not stop in
Mr. Pankowski's office. Instead, Carol took me to the side of a
first floor staircase. Behind it, opposite an outside entrance, was
a blackened door I supposed only janitors used. I was mistaken.
When Carol opened it, I looked down a flight of wooden stairs
at the bottom of which stood Mr. Pankowski and Rudy. They
were arguing.

"No, man, let me stay," Rudy was protesting. "If you gonna
talk to Sue, I want to be here!"

"Rudy, go back to rehearsal."

"Aw-w-w-w, Mr. Pankowski! Come on, now, let me stay
and hear. I got to stay!"

"Rudy," Mr. Pankowski shook his head. I walked down the
stairs and put my hand on Rudy's arm to let him know I was
aware of his concern. He squeezed it, turned to leave, and
disappeared up the stairs with Carol.

Mr. Pankowski led me through a small room piled high with

stuffed animals and science equipment into another larger room where exposed pipes bisected the dim light. A couch and two chairs were neatly arranged in a small circle around a coffee table.

"You've never been down here before, have you?" he asked, noting my obvious surprise.

"No," I answered.

"Have a seat," Mr. Pankowski suggested with a smile. "This is where we hold the secret conferences. We can have more privacy."

I nodded and sat down. Mr. Pankowski began to explain his reason for calling me in. He was concerned about my class rank and wanted to know how I felt. He thought I was angry and disappointed because I was not Salutatorian. He told me he felt guilty about my position. I assured him that I was neither angry nor disappointed and that there was no cause for him to feel badly.

"I have no intention of hurting Helen," I told him. "And I don't care about the prestige. It means much more to her than it does to me. She sweated for four years to get where she is, and I just came in. It isn't fair. Really, Mr. Pankowski, don't worry!"

Mr. Pankowski smiled. He was relieved that I was not upset. "Well," he said, "a compromise has been worked out. Helen already knows about it. She will be Salutatorian in the ceremony while you will be listed as number two on all official school records. Being number three won't hurt her chances for college scholarships, and being number two isn't going to make or break yours."

We chatted a few minutes longer, but we were both satisfied with the plan that had been worked out. Mr. Pankowski led me back upstairs and I returned to the auditorium.

As is the custom in most high schools, Marshall seniors signed each other's yearbooks and wrote personal messages of remembrance. There were three entries in my yearbook that I particularly cherish:

Dearest Susan,

I knew that when I started to sign this it would turn into a long story, but yet I want to write it. Our friendship has grown only because we have learned to accept each other as people. That I feel is the most important thing to happen this year.

Friends Always,
Carol

To Sue

It is nice to know that in a world filled with apathetic people, there is still someone who cares. You are *tops* in my book even if you don't have *Natural*.

Love,
Andrez

To Sue

Someone who means the most to me, someone who has helped greatly. Sue I wish I could think of something to express myself and the appreciation. The best way I know is to say Thank you heavenly Father for this Blessing of knowing Sue. You see Sue I believe the God is watching me and taking care of me. And He has sent you to help me. There aren't many girls with a warm, receptive understanding that you have.

These are things that I love you for. One day you will make some lucky man a wonderful wife.

I hope our closely knit cord of understanding shall never be cut. May God for ever Bless you. With my deepest *love,*

Rudy

Roosevelt left for his summer work project in Africa the Saturday before graduation. I went with several other Order members to see him off on the plane that would carry him to Europe and then to Swaziland, a tiny country on the border of the Union of South Africa. It was not easy to see him leave. When the final moment of parting came, there was a kiss and and a whisper of "Be good." There was a smile and a wave— and then he disappeared into the plane.

"Sue!" Rudy called to me in the hall. "Sue! I got something to tell you!"

"What, man?"

"I've been accepted in college! I'm going to Hope College!"

"Hey, that's wonderful!"

I had no idea that Kalamazoo College, where I would be going, was only forty miles from Holland, Michigan, where Hope was located. When Daddy told me, I planned to surprise Rudy and caught him in the lunchroom sixth period.

"Hope is in Holland, Michigan. Right?"

Rudy nodded.

"Well, I'm going to be at Kalamazoo College, forty miles away!"

"Girl!" Rudy howled, running around several tables in complete ecstasy. "Girl! We can go to Detroit and see the Tempts!" He took my hand and raced around a post. "We can visit each other!"

"Yeah, Rudy!" I was so excited. Rudy scribbled an address where I could write him. I was relieved that I would not be completely cut off from my Marshall friends after graduation.

Daddy and I walked through a little courtyard and down a narrow sidewalk to the glass door of Rudy's brown, brick apartment building. It was the second time we had been to his home, and we did not hesitate as we entered the hallway, climbed the dirty, littered stairs, and stopped in front of the plain, wooden door that was the apartment's only entrance and exit. Knocking, we heard a stirring and Mrs. Harris appeared, big and heavy and old, but glad we were there.

"Little Susie's come back to see me again," she said, putting out her arms and embracing me in a motherly bear hug. She eased her weight into a small chair and urged us to have a seat.

The wooden floors of the small apartment were completely bare. One wall in the living room was covered with Rudy's trophies, photos, letters, and pennants from Marshall—the most striking bit of decoration in the apartment.

"Rudy's at Marshall," Mrs. Harris told us. "He ain't home yet. . . ." Rudy was the youngest of her children. Her other children had left home or gotten married. She lived alone except for Rudy and her cat, who rubbed Daddy's legs as we talked, and scampered across the wooden floor into a bedroom when Mrs. Harris sent it away with a swat.

Mrs. Harris stared into space for a moment, her eyes watery, shadowed in wrinkles. Her age seemed impossible to determine, and I wondered what occupied her time, now that she couldn't work and was alone during the day.

In the room to the left, there was a scrubby plant sitting on a windowsill. A mop stood in a corner and was visible from the living room. A drawing I had done for Rudy was taped over a bureau that was littered with framed prom pictures. Mrs. Harris said people always asked her who had done the drawing.

"I jus' tell 'em little Susie did it and she's one of my own, too. . . ." She told me I could make a lot of money drawing, but I explained that I only drew to make other people happy. "Rudy . . . he'll jus' have a fit. . . ." She was staring into space again, speaking slowly. "He'll jus' have a fit, 'cause you came and he was gone. . . ."

I handed Mrs. Harris a collage I had made as a graduation present for Rudy. It was a series of drawings depicting different facets of Rudy's personality. The drawings were mounted on a large piece of black cardboard. It was wrapped in tissue paper and tied with pink ribbon. Mrs. Harris shook her head, as her eyes moved over the package.

For a moment there was silence. Daddy mentioned the weather. Mrs. Harris looked at the floor, then fingered her dress. She said she didn't care if it rained, but dreaded snow. "But, long as I'm alive," her voice was tired, "if I can wake up in the mornin', be alive, then I'm happy. I thank the Lord. . . ." Again her eyes became distant and the room was silent. I felt speechless in the presence of this woman who so easily slipped away into her world, a world that had undoubtedly tried to destroy her, but of which she was grateful still to be a part. I felt utterly sad in the face of her melancholy. It was as though she were with us in thought and time for a brief moment, and then her eyes would indicate that she was far away. Daddy and I exchanged glances. What could we say in that cramped room to this woman whose experience and knowledge of life were unfathomable? What could we say as we stood up to leave her alone again to the quiet of her mind and her age?

Mrs. Harris looked up at us as we rose. Then she stood and shook hands with Daddy, telling us to come again. She hugged me. "Be sweet," she told me and I nodded.

"We really must be on our way," Daddy said, smiling.

When the door closed, he and I walked through the courtyard again, past the broken windows, out onto Warren Boulevard. Neither of us spoke.

Then, almost abruptly, it was all over. I sat numbly through the graduation ceremony, watching my classmates file forward to receive the certificate that was their passport into an uncertain future, so subject to change without notice. The graduation speeches did not mention the reality of the ghetto, which hung over our aspirations. Nor did they mention the difficulty of facing the white world as "adults" for the first time. They did not touch on the significance of the diplomas handed to those of us fortunate enough to walk across the stage. The speeches covered the familiar, superficial words of praise for the four-year journey we seniors had traveled and a summons to the glowing future successes that were ours to work toward.

When Rudy walked across the stage, he had difficulty containing his natural exuberance under the cloak of solemn dignity. In the hall before the exercises began, Mrs. Harris told me he had cried in the kitchen when he unwrapped my collage. He thanked me and kissed me on my forehead as we stood in line in our caps and gowns for the processional.

Dr. Bronski called out my name when student awards were presented. He handed me a small trophy engraved: "Marshall

H. S. Salutatorian, June, 1967." He told the audience it was a special award.

The year had passed so quickly. Was it really over? Had I seen my Marshall friends for the last time? Were there to be no more walks down Fifth Avenue, no more singing for Miss Ellis, no more evenings with Roosevelt? It was hard to let go and move on.

Graduation marked the end of the school year, but it did not mean the end of my life on the West Side. It did not mean the end of my learning about the black man in the city. The summer brought new experiences that were followed in the fall by college and a turning point in my whole philosophy of race relations.

The Conclusion

CHAPTER 12

Several afternoons a week during the summer after I graduated from Marshall, I stood in front of a microphone in the playground of an elementary school or on the sidewalk of a West Side street.

"Welcome to Theater in the Streets," I would announce to the crowd of children gathered around us. "We are a group of John Marshall High School students. Our one and only function is to entertain you. We hope you will enjoy our production. Some of the students have passed out evaluation sheets. Please complete them and return them to us. And now . . . on with the show—The Sounds of Soul!"

Mr. O'Bara organized our traveling troupe. We met at Mar-

shall every morning to rehearse, traveling by bus to performance locations in the afternoon. Several Madrigals were involved in Theater, as well as numerous other Marshall students
who wanted a worthwhile summer activity. Our show con-
sisted of dancing, reciting poetry, a skit, several songs that included two spirituals and an African number, and an ensemble
that played everything from Mozart to the theme from "The
Magnificent Seven."

Marshall was the only school sponsoring a street theater in
the city, and we were publicized in the local black newspapers.
For the most part, our shows were well received. The younger
children, particularly, enjoyed us and often joined in the dancing and hand clapping of our finale.

Despite my involvement with the Theater, the summer was
a lonely one for me. Letters from Roosevelt in Africa lifted my
spirits, which were heavy with the thought of leaving the
West Side. Rudy was working in the Young Life camp in
Colorado, and I wrote him of a new development—family
plans to move. The family's decision to leave the West Side
demanded as much thought as the initial decision to join the
Institute. There were many reasons for the new plan.

It had become clear to us that the attitude of the suburb was
an important key to progress in racial justice, and that the local
churches could benefit from the insights we had absorbed
through the Institute's training program. Then, too, Daddy
decided that developing a curriculum that would better edu-
cate high school students to function with a comprehensive
picture of the world was more feasible in a school unhampered
by an inflexible bureaucratic system. It would take years to
change the Chicago public schools radically. New Trier, with
superior facilities and community support, was more open to
progressive movement. Life at the Institute was rigorous, and
my parents found that problems of health limited their effec-
tiveness. In view of all these factors, the family decided that,
although its goals remained the same, the arena of its activities
would again become the suburban community.

In August, at the close of a year on the West Side, the moving van returned to carry our furniture to a small brick house
in Wilmette. I cried the day we were "sent out" by the Order.
I cried as the VW traveled north on the expressway, and the
familiar streets slipped from view.

During the two weeks before I left for college, I returned
to the West Side to share those final moments with Roosevelt,
who had returned from Africa a proud black prince. The Institute hoped to send him away to school, and for several days
we waited for the final word about where he was to go.

On a sweltering day in August, I first felt the pathology of
summer in the ghetto. Roosevelt's suitcase was packed to leave.
While waiting for news, we went outside and sat on the chapel
steps. Roosevelt read *Manchild In the Promised Land*, and I sat
behind him, rubbing his back as he bent over the book. A group
of neighborhood kids wandered into the yard. Among them
was Moe, the same little boy I had first noticed a year ago
playing on the Institute campus. He had a clubfoot, and his
legs were often bruised and covered with open sores. He was
retarded and spoke with great effort. His eyes didn't focus
properly either. I often wondered where he lived and who
cared for him.

Moe was arguing with several young boys. We could hear
the angry voices in the heat of the afternoon. Looking up and
through the gate onto Van Buren Street, I felt a heaviness
about the neighborhood. Here we were, Roosevelt and I,
caught in limbo, waiting. Here was the rest of the West Side,
struggling to live through another day—a sweltering summer
day when you moved out onto a porch because your flat was
stifling hot, and there was no place but the street to play or to
carry on your business.

I saw an arm swing and heard the cheering of the group of
boys. Moe and another tiny dude were facing off in a circle.
Moe's leg was horribly bent, and I was fascinated with the ease
with which he moved. Because of his affliction he surely had a
more difficult time surviving; he must have been forced to de-

fend himself more often against ridicule and mockery. The two boys grappled and fell to the dirt of the yard. For years Order men had made futile efforts to plant grass and nurture its growth. Dry dirt, easily kicked up, was all that covered most of the campus now.

The boys witnessing the fight jumped up and down, screaming their encouragement. Roosevelt glanced up from his book, then returned to his reading.

What are you doing reading *Manchild*, baby, I thought of asking him. What Claude Brown writes about is all around you. All you have to do is stop and look. But you know that, don't you! Claude Brown has just put it on paper, that's all.

The fighting became rougher. Moe and the little boy rolled over and over on top of one another, and the smaller boy tried to shove dirt into Moe's mouth. Somehow Moe managed to break the boy's grasp and get up. A tiny girl who had joined the spectators began sparring like a boxer. The little dude bowed out of the fight as the girl attacked Moe. She was a monster of energy and even when her blouse got torn, it didn't hamper her. She flung off the piece of clothing like a champion and fought bare-chested.

My mind whirled, and I felt sick. The sun bore down unmercifully as I rubbed Roosevelt's muscles and wondered how I could stop the battle.

Finally Roosevelt's temper was aroused and he put his book down. He walked over to the group and chased the kids out of the yard. Even that didn't stop their fight. They simply reformed on the sidewalk outside the gate.

"All these people's lives," Roosevelt said bitterly, sitting down again on the chapel steps. "All these people's lives . . . wasted . . . and mine's wasting away, too. . . ."

That was the afternoon I felt the frustration and despair of summer in the ghetto. That was the afternoon I felt the pathology, the sad heavy hopelessness that permeated every house on every street around me. That was the afternoon, one of my last on the West Side, when I, too, felt as though I would burst with a force that could do nothing but cry out at "these people's lives" and the poverty of their hope. That was the afternoon when I began to understand a summer riot. The tension was unbearable. Without a concrete sign of change, an explosion, if not today, seemed imminent and inevitable.

Roosevelt went to Pittsburgh where he lived with a family previously associated with the Order. He graduated from Oliver High School in that city and began studying at a junior college.

Rudy took the Hope College campus by storm, but he experienced difficulties his first year learning how to study and adjusting to the small-town atmosphere of Holland, Michigan. As a sophomore at Hope, he found many opportunities for his capable leadership.

Mella spent one year at University of Illinois, Circle Campus, before leaving school to work at a day-care center. She had problems with her science courses and disliked the cold atmosphere of a commuting college.

Through the government's Upward Bound program, Carol studied at Barat College north of Chicago. As a sophomore she won a teaching position there in a black literature course over four competing senior girls. Her future was linked to a soldier in Viet Nam.

Many Marshall students did not go on to college. Others who did, flunked out or did not return after one year. There were marriages, subsequent separations, and divorces. There were deaths in Viet Nam and students losing or quitting jobs. There were babies born and drinking problems that hadn't been apparent before. There were also the students who attended Marshall four or five years without qualifying for a diploma. There was the friend who schemed and tricked his way out of the Air Force. And there were the boys in my senior class who walked the street, still hanging out, still trapped.

My own adjustment at Kalamazoo College in Michigan was difficult. Images of the city haunted me. I couldn't separate them from the academic world I found myself in. I couldn't erase them from my mind. They had become a deep part of my subconscious. The culture of the ghetto was so far removed from the white, middle-class value system of the college. In writing to Roosevelt, I poured out my frustrations, the images that contrasted with the isolated realm of the college campus:

> I see Jessie in my mind. I see the scar on his shoulder left by a dude with a knife. I see your room in Mack Hall, so dimly lighted. I see us sitting in the lounge or strolling around the chapel. I hear you talking about getting drunk. I hear "shit," "kiss my ass," "motherfucker." I see that little boy shoving dirt into Moe's mouth. I hear WVON, somebody saying "What's happenin'!" I see us riding the El, eating ice cream, stopping at the joint on Fifth Avenue for something to eat. I see Garfield Park, the snow, you pulling that piece of glass out of my foot in the summer when I stepped on it. I see the way you smile and dance to Jimmy Smith. I hear a police siren, the sound of a key turning in our apartment door. I see us sitting on steps —and the many we sat on—talking. I see a softball game in the Institute yard, and hear a girl say, "Oooo, white girl, colored boy."

They were the kinds of memories a black person from an urban ghetto might bring with him to an all-white campus. They were difficult to reconcile with the routine demands of classwork and lectures.

One of my first letters home indicated my struggle to adjust to the drastic change of college life:

> Last year I lived life. I was aware of my surroundings and what was happening, and I let my senses go and allowed my feelings to control me completely. I submerged myself in the humanity around me. When others cried, I cried with them. When others sang, I rejoiced, too. The whole meaning of my existence was wrapped up in relationships with people, wrapped up in black human beings on the West Side of Chicago. I learned how to respond to the moment. I exhausted myself with highs and lows of intense feeling, but I

always knew I was alive. I lived every minute of the
hell and the drama and the guts. My whole life was reacting to people, being sensitive to them, trying to
help them. I lived life at its deepest level. I experenced
new places, new situations. But I was not unhappy to
be where people were suffering—they needed me and
I needed them.

God, the things I did . . . the streets I walked . . .
the laughter I heard, the profanity, the apathy I saw!
It hits me over and over again. I gave my soul to the
city and its people. I gave my being to the tenements
and the alleys and the lives that were dying there, and
the lives that were still fighting for breath. I was
keenly aware and responsive to every minute.

Where am I now? Where are the people? Suddenly I am boxed in by books and assignments. My
emotions haven't been stirred for days. Everything is
at surface level. Essays on science and mysticism swirl
in my mind. The professor's voice, in so many ways,
says, "I hate teaching freshmen! This course is impossible!" I make lists and lists and cross items off and
make more lists. I go to class and to a meal and to
work and back to the dorm and sit down for ten minutes. And I go to sing and to listen to a lecture and to
read and to try to write. And then out of nowhere, in
a passing moment, an image comes to my mind and I
am paralyzed. I want to scream or cry or be swallowed
up. Because the image is from a window. The sill is
dirty and I am looking out. I see a street somewhere
and on that street people are fighting to survive.

What am I doing here? Walking the same sidewalks
of a college campus day after day. I want to live again!
I want to feel my life. I want to bum. I want to experience the deeps. I want to wear old clothes—jackets
and pants, and I want to put my hands in my pockets
and walk the ghetto again. I want to talk to people. I
want to fight for them. I cannot exist in a world of
grades and averages and numbers and books. I am separated from the very meaning of my presence on

earth. I am stifled with middle-class morals and values,
rights and wrongs, rules and regulations. The grades,
the facts, the tests all seem unimportant.

I want that unregulated life again, with the unexpected, without appointments at ten or meetings at
twelve. People are what existence is all about. In the
city I found beautiful black human beings with incredible gifts. We gave to each other. I miss that. I am
hungry for last year's "living," last year's immersion.

During Christmas vacation, I visited Marshall and the West
Side. At school I ran into Andrez in the lunchroom, and he
asked how I was doing in college.

"All right," I answered.

"Are you making it?" he pressed.

I said I guessed so.

"Even with the second-rate education you got here?" he
asked, with a bitter smile.

"Even with the second-rate education!" I flung at him. "My
experience here is what's keeping me alive." He laughed. I
laughed, too, knowing there was no other way to react to his
cynicism and bitterness. As we began to part, he stopped.

"Of course," he said, "it all depends on what you want to
learn. After all, we have some of the best pot smokers in the
city at this school!"

He turned then and walked away. Again I realized how deep
were the scars of the ghetto.

The reality of the danger in the city was ever present.
Several days before Christmas I called Hosea on the phone.

"Hi! How you feelin'?" I greeted him.

"Not so good."

"What's wrong? Are you sick?"

"Sue, I got beat up and robbed last night. . . ."

How like the ghetto, I thought, and just before Christmas!
How like it to happen that way!

"I was walkin' home from work Friday night," Hosea went

on, "I jus' got paid, you know. At an alley around Fifth and
Homan a dude stuck a gun in my back. 'Gimme your dough,
man,' he said. 'I know you got some bread. Lemme have it!'

"I said, 'No, man, I ain't got any.' The dude was scared, you
know. I didn't think he would pull any jive . . . he didn't have
the nerve. But then his three buddies came outta the alley.
'Come on, man,' they said. I said, 'No, I ain't got any. . . .'

"Then one of 'em slapped me. The next thing I knew the
dude hit me in the head with a lead pipe. I fell down, holding
my head. I could feel their hands in my pocket . . . I could
feel 'em take my wallet, but I couldn't do nothin'! I was jus'
holding my head . . . I couldn't let go. They kicked me a
couple of times and then they ran.

"This woman from an apartment along the alley took me inside her place, let me lie down, put an ice pack on my head.
She called the police. I was so mad I cussed 'em out! I told 'em
they ain't doin' shit . . . they don' never catch the people who
jump on you like that.

"The next nigger who come up to me and even ask for one
penny—I'm gonna shoot 'em! Ain't even gonna answer . . .
gonna shoot 'em! They always be jumpin' on folks . . . even
little kids. 'Gimme ten cent,' and if you don', they on
you. . . ."

Hosea was bitter, lashing out with a deep frustration and a
sense of the injustice at the blows life had dealt him. He was
still caught in the grip of the city. Rudy, on the other hand,
participated in two different worlds—college and the West
Side—and was able to travel between them with comparative
ease. He was reconciling his past with the present.

When Martin Luther King, Jr., was assassinated in April,
1968, Rudy was on his way home for Easter vacation. He
walked right into an inferno on the West Side.

King's death was, for me and for the black community, the
most traumatic event of my freshman year in college. It
brought about a radical change in the mood of the country,

which, in turn, affected my relationship with all my black friends.

On the Thursday evening the news of the murder reached our campus, I felt a polarization of the races. Most of the black students at Kalamazoo College joined the black students at nearby Western Michigan University for a sit-in at the student union. Immediately afterwards, they formed their own black student organization on campus, and I felt torn from their friendship and unable to communicate with them.

That week end my radio brought the horrifying news that the West Side was in flames. Nowhere on the campus could I obtain exact information about where on the West Side the burning was taking place. I wanted names of streets, numbers of houses. I had to know if any of my friends had been injured. I was worried about Rudy, knowing he would be out in the street trying to control the crowds and cool tempers.

In a frenzy of concern, I walked downtown to a news agency and purchased several Chicago newspapers. There, on every page, were pictures of streets in Fifth City and around Marshall, streets I knew, gutted and in ruins. The West Side was a huge area, but the streets in the photographs were familiar. The burning was highly selective in many places. A drugstore run by whites and known for atrociously high prices, was in rubble. On one block I passed every day on the way to Marshall, only a black-run barbershop remained. The dry cleaning shop, the Certified Grocery, and the liquor store were completely destroyed.

Confusion, anger, and bewilderment swept over me. The following Monday, I received a letter from Mella, written at the height of the riot:

April 5, 1968

Dear Sue,

What an exhausting, tension-filled twenty-four hours this has been! After the initial shock of Dr. King's assassination yesterday wore off, there was disbelief. Now there is hell!

This morning when I got to the university for my eleven o'clock class, a number of black students were leaving the campus. They said there was a sign in the student union that said, Memorial Rally at Roosevelt University—No Whites Allowed. I didn't follow. I went to class. Dr. Segal, our psych lecturer, talked about her feelings toward the sign. So did the students. During the discussion, Negro students walked out. Near the end of the hour this one white guy wanted to know "Why is everyone upset over King's death?" I could only cry.

Earlier this morning my sister Gayla came home from Marshall. They—some of the students, I believe —set the first and second floor washrooms on fire. As she was leaving, Hosea was coming in. He wanted to know if she had seen Rudy. I just know he's in the middle of things.

About noon I went to the Young Life office downtown. From there I called Rudy, but his mother said he "was out in the streets." It seems as though a number of kids had assembled in Garfield Park. Rudy had gone over to talk to them.

While downtown I ran into a girl named Ellen, from a suburb. She said the people there really don't know what's going on in the city.

Right now my sister and I are watching West Madison burn down. Pulaski and Roosevelt have already gone. All we can do is sit and watch the smoke, clouds, and flames, and the troops move in. Someone in our gangway dropped a lead pipe, and everyone fell to the floor at the sudden sound. There was silence at first, then nervous laughter. All my mother said was, "This is ridiculous."

I just learned that Rudy and his mother have been forced from their home. There were fires all around it. Hosea says things are terrible in his neighborhood. I have an answer to that guy's question, "Why is everyone upset . . . ?" He should come out and take a look at my neighborhood, my friends. They even burned our church.

> So where do we go from here? What do we do
> now? Stokely Carmichael has called for "revenge."
> Has King's work been in vain?
> Now everything's in God's hands. Now my faith in
> him is stronger than ever. I've lost faith in man, but
> maybe this is only temporary. I hope so. Faith is essen-
> tial in any good relationship between people. . . .

Mella wondered what was going to happen next, and so did
I. I felt a definite shift in the focus of the black man's struggle
for freedom. In the aftermath of King's death, the black man
began to stand up for himself in a way the world had never
before witnessed. Black people were rising up to their identities, affirming their heritage, and demanding to be respected as
human beings. Black people were determined to decide their
own destinies. "Black Power" represented a need for unity, a
need for new race awareness and consciousness. "Black Power"
demanded the development of a black political and economic
base, without white people in positions of ultimate authority.

Having seen black self-hatred on the West Side and its devastating effects, having noted the white man's position of power
in the ghetto, and the need for the black man to have a positive
self-image, I was thrilled by the new thrust of the Black Revolution. The realization of black as beautiful was a significant
step forward, one I endorsed and rejoiced in. The discovery I
had first made in Knoxville, confirmed by my experiences at
Marshall, was finally becoming nationally recognized as a focal
point of black pride and identity.

But while I was thrilled, I felt cut off from the struggle. For
the first time in my life I felt in limbo, between both races.
Black consciousness did not include me. The integrated meetings I had attended when working for King no longer existed.
Black students met separately from white students on campus.
It seemed as though a line was being drawn with black people
on one side and white people on the other. Everyone was being
asked to make a choice, to step over the line. How could I take
sides? How could I face complete separation from either my
white or my black friends? How could I decide to stand up for

one group and not the other? Wasn't I being asked to negate a part of myself? Confused and upset, unable to choose, I found myself alone, straddling both sides of the line.

Later in the spring, a group of students from Fifth City came to Kalamazoo to present a black drama at the YWCA. Several of them were friends from Marshall and the Institute. One girl friend warned me I no longer would be safe on the West Side. "I want to see you again, alive," she stated, as she urged me not to visit the area. Was the hatred that devastating that I couldn't walk in my old neighborhood? Were black people really telling white people to stop their involvement? What, then, was the concerned white person to do?

All my questions came into sharp focus with the formation of the Black Student Organization on campus. Here again I could have no part, for I had become "white" once more—only a skin color. I felt robbed of my true identity and rebelled against being seen not as "Sue," but as "Hey, white girl!" I wrestled with what the new mood of the black community after King's death meant. I felt blinded by my selfish memories of Marshall and the way I had previously been accepted.

I was forced to rethink my role as a white person and to come to terms with what the black mood was saying *now*. It was not the same message as that of Martin Luther King. It was not the same message I had heard at Marshall. It was born of frustration over the fight for integration. It was born out of disillusionment with past progress—progress that was only token in effort and had not significantly altered the black man's life in America. It was born out of a new awareness of being black and the need for affecting one's own destiny. I was pushed to grapple with my turmoil until a rational perspective could take shape. As at Marshall, I knew that some form of love was my only stance—some kind of compassion and sensitivity.

Now I see that the white man's role must be radically different in the Black Revolution from what it has been in the past. In order for the black man to come into his own, he must do so through his own leadership. The ideas of paternalistic well-intentioned whites can no longer be imposed upon him.

The white man's knowledge, technical assistance, and financial support *will* be needed in the ghetto. It is important that the white man hear the voices of the ghetto and work sincerely, side by side, with the black man *if allowed to do so*. But the black man can no longer be allowed to see himself as a victim. He must learn how to organize, to support himself, to make decisions about his own life. And he can't achieve a positive self-image, he cannot begin to build and make decisions about his own life if white people are involved in his organizations, once again being the "masters."

In the eyes of many blacks today, the white man has been given his chance to demonstrate his alliance with the black man as common members of American society. He has been given his chance to treat everyone equally, to show concern for minority groups. But the black man has seen the white flounder and evade his responsibility. The black man now knows that no one will protect his interests but himself. The black man has begged for his rights long enough. Black Power is his answer to white apathy and indifference. If the white man will not care about the black community, the black man will obtain the power to direct the changes he wants. Indeed, the white man has created the necessity for the black power movement he is so afraid of.

I am not suggesting that all dialogue between races be discontinued. The road to dialogue must stay open! I am not suggesting that black-white friendships can no longer exist. I believe in meaningful personal relationships. An individual's attitudes are changed most basically through deep personal experience. Sincerity and honesty can and will continue to break down the barriers of suspicion and distrust that exist between the races. No, communication dare not come to a halt.

I know of many individual members of both races who have proved their ability to accept and love one another. They are secure in their identities and their knowledge of themselves. They are building on a small scale the society of the future.

These intimate relationships should continue to operate wherever they are possible. But on a national scale, we as a country have not proven we are ready. The white man has consistently run from integration and the black man has despaired of chasing him. Now it is essential that the black man be allowed to come into his own through his own leadership. The coming together of black and white will occur only when the two can meet on an equal basis.

The period in-between will be a difficult time for many of us. We will feel the pain of separation. Many whites will feel rejected. But they must understand what has driven the black man to his present stance. And they must continue to fight for social justice, to be aware of the mood of the country, to be concerned. We as whites must maintain our compassion and understanding. There has been so little significant and constructive action on the part of white people, so many unkept promises and unenforced legislation. The result is this state of seeming separation. I believe this is only a transitional period, however. And it is up to us now, as white people, to help this period be creative and not violent. When black and white can meet as equals, integration will result naturally.

Our efforts should be focused on our own communities. I have long avoided my own suburb in that respect. I have blotted out the need for changing attitudes there, because I knew change would be difficult to bring about. But the need for white education is overwhelming. There is so much fear because of ignorance. One father on the North Shore bought a machine gun. Now he sits at home, content to say, "I'm ready, let 'em come!" This kind of frightening attitude must be changed or we will all be swallowed up in one tremendous and horrible misunderstanding.

Malcolm X wrote in his autobiography:

> I tell sincere white people, "Work in conjunction with us—each of us working among our own kind." Let sincere white individuals find all other white people they can who feel as they do—and let them form

their own all-white groups, to work trying to convert
other white people who are thinking and acting so rac-
ist. Let sincere whites go and teach non-violence to
white people!

We will completely respect our white co-workers.
They will deserve every credit. We will give them
every credit. We will meanwhile be working among
our own kind, in our own black communities—showing and teaching black men in ways that only other
black men can—that the black man has got to help
himself. Working separately, the sincere white people
and sincere black people actually will be working together.

In our mutual sincerity we might be able to show a
road to the salvation of America's very soul.

The black student organizations on college campuses across
the country represent attempts to achieve black power bases.
They are honest expressions of black students finding themselves, resurrecting their beauty and greatness. It is important
that white students see how necessary these organizations are.
We cannot look at the ghetto, cry out at the deprivation, and
then deny the formation of groups trying to create the black
consciousness the white man has systematically destroyed.

My experience at Marshall gave me many new friends and a
love for the city. I have lost neither of these. I visit the West
Side whenever I am home, and I will never tire of the streets
and never stop loving the people whose lives I shared. But I
also know that the most crucial role for any committed white
person is to get his own people together. We, as white people,
need to face our history. We must come to grips with what it
means to be white. We must confront our past deeds. We cannot afford to be destroyed in our guilt, but we should turn that
guilt around into constructive, positive energy and action.
Most of all, however, we must view the coming together of
black people with compassion and sensitivity. We must try
harder to understand black anger and frustration. We must
stop being afraid because we are ignorant.